D1527242

The Frisco Detective;
or,
The Golden Gate Find.

San Francisco, California, 1875

The Frisco Detective;
or,
The Golden Gate Find.

A Story of Five Millions of Dollars

By Albert W. Aiken

Published 1885, Banner Weekly
Edited and Annotated 2018 by Mark Williams

Cover Design and Cover Illustration by
John Coulthart

Dark Lantern Tales
Charlotte, NC

Copyright Information

The Frisco Detective was originally published by
Beadle and Adams in 1885.

Dark Lantern Tales has edited this story and added new
material, including historical information,
a glossary of slang and period terms, and illustrations.

TABLE of CONTENTS

Joe Phenix, The Bat of the Battery,
Free Sample Chapters

Joe Phenix Detective Series
Advertisements begin on page 286

Editor's Introduction

On the day after Christmas in 1885, a new story by Albert W. Aiken began in the Banner Weekly. *The Frisco Detective* was a serial and would appear in weekly segments of several chapters each, extending nearly three months into the new year.

With his parallel careers as a fiction writer, playwright, and actor, author Aiken delivered authentic scenes behind the scenes of the sleazy music hall in *The Frisco Detective*. And with a search by competing parties for the lost heir to "Five Millions of Dollars," the plots split and intertwine all the way to the surprising conclusion.

The Banner Weekly was a "story paper," meaning that it contained a number of serialized stories, overlapped so that readers were held by reading some story segments in every issue. Beadle and Adams were the publishers, and their best writers were available to write the content.

Story papers can be traced back to at least the 1850s, and by the 1880s the format was somewhat standardized to be about eight pages in any size from a large tabloid to the size of a daily newspaper. The Banner Weekly was newspaper sized. Illustrations (originally wood engravings) ornamented the front cover and usually a few pages internally.

The story papers have been described as the 1800s equivalent to prime time television, with certain stories expected to catch the especial interest of certain family members while not offending any of the others. *The Frisco Detective* certainly has some adult situations and was for an adult reader, but like modern prime time television, sexual activity is at most suggested and not portrayed.

About five years after the serialized version of The Frisco Detective appeared in the Banner Weekly, it was published in Beadle's New York Dime Library, complete in the one issue.

Duels between men are featured in several of author Albert W. Aiken's stories. In practice, a man who felt that his honor was impugned in some way by another man could seek redress by asking for a public apology or a duel.

The offended person would typically select a friend as his "second" to make the request of the offender, and to generally look out for the rights of the offended. His request might be made by his second to the offender directly, then the offender would either tender his apology (which could make his professional and social positions untenable), or send his own second to negotiate the details of the duel. The offender in this situation had the right to choose the weapons for the duel.

Years before his presidency, Abraham Lincoln expressed his opinion about an Illinois attorney in a newspaper, and used some very colorful language. The attorney was insulted and sent his second to demand satisfaction.

The choice of weapons was Lincoln's, and considering his long arms, he chose broadswords. The prospect of a gruesome personal battle with medieval weapons may have helped in the negotiations that led to Lincoln's apology being accepted by the offended attorney.

Certainly duels were still fought in the 1880s, but more occasionally than in the years before the American Civil War.

In the early half of the 1800s, there was concern expressed publicly that duels were removing some of the best and brightest from the U.S. population. Laws were passed to the effect that the survivor of a fatal duel would be arrested for murder. In the northern states, the practice was gradually diminishing before the Civil War, but in the southern states it seems that it remained a way for gentlemen to resolve a serious difference.

After the war, the astonishing number of lives lost in the conflict is said to have contributed to a reduced appetite for bloody "satisfaction" on the dueling field. The courts were increasingly the place to seek redress for an offence and duels were rare by the turn of the century in 1900.

The time of *The Frisco Detective* story could be in the early 1870s, but placing some character's ages next to historical events like the 1849 gold rush, makes that less specific.

For the sake of the story, suffice to say that it transpires in the years after San Francisco had matured somewhat as a city and some years before the story was published. Using 1872 as a possible time, $1 in that year would be worth about $21 in 2018. This makes the amount of an inheritance mentioned in The Frisco Detective all the more impressive.

But enough background - one of Albert W. Aiken's most rollicking stories is just a page away!

The Frisco Detective;

or,

The Golden Gate Find.

A Story of Five Millions of Dollars

By Albert W. Aiken
Edited by Mark Williams

CHAPTER I.
A STRANGE GUEST.

San Francisco, on a bright May morning, and the time not over a dozen years ago.

The chief of police was seated in his private office and in bad humor.

Things had not gone as well as they ought to have done.

He had been engaged in a little game of poker at one of the principal hotels until daylight had peeped in through the heavily-curtained window. Either luck had been against him, or else he had "struck" some gamesters who were more expert in handling the "papers" than himself.

Whatever the reason, the chief had quitted the game a heavy loser, and as he happened to be short of money just then, the loss bothered him.

In his embarrassment he had applied to one of the millionaires of the stock market, a man whom it had been in his power to oblige on several occasions, for a "pointer," that he might be able to pick up a few hundreds by

1

an operation in stocks.

But the wise-head replied that a "pointer" of that kind was just what he was after, yet, as far as he could see, the whole bottom had dropped out of the market, and if the chief was wise he would keep out of the speculation. As things looked at that time, he stood far more chance to lose a "few hundred" than to acquire them.

As a rule when the chief of police of such a city as San Francisco is in this fix, he quietly summons the confidential officer who attends to his private business, and who is generally known as the chief's "shadow." The chief tells him that he wants funds, and that individual proceeds to raise it by calling upon the gamblers and such like trades, prohibited by law but flourishing in secret and winked at by official eyes, to "come down."

And "come down" they must, or else the police will suddenly become so active in their particular direction that their business will be ruined.

But in this case this game could not be worked, for, as the shadow recalled to the recollection of the chief, it was only a week since a "pull" had been made in that direction, and as they had all contributed pretty liberally, it would not be expected that they would be able to stand a second draft within so short a time.

The chief assented to this and became more gloomy than ever.

The shadow endeavored to cheer the "boss" by announcing his intention of trying to effect a "loan" from some of the prominent sporting men who might in time come to profit by being in the good graces of the head of the police department.

The chief said that he didn't "take much stock in this way of raising the wind," for his experience had been that when he was short, and wanted to borrow a little money, almost everybody else of his acquaintance was in the same predicament.

This chief of police was called Alexander Kettleton, originally from the East somewhere, but he had been on the Pacific slope so long that he was regarded as a native.

In person he was a rather short, thick-set man, muscularly built, with a big head, and a thick neck.

Kettleton had coarse features and a square, bulldog-like chin, hidden, however, by a tawny beard. But as he wore his hair long and brushed back of the ears after the fashion common to some parts of the southwest, he did not look as ugly as he certainly would have done without these hirsute adornments.

While the chief sat in this decidedly disagreeable mood, one of the policemen who attended to the door entered with the intelligence that a man wanted to see the chief in person upon particular business.

"Oh, bosh!" exclaimed Kettleton, impatiently, "I am sick of these yarns! Every pilgrim in the town that loses his dog or gets his pocket picked thinks that I haven't anything to do but to listen to his story.

"Tell the galoot that I am busy and that you reckon you'll do as well."

"I tried that on him but he wouldn't have it; said that he must see you in person."

"Try and get rid of him, and if you can't, run him in and I will make short work of his request."

The officer retired, and in a few moments ushered in a stranger.

A typical Englishman, round red face, yellow mutton-chop whiskers, a tweed suit, "billy-cock" hat, and the inevitable eye-glasses and umbrella.

"Good-morning, sir! Have I the honor of addressing the chief of police?" the new-comer asked, with a decided English accent.

"Yes, sir, I am the chief," said Kettleton, perceiving at once that this visitor was something out of the common run.

"I have come, sir, to see you on a matter of important business—very important business I may say, don't you know; so, in the first place, allow me to introduce myself.

"My name, sir, is Macarthy, Maximilian Macarthy, specifically, and as you have probably guessed from my appearance I am not an American.

"No, sir, I am an Englishman, don't you see, a Londoner, sir, and I have come to this country on very particular business. As the head police official of this city of San Francisco, I have come to see you in regard to this business."

The Englishman had a rather pompous way with him, but as he was evidently a man of substance and of standing, he impressed the chief favorably.

"Well, sir, I will try to do what I can for you," Kettleton said.

"I come, sir, to San Francisco on an important quest," the Englishman announced. "Of course, sir, you will at once perceive that it must be important when I state that it is solely on account of this business that I have crossed the ocean and journeyed all the way from London to San Francisco."

The chief nodded.

It was his experience that every man who sought his advice thought his business was extremely important.

"I come, sir, to ask your aid to find a child lost here in San Francisco twenty years ago."

"Twenty years ago—that would bring it to about 'fifty-five," said the chief, reflectively. "Yes, sir, that is the date."

"What was the child's name?"

"I am ignorant of that."

The chief looked surprised.

"Again, sir, I must plead my inability to answer."

"Hang it, man, how can you find this lost child when you know nothing about it?"

"The child must be found, for it is heir to five millions of dollars."

01. The Frisco Detective serial began on December 26, 1885, in Banner Weekly Vol. 4, No. 163, and ran to the issue of March 20, 1886. The original size was about 14 inches wide and 21 inches tall.

CHAPTER II.
THE MACARTHY.

The chief of police pricked up his ears immediately at this statement.

"Five millions of dollars, you say?"

"Yes, that is the figure; a very tidy one, is it not?"

"Well, I should smile!" cried Kettleton.

"And as five millions of dollars don't grow on every bush, at least in England, it strikes me that this matter is worth some little trouble."

"Oh, yes, there isn't the least doubt about it, and I shall be pleased to give you all the assistance in my power, although from what little you have said it seems to me that the case is a difficult one."

"I will put you in possession of all the facts, and then, of course, with your large experience, you will be able to judge what is best to be done.

"And, to begin at the beginning—I must state to you a slight portion of my family history."

The chief signified that he would be pleased to listen.

An idea, which seemed to be a particularly brilliant one, had entered his mind.

If his visitor was all right, and there was truth in his story—and certainly he did not appear like a crank—there might be a chance to get some handsome pickings out of the affair.

A job with five millions of dollars in it would stand a good many pulls.

"The Macarthy family," began the stranger, "is a good, old Scotch-Irish race, although we have been domiciled in London for the last hundred years.

"We have been engaged in trade, son succeeding to father, until our house ranks as one of the oldest in the city.

"In fact, I am not boasting when I say that the fame of Macarthy's Peerless Pickles is world wide.

"My grandfather established the house: my father, an only son, succeeded him; but my sire, having two boys, was, when we were growing up, somewhat perplexed about how he should divide the business when the time came for him to retire.

"My brother was named Archibald, and being from early youth a wild, reckless fellow, gave my father a great deal of uneasiness.

"Archibald was three years older than I, and this made the matter worse, for being the eldest my father expected more of him.

"They did not get on together at all, and when Archibald was fifteen years old he ran away from home to seek his fortune. For twenty years no one at home ever heard a word from him, and of course we all came to the conclusion that he was dead.

"In the interim my father paid the debt of nature, and I succeeded to the business. Then, one day, just twenty years from the time that my brother had fled from England, he appeared without any warning, a hearty, bearded, bronze-faced man.

"He had been in the wilds of the New World—had been one of the fortunate gold-seekers, don't you know, and had made a mint of money.

"I of course offered to give him the share of the family property rightly his due, but he laughed at the offer.

"'I am worth millions,' he said, 'and what care I for your paltry thousands and your miserable pickle trade?'

"After a brief visit he returned to America, and for

ten years I neither saw nor heard of him again, and then he made his appearance as abruptly as on the occasion of his first visit.

"But during this interim there had been a great change. He had come back to England a broken-down wreck, the victim of strong drink.

"'I am utterly ruined, and played out,' he said, in his strange way. 'And I have come home to die.'

"With the Macarthys, blood has always been thicker than water," continued the Englishman, with a touch of pride. "And my unfortunate brother did not lack for anything that money could buy to the time of his death, which took place in a short time.

"He was averse to saying anything about what his life had been abroad, except that from great wealth he had suddenly been plunged into the deepest poverty. And in his despair, he had given way to drink and so brought himself to death's door.

"His mind seemed a little affected on this point, and his conversation was vague and incomprehensible at times.

"But on the night of his death, just before the fatal stroke came, his mind seemed to clear.

"He took my hand in his.

"'Brother Max,' he said, 'I have been a wild, reckless fellow, and in my time I have committed some awful sins, and now, as a punishment, I am stricken down right in what should be the prime of my life.

"'There was a poor girl in California whom I have bitterly wronged, and I suppose I am being punished for that crime now, but fortune stood my friend so stanchly in the past that I believed I could do anything and yet escape the consequences of my acts, but it is coming home to me at last.

9

"'When I saw you last I told you that I was worth millions, and so I was, but when I made my strike in the mines, knowing how uncertain all such things were, I invested all I made in land situated in Southern California.

"'It was my ambition to be the greatest cattle-king in the South, and at one time I bid fair to become so; I was on the topmost wave of prosperity, when there came a sudden blow.

"'My title came through the old Spanish land-grants so-called, and one of the sharp Frisco lawyers discovered that there was a flaw in all these old deeds, and so the matter was brought into the courts.

"'A long and weary struggle ensued, but in the end all we cattle men were beaten. At a single blow I was stripped of all that I was worth, and from being able to call myself the owner of millions I was reduced to absolute beggary.

"'When I was thought to be wealthy I could count my friends by the hundreds, but when poverty stared me in the face, the acquaintances who were not ashamed to acknowledge me could be numbered on the fingers of one hand.

"'Then I fell sick; in disgust at the bad fortune which had fallen upon me I had taken to drink, and soon I became a wreck.

"'Penniless and friendless I appealed to the English society known as the Sons of Saint George. They, because I was a brother Englishman, raised a subscription to send me home, so that I might be able to die in my native land.

"'And now, brother Max,' he said, his voice beginning to grow fainter, his strength evidently failing, 'I want you to do an act of justice for me.

"'I have a child in California—a child whom I

abandoned in San Francisco when it was an infant. You must find it, brother, and make amends for its father's cruel neglect. And if you will look after it there is a chance that, with your aid, the fortune I lost may be recovered for my child.

"'According to the terms of the treaty with Mexico, under which Lower California was ceded to the United States, it was agreed that all these old Spanish land-grants should be recognized, and an appeal has been made to Congress to see that the terms of the treaty are respected. But there has been powerful influence brought to bear in the opposite direction by men who were anxious to secure these lands now rendered valuable by the rapid settling up of the country.'"

"Yes, I know all about that," the chief of police remarked, at this point. "Congress has decided that the terms of the treaty must be respected, and under that decision, all those who had claims based on the old Spanish land-grants have been put in possession of their property,

"When I say all, I mean all those who have tried to regain their lands.

"Human nature out here in California is just about the same as it is all over the world, and most people are certain to hold on to what they have got, whether their claim is just or not until they are forced to let go."

"I comprehend that of course," the Englishman remarked.

"But to conclude my recital; my brother asked me to promise that I would see justice done for his child, and I said I would, of course. Under the circumstances it would have been hard for me to say anything else, although for the life of me I didn't see how I was going to leave my business and go off on this wild-goose chase half across the world.

"The moment I gave the promise, the strength which had supported the sick man seemed to suddenly give out, and with a gasp he turned over on his side and died.

"Then, too late, it suddenly occurred to me that I possessed no clew to the child; he had not even said whether it was a boy or girl. All the information that I was in possession of was that he had lost a child in San Francisco some twenty years ago.

"Now I have delayed doing anything about this matter until now, allowing five years to elapse. But at last I have crossed the ocean, and I am determined to find the lost child if such a thing be possible."

"I suppose the reason why you started to take a hand in the game now has nothing to do with the fact that it is only two months ago that Congress passed the law that the old Spanish land-grants must be respected," observed the chief of police, with fine sarcasm.

"Oh, yes, of course that rather impelled me to look into the matter," the other replied, coolly. "Ever since my brother's death I have taken one of the leading New York newspapers, and in that way have kept posted on American affairs.

"It is quite a different matter, you understand, to interest oneself in a child to whom a heritage of five millions of dollars is coming, from spending good cash to hunt up one who will only be a burden to the party who finds him."

"This heir must be about twenty-seven years old now."

"Yes."

"I don't see as I can do anything for you," declared the chief. "It is out of my line entirely. Hire some private detectives to look into the matter. There are plenty in the city who will gladly undertake the job. There isn't anything criminal about the matter, and I can't act."

And with this cold consolation the Englishman was obliged to be content.

But the moment he left the room the manner of the chief changed.

"By Jove! This five-million business is worth looking into!" he cried. "I knew Archibald Macarthy well, and he once was worth the money.

"I'll find that heir if he is on top of this footstool, and then take my whack out of the five millions."

CHAPTER III.
LA BELLE HELENE.

It is near midnight, and yet certain parts of the city of San Francisco are more full of life and business than when the daylight reigns.

It is of the quarters devoted to dissipation and vice that we speak.

One of the most noted resorts on the Pacific slope at the time of these events, was the notorious Bella Union Concert Saloon, a variety theater where all sorts of "spiritual" refreshments were sold openly in the auditorium, while the performance was in progress on the stage.

The entertainment was of the same order as that usually given in variety theaters—singing and dancing by both American and foreign performers, interspersed with feats of strength and agility by circus performers.

But the bright particular star of the variety saloon at the time we introduce this "dive"— for it was nothing more—to the notice of our readers, was a performer who in the announcements of the establishment was heralded as La Belle Helene.

She was a vocalist who was wonderfully popular with the frequenters of the establishment.

"A dainty duck, betcher life on it, and she stands me in two hundred chucks a week," Mister Billy Macduff, the red-faced proprietor of the variety saloon was wont to declare, and then he would supplement the speech with the declaration:

"And she's wu'th every blamed ducat of it, too, fer thar ain't any woman in the world w'ot kin sing with her, and when it comes to beauty, why, she takes the rag off the bush every time!"

There was some foundation for these statements, for the lady possessed an excellent voice, which had been well cultivated, and she had a sweet, sympathetic way with her that went through to the hearts of the rough and decidedly "mixed" audience who patronized the Bella Union.

In person she was a tall, queenly girl, with a well-proportioned form and a beautiful face.

As one of her greatest admirers, the burly manager of the Bella Union, declared:

"She's a lady, too, you kin bet yer boots on it! Got more style to the square inch than any heifer in Californy today, for money!"

By this last rather misty remark meaning that he was willing to wager his loose change upon the truth of his assertion.

She had finely cut, regular features, large dark-brown, almost black eyes, and the most beautiful blonde hair imaginable. Possibly it was this rare combination of dark eyes and light hair, which gave the charm to her face.

She was a lady, too, a girl who had been well brought up. And despite the fact that she sang on the stage in one of the worst places of amusement that could be found in all America, yet she would not permit the slightest familiarity from any one, either performers, officials, or the prominent men who had the right to come behind the scenes.

Like all places of its class the Bella Union boasted an apartment known as the "wine-room," and all performers, both male and female, were expected to sit in the wine-room when not occupied on the stage, so that the patrons of the house might make their acquaintance and invite them to partake of "refreshments."

It cost the patrons of the house a dollar apiece to get into the apartment, and all drinks ordered there were just double price.

The glass of beer, which cost two bits in the auditorium, called for four bits in the wine-room, and everything else in proportion.

The whole idea of the "scheme" was that by payment of these extra charges the patrons of the place were enabled to make the acquaintance and enjoy the society of the artists engaged on the stage.

And it was astonishing what an amount of callow youths and country pilgrims taking in the sights of Frisco were to be found there every night, to say nothing of the sports and the men about town who thought it the "proper caper" to take in the wine-room of the Bella Union.

But, from the first, La Belle Helene wouldn't have anything to do with this apartment.

The way she secured her first engagement at the place was odd in the extreme.

As a rule, the performer who desired an engagement either wrote and enclosed programmes showing what he or she could do, or else applied in person with the programmes as proof that the applicant was an artist and not an amateur.

La Belle Helene came personally, and said she would like to come and sing. When questioned by the manager in regard to where she had "worked," she said frankly that she had never sung in public, but felt sure she could please the audience.

At first Macduff did not know what to make of her, for she was so different from the usual "fool girl who thought she could paralyze the duffers," as the manager was wont to phrase it.

She proposed, too, to sing songs, which to the

experienced "main guy" of the variety show seemed simply ridiculous--"The Last Rose of Summer," " Home, Sweet Home," and "sich trash."

He told her without the least hesitation that the audience would guy the life out of her, but as she smiled in disdain, Macduff, nettled by her apparent contempt for his judgment, told her he "was willing to risk it if she was, and she might go on and sing that very evening if she chose."

She promptly replied that she was quite ready.

Rehearsal was just about at an end, and the manager sent word for the leader to wait, as he wished to see him.

Then when the stage was unoccupied he conducted the girl and introduced her to the leader as a "party" that would do a turn that night.

The musician, a fat, middle-aged Englishman, was a man of fine ability, but so wedded to the love of liquor that to conduct the orchestra of a variety theater at a miserable salary was the best he could do. He looked rather askance at the new-comer.

The conductor had had the usual experience of all leaders with amateurs, who, when they break down or make a failure in any way, always try to throw the entire blame on the music.

But, after trying the songs with the girl, he saw that she was different from the usual run.

Although she was dressed very plainly, not displaying any of the little trinkets that young ladies delight to wear, yet to his experienced judgment it was evident that she was very much of a lady. And what was more, she had a fine musical education as well as being possessed of more than the usual musical abilities.

"I think you will pull through all right, my dear," he said, with the easy, unconscious familiarity that comes from the stage life.

"The boys will probably guy you a little, but you mustn't mind them; the down-stairs will stand it if the gallery won't.

"The gang that comes here knows what music is when they hear it, rough as they are, so keep a stiff upper lip, and I will do the best I can to pull you through."

"Thank you," the girl had replied. "I am singing that I may live, and a mortal will struggle hard for life, although oftentimes death perhaps would be a welcome boon."

And, bowing to the manager, she departed.

"She's a rum one, eh, Uncle John?" asked Macduff of the veteran leader.

"Yes, rather odd."

"I expect the boys will make a holy show of her to-night!"

"Well, sir, you can't most always generally tell," the musician replied, placing his violin carefully in its box. It was the only treasure that he possessed.

"It may be that she'll hit 'em. The girl can sing, and these little simple songs sometimes catch an audience, and as we have never had anything of the kind in the place the novelty may take."

"Oh, you're getting clean off your nut," was the manager's contemptuous comment.

"I'll bet you ten dollars to one that the boys guy her off the stage before she gets half-way through one song. Come and have a drink to clear your brain."

That night the girl came to the theater ready to go on, and when the stage manager discovered that she hadn't any stage costumes, but intended to go on in her plain black street dress his amazement was great.

The stage-director was a veteran actor, Jack Batcliff

by name, whom cruel fortune had condemned to the stage management of the variety dive. Like most of the regular actors, he was disposed to do what he could for the debutante.

"Well, if you haven't got any dress you'll have to go on in that, of course, but it will knock blazes out of your act," he grumbled. "But you must have some paint on your face!"

"Oh, no, I would rather not, please," she replied.

"But you must. You don't understand; it isn't to make you look any prettier—you are good-looking enough—but the yellow glare of the footlights causes a death-like pallor in your face, and without a little vermilion on your cheeks you will look like a ghost! So come in here, and I'll fix you in a twinkling."

The stage-manager had a little room right off the stage, and as the girl stood in the doorway, he put the vermilion on with a hare's foot, causing her pale cheeks to assume the rosy blush of health.

"There, now, you'll do. Here, take this roll of music to carry in your hand," and he rolled up a piece of music, which was lying on his dressing-table, and placed it in her hands.

"I will have to announce you to-night, for your turn is not on the programme. How shall I word it—what is your name?'

"My name—" and the girl hesitated, while a vivid flush came over her face.

It was plain that this was a contingency she had not expected.

"Yes, I've got to give your name to the audience when I announce your turn!" the old man exclaimed, testily. "I can't say, 'Ladies and gentlemen, I will now have the pleasure of introducing Miss Nobody in a bouquet of pleasing melodies to your notice.' That will not do at all, you know."

"Oh, I cannot give my real name!" the girl replied.

"Take any one then, quick!"

"My middle name is Helene."

"Capital, Jack!" exclaimed a young man who was lounging in the wing. "Say La Belle Helene, from the Folly Theater, Paris, the world-renowned French vocalist!"

The delighted audience began to "chuck" pieces of money upon the stage, both silver and gold.

02. The delighted audience began to "chuck" pieces of
money upon the stage, both silver and gold.

CHAPTER IV.
A JACK OF ALL TRADES.

The bell rang for the next turn, and before the girl could open her mouth to object the old actor was on the stage and the announcement was delivered.

There was a hum of applause in the house, for of all audiences in the United States, those of San Francisco are most prone to welcome strangers warmly—especially those from abroad with European reputations.

The stage-manager, like an old actor, was quick to perceive the temper of the audience, and he saw that the announcement had "caught them," to use the common phrase, and on the spur of the moment he ventured a few more words.

"It gives me great pleasure to announce that this is the first appearance in any theater in America of the sweet singer upon whose silver notes kings and emperors have hung with delight," he continued.

"This great and incomparable artist is engaged at a salary which is the largest ever paid by any theater in the United States for a single turn, which is all she will consent to do. One hundred dollars a night in gold, and the money has to be deposited in the bank every morning before her manager will allow her to rehearse her songs.

"And now, ladies and gentlemen, I will leave this beautiful stranger to the kind consideration of this audience which is noted the world over for its hospitality and justice!"

Amid a storm of applause from the gallery, which highly appreciated such bombastic stuff, the stage-manager bowed himself off, only to be collared in the wing by the infuriated Macduff, fairly purple in the face with rage.

"You blessed idiot! Now you've gone and done it!" he exclaimed. "If she is a duffer and no good, they'll tear the blamed place down after sich a lay-out as that!"

By this time the girl was on the stage and was welcomed in the most hearty manner.

The strangeness of her plain black dress, unrelieved by a single ornament, so different from the usual gaudy attire worn by the so-called, serio-comics—as the lady vocalists are termed professionally—seemed to the minds of the audience to carry out the idea of her foreign origin, and then her rare personal beauty made a profound impression upon them.

As it happened, her features being strongly marked, she had what is called a good stage face.

She was not a "fraud" or a "duffer," as the manager in his terse way had expressed it, but a most excellent vocalist, far surpassing any one who had ever trod the boards of the Bella Union, and the success she achieved was great.

The house rose en masse at the end of her first song, and never had the walls of the place listened to a more tumultuous recall.

And then when she sung the simple melody of "Home, Sweet Home," the house was hushed into such a profound stillness that a pin might have been heard to drop.

The applause at the end of the second song was even greater than that which had attended the first, and the singer was obliged to repeat it.

Nor was the audience satisfied when this was done, and in the midst of the storm of applause, Batcliff was obliged to lead the lady upon the stage and explain to the enthusiastic people that, as the vocalist had only rehearsed two songs, it was impossible for her to reply to any more encores, but if they would excuse her tonight on the following evening she would be prepared to respond.

And then, in the glorious fashion common to the audiences of the Pacific slope—a fashion which came in vogue in the old flash mining days and had not entirely disappeared—the delighted auditors began to "chuck" pieces of money upon the stage, both silver and gold, but no nickel or copper, for the proud people of the Pacific slope reject in disdain the baser metals.

The pair upon the stage retreated from the footlights when the shower began, and when it ended, the stage-manager, in obedience to the demands of the audience, gathered the money in his handkerchief, and presented it, with a low bow, to the singer, who was amazed at this novel bouquet.

Then, bowing their acknowledgments, the pair passed from the stage, and the bell rung for the next act to go on.

"By hookey, my dear, I'll bet a week's salary that you have got at least fifty dollars in this haul, and that is the biggest thing of the kind I have known in years, for this sort of thing has been going out of date lately."

Macduff was in waiting, all excitement, for he now understood what a prize he had in the young girl.

"Batcliff, draw up a contract at once with La Belle Helene for one month with the privilege of another at my option," exclaimed Macduff, laying hold of the stage-manager and fairly pushing him in his room.

"Fifty dollars a week, usual performances, and twenty-five per cent on all wine room business!"

Batcliff was hustled into his room and toward his

desk, Macduff at his back, while the girl following, still flushed with her triumph, halted on the threshold of the room.

"Charge him two hundred dollars per week and no wine-room business at all," the young man who had suggested the name of La Belle Helene said in the ear of the girl. "I can get that sum for you if he will not give it, but he will."

The girl was no innocent child, but one who had seen a deal of the world. She knew that the counsel that had been given her was good, and she adopted it at once.

Macduff was amazed. The girl was worth the money to him, but he fancied that, with such a novice as she was, he could make his own terms.

He expostulated, but she was firm, and finally he gave way and the contract was signed.

"You are throwing away twenty-five or fifty dollars a week by not going into the wine-room," he groaned.

But on this point she was decided, and so it happened that the patrons of the saloon were debarred the privilege of making the acquaintance of La Belle Helene at so much per drink.

But, in such a place, it was impossible for the girl to keep from being introduced to strangers. There was a certain set who had the right of entree behind the scenes—friends of the manager, influential politicians, city officials, men high in the police department, members of the "press" gang, and such like.

All these persons were well dressed—were supposed to be gentlemen, whether they were or not—and the girl was obliged to treat them politely when they were introduced to her.

But, out of them all there was only one man with

whom she was at all familiar, and that was the young fellow who had given her such good advice on the night when she first made her appearance in public.

And an odd sort of a fellow this young man was, too.

He was called Andrew De Lormé. It was said that he was from the East, and was supposed to be a graduate of one of the great Eastern colleges, although no one knew anything certain about this, for when questioned upon this point he always evaded answering.

One thing was certain; he had a most excellent education, having Greek end Latin as well as three or four modern tongues, at his command.

By profession he was a lawyer; by occupation a journalist; and in reality he was a jack-of-all-trades, who did not make much at any of them.

Yet he could discover the fine points of a difficult law case, and argue the matter to the satisfaction of judge and jury better than nine-tenths of the lawyers who made boast of their excellent practice.

He could write an editorial that would go as straight to the mark as a bullet from a crack sharpshooter's gun; he hashed up a column of wit that would pass muster with ease, and in an emergency could throw off a poem full of the true ring of poetry.

In this line he had once written a thirty-minute burlesque of a popular play which had been a great "go" at the Bella Union, and though he generously let Macduff off with a champagne supper for the "boys" in lieu of payment, yet ever after he had the free run of the theater.

Andy De Lormé, as every one called him, was a genius. There wasn't any two ways about that; and, like a great many other geniuses in this life, he had some besetting sins, which seemed likely to prevent him from ever making any good use of the glorious gifts, which Dame Nature had bestowed upon him.

He was a hard drinker, liked the excitement of gambling, and, apparently, totally lacked the application necessary to enable a man to do hard work in any particular direction.

But he seemed to be a lucky fellow, and though he never appeared to do much work, yet he contrived to make money enough to rub along in a comfortable manner.

His intimacy with La Belle Helene was a source of annoyance to the other suitors who sought her smiles; and yet De Lormé told the truth when he said that he had nothing to boast of.

"I am just dead in love with the girl," he was wont to say in his frank way, "but upon my word I do not think she cares the snap of her finger for me.

"She makes a convenience out of me, and that is all. I escort her home at night from the theater because she doesn't like to go alone. She graciously permits me to pay for a supper or a buggy for her once in a while, and that is all the good it does me.

"No, no, the prize is not yet mine—the race is open to all who desire to try their luck!"

On this night of which we write, De Lormé as usual waited for the actress.

She lived on a small side street about a mile away from the theater, and as it was a lonely walk, it was not strange that she was glad of the young man's escort.

It was after eleven when the two set out.

La Belle Helene had now begun upon her second month at the theater, and her success was as great as ever, the audience never seeming to tire of her songs.

She could boast of jewelry now, for, with a woman's love for such things, she had bought trinkets. And then, too, admirers, known and unknown had laid their offerings at her feet.

In going to and from the theater she carried her treasures in her hand-bag, and De Lormé had often told her that the custom would lead to their being waylaid by footpads some night.

And though he spoke only in jest, on this particular occasion his words came true, for, on turning the corner of the street in which the vocalist lived, two disguised men sprang out in the way and the ominous words, "Hands up!" rang out on the air.

THE FRISCO DETECTIVE

BY ALBERT W. AIKEN

"Hallo, hallo! what does this mean?" De Lorme demanded.

03. "Hallo, hallo! What does this mean?" De Lormé demanded.

CHAPTER V.
AN OLD ACQUAINTANCE.

The fellows were two slouchy-looking customers, shabbily dressed.

The street was deserted; not a person was within sight: not even the sound of a distant footfall broke on the stillness of the night.

"Hallo, hallo! What does this mean?" De Lormé demanded.

He did not throw up his hands in obedience to the command, for the lady's arm was interlocked with his, and in the other he carried his sachel.

"W'ot does it mean? Ain't it plain enuff to you, boss?" cried the taller of the ruffians, who, by his assuming the rôle of spokesman, seemed to be the leader.

"We are toll-gatherers, we are, and we are axing you perlitely for to shell out, and if you don't do it to onc't, we shall be obligated to drill some holes right through you, warranted for to keep open till the grave-worms fills 'em up."

"Well, really, my friend, as far as I am concerned you have waked up the wrong passenger unless you will be content with a sum of money representing about four bits," De Lormé remarked.

"To blazes with your four bits!" cried the ruffian, in disgust. "W'ot sort of cattle do you take us for, anyway? Do we look like four-bit men? Nary a time!

"We are on the biggest kind of a lay-out! We don't trouble our heads with any sich small-fry as you are, anyway. This hyer gal is our antelope, and we are jist arter the little diamonds that sparkle so on her neck and in her ears, every night.

"My pard and I have blowed in a good many dollars at the Bella Union for to see the show, and now, as turn about is only fair play, we want a hack at the profits. The sparklers are in that 'ere bag, I take it, so jest have the kindness to hand it over."

"Oh, certainly! Of course! Anything to oblige so persuasive a gentleman," and, as he spoke, De Lormé extended the hand which grasped the bag toward the ruffian.

Thrown off his guard by this seeming prompt surrender, the ruffian advanced to take it, changing his revolver into his left hand, but as he did so, with a sudden spring, De Lormé darted forward and caught the man around the middle, before he had any chance to use his revolver.

At the same moment, out came the hand of La Belle Helene, which she had thrust within her cloak at the first sign of danger. In her hand was a revolver, a double-acting tool, as it proved, for without stopping to raise the hammer, she leveled it at the second ruffian and fired.

The bullet whistled within a half an inch of his ear, so near that he thought it had winged him. This circumstance took all the fight out of him, for without waiting to see what was to be the fate of his comrade; he turned and ran for dear life.

The other ruffian was made of sterner stuff, and he struggled like a professional wrestler when gripped so stoutly by De Lormé.

Although a bigger man, weighing fully twenty-five or thirty pounds more than his antagonist the footpad yet was no stronger, and in no respect was he a match for the ex-college athlete.

He found himself in a grip of steel, and as there was no chance to shoot this Bohemian champion, he endeavored to use the revolver to club his opponent's head.

But with a sudden twist he was lifted bodily from the ground and thrown upon his back, his adversary dexterously adding his weight to the fall.

The concussion sent the revolver flying from the toll-gatherer's hand, and he was now at De Lormé's mercy.

The young man took advantage of the footpad's stupor from the shock of the fall, to plant his knee upon the breast of the fallen man and take him by the throat.

"Gosh!" cried the ruffian, opening his eyes after a moment, and staring into the face of the victor—"cuss me if you ain't 'bout cracked my head!"

"Well, who began this, anyway?"

"I reckon you have ended it, pard, no matter who began it," the fellow replied ruefully. "Yes, it does look a little that way now."

"And that 'tarnal hound has cut and run, I suppose, and left me for to bear all the blame," the rough remarked, seeing that his companion had managed to disappear.

"Yes, he has deserted—a firm believer evidently in the old couplet:

"'He who fights and runs away may live to fight another day.'"

"Say, Andy, what are you going to do with me?" the fellow asked, abruptly.

"Hallo, hallo! So you know me, eh?"

"Oh, yes, I've seen you before."

"And now I look at you it seems to me that your face is familiar."

"Oh, yes; you kin jest bet on that! I'm an old pard of yourn, Andy; so I hope you'll jest let up on me this time.

"I sw'ar if I hadn't been strapped clear down to

bed-rock I never would have thought of going for an old pard; but, Andy, I wish I may die if I had a cent to brace up on, and I happened to run across that durned galoot who war in the same box. He jest laid out this riffle, and then the moment thar's a hitch in the programme, cuss me if he warn't a-trainin' for a foot-race.

"I tell yer, Andy, sich an ugly deal as this ain't been rung in on yer humble servant to command for a dog's age."

"Oh, that is a likely story!" the young man exclaimed, "you have fallen by the wayside, and lay all the blame on your comrade. I haven't the least doubt that if he had been captured instead of you he would have tried to get out of the scrape by throwing all the blame on you!"

"Sart'in he would, durned miser'ble hound. That is the kind of a yellow dog he is."

"Call the police and hand the fellow over to them!" exclaimed the lady, wearying of the conversation. "Either one of the wretches would have shot us in a moment, if by so doing they could have succeeded in their purpose, so don't have any mercy upon him. I wouldn't!"

Cruel and vindictively came the words from the beautiful lips, and the young man looked up in astonishment, for this was a new and unexpected phase in her character.

"No, don't, Andy, old pard! Don't do it for sake of old times!" the ruffian pleaded. Don't mind w'ot she says; she is only a fool woman, and w'ot do women know, anyhow?"

"'Only fit to comb their hair and look at themselves in brooks,'" quoted De Lormé. "'Were I a god and had a world to make, I'd make no women.'"

"Neither would I! Durned set of cats; allers getting

men into trouble!" the ruffian said. "I've seen more good men fixed for planting in mining-camps all on account of some yaller-haired heifer like this one than you could shake stick at in a week."

The words struck De Lormé ominously.

Was this rough fellow a prophet?

"I say, Andy, lemme go, and I'll do as much for you some time; honest Injun, I will. Say! Don't you remember when up in the Feather River country how you got me off for hoss-stealing onc't?"

"Scotty Bilk, as I'm a sinner!" ejaculated De Lormé, releasing him and rising.

The rough was quick to jump to his feet.

His first act was to secure his revolver.

"Can't travel without weapons in this country, you know," he said, with a grin. "So long! Much obliged! See you ag'in some time, and you, too, 'betcher life!" He scowled as he addressed the girl, then hastened away.

CHAPTER VI.
AN INVITATION.

"You acted very foolishly in letting that wretch go!" she exclaimed, as she looked regretfully at the figure of the tall ruffian fast disappearing in the gloom of the night.

"Oh, no; I think not," he replied carelessly. "Of what possible use would it have been to have given the fellow up to the hands of justice?

"He would have been tried, and you and I would have had to appear in court as witnesses against him. It would have been a terrible bother."

"On the contrary, I think I should have enjoyed it," she replied as she took his arm and they again proceeded on their way.

"It would have been a capital advertisement," she continued. "Yes, an excellent advertisement for me; and then, you could have made a burlesque out of it for the Bella Union, and I could have played the principal part."

He shook his head.

"Oh, no; no more burlesque for me."

"But you wrote one once; a great success it was, too, they say; but, perhaps I am not as pretty as the woman for whom you wrote the principal part," she suggested with a sly glance at his face.

"Oh, yes; you are a far prettier woman in every way, but my burlesque didn't seem to bring her lack, for in it she managed to fascinate the man whom she afterward married.

"He was a jealous brute. It wasn't any of his business what love affairs the girl had had as long as he was willing to condone the past by marrying her.

"She led a dog's life after the marriage, for when he

got in liquor, he always became jealous and beat her," and the hands of the speaker involuntarily clinched, while a peculiar glint of fire shone in the usually quiet eyes.

"Not a word of complaint ever escaped her lips, for she really loved the beast, and thought she could never do enough to reward him for having married her, a stage beauty against whom some ugly scandal had been whispered; but she drooped, and sunk, day by day, until at last she died.

"And that very night, in the midst of a crowded saloon, he had the insolence to boast 'that his beauty was now in her grave beyond the reach of her lovers.'

"The taunt was intended for a single man in that crowded room—a quiet, easy-going fellow, who, since his advent in San Francisco, had never even seen a blow struck, much less been mixed up in any personal quarrels.

"But, the words had hardly left the mouth of the boaster, who was a professed duelist, and proud of recounting the number of men whom he had killed, when a glass tumbler shattered itself on his teeth, gashing the lips which had so cruelly defamed the dead.

"Pistols were out in a moment—the two men were not twenty feet apart—it looked certain that neither one could escape a mortal wound.

"Both pulled at the same time, but the bully's pistol missed fire, and the bullet of the avenger cut his heart in twain.

"It was a fair fight; there were plenty of witnesses to the affair, and public opinion was so strongly against the bully that, when the case came before the courts, the slayer was acquitted on the ground that he had acted in self-defense, without even the jury taking the trouble to leave their seats.

"But the disturbance all sprung from my burlesque, and therefore I shall write no more."

"You were the man, too, who avenged the insult flung upon the dead," said the girl, who had listened with a great deal of interest to the sad story.

"Oh, no; there isn't anything of the duelist about me."

"No use for you to deny it, for some of the women at the theater told me the story, and congratulated me upon having a lover who was not only willing but able to take care of my reputation."

"Well, I am glad that there are some who believe that you favor me, because I don't. And as the interested party, I ought to know something about it," he observed, with a grimace.

"Well, don't you consider yourself my lover?"

"As far as I am concerned, it is no doubt true enough, but you don't look upon me in that light."

"I certainly do," the girl declared. "Is there any other gentleman whose attentions I receive or permit? Do you not act as my escort at all times?"

"Oh, yes; I play the lackey to perfection," he replied, dryly.

By this time they were at the door of the house where the girl dwelt. It was a small, two-storied dwelling, occupied by a widow lady with a half-grown boy, who took in the boarder to aid a small income.

"And since you have played the lackey, as you term it," she said, mimicking his tone, "your wages have been sadly in arrears, but it is not too late to make amends.

"Shut your eyes for a moment."

He obeyed the command, not knowing exactly what to expect, so capricious was her humor.

Then he felt a pair of soft arms close around his neck, and a couple of moist lips pressed a long, lingering kiss upon his mouth.

The close contact of the woman he believed he loved should have intoxicated him with joy, but it did not, for some subtle instinct seemed to whisper that it was not a true caress, springing from the heart, but a false one, intended to deceive.

But, for all that, he was but man; so he returned the kiss, and drawing the girl to him pressed her closely to his heart.

"Now, then, do you believe that I love you just a little?" she whispered.

"Yes, just a little," he repeated.

"And it depends upon yourself whether that little will grow to be more or not," she said, just a little petulantly, as though his repetition of her speech annoyed her.

"But now, having given one proof, I will give you another. I am hungry, and I will let you come in and have supper with me if you will provide the viands," she continued.

"I want some fried oysters and some champagne. There is a saloon at the corner where you can get both. I will spread the table in the dining-room, and be all ready when you return.

"Mrs. Briggs and her hopeful are sound asleep long ago, and as their rooms are up-stairs, we will not disturb them. We can enjoy a delightful tete-à-tete and no one will be the wiser.

"I have the latch-key and the dining-room is right here, so I can watch for you and let you in when you come back.

"Hurry, now, for I am as hungry as can be."

"'I'll put a girdle round the earth in forty minutes!'" quoted the young man, and with a pigeon-wing he immediately set out to where the lights of the saloon at the corner shone out on the pavement.

The girl watched him for a moment, as he hurried down the street, before she entered the house.

"I sometimes think I do not know this man," she murmured, communing with herself. "Has he two characters? Is this which I have seen his real or his assumed one?

"A light-hearted, foolish fellow, so careless with his money that any one almost can have it for the asking—a man of genius, yet who seems incapable of any serious work. He drinks, too, more than is good for him, so they say, and yet I have never detected that he had been over-indulging in stimulants.

"A gambler, too, I am told; a man who nightly sees the gray light of the dawn creep in through the curtained windows. But when I meet him in the morning, no matter how early, he seems as fresh as a daisy.

"And then, that story of standing almost breast to breast with the duelist who was the terror of all San Francisco, courting almost certain death—how does it agree with this butterfly of a man who is a better authority on a woman's dress than any modiste I have ever seen? To-night, too, how quickly and easily he overthrew the ruffian who looked to be a match for a man twice his size!

"And now comes the most important question of all: will he do as I want him?

"Is this love which he professes to feel for me strong enough to carry him through all the obstacles in the path until the goal of success is reached?

"That is a question which I must have answered ere this night is over, and I will know the truth, too, if 'woman's witchery' is of any avail."

Then her thoughts took on a lighter cast as a sudden idea came to her.

"Here I have sent him to get oysters and champagne, and I do not believe the fellow has a dollar in his pocket! In fact, he said at the theater that he was reduced to his last four-bit piece."

And she laughed heartily at the idea.

"Well, I suppose he will arrange the matter somehow, though I haven't the least idea how, for I do not believe he is acquainted in the neighborhood."

And, musing over the dilemma into which her request had plunged the young man, she entered the house.

A small lamp was always left burning on the dining-room table for her accommodation, but placing this on one side, as well as the cold lunch which was always set out for her—she paid a liberal sum for board, and the landlady did everything in her power to make her comfortable—she proceeded to arrange the table for the "little supper" soon to come.

Following the footsteps of Andrew De Lormé, he went on happily enough until he arrived at the saloon, and then just as he was about to enter a sudden thought occurred to him.

"Oysters and champagne!" he muttered. "Champagne and oysters, and all I've got in my pocket is a single half-dollar! Four bits won't go far for such a lay-out as this!"

CHAPTER VII.
A NOVEL PROPOSITION.

It was a rather awkward position.

As the young man justly observed, fifty cents will not go far toward providing an oyster supper for two, with champagne attachments.

"Let me be certain there isn't any mistake about this matter," De Lormé soliloquized, as he halted outside of the saloon which was restaurant and bar-room combined. "Let me be sure I haven't a ten-dollar bill stowed away somewhere in the recesses of my clothing.

"It is possible, of course, that I might have put such a trifle away and forgot all about it, although the odds are about a thousand to one against such an event. Ten-dollar bills are not so plentiful with me that I would be apt to stow one away and forget all about it."

The conclusion at which De Lormé had arrived was correct, for an exhaustive search only revealed the four-bit piece.

"Clearly, then, the committee on ways and means must meet and deliberate," mused the young man.

"Now, if this was one of the regular shebangs where I am known and the color of my money has been often seen, there wouldn't be much trouble in 'hanging' the man up; but as near as I can remember, this fellow is a perfect stranger to me. In fact, I don't think I was ever in his place even to get a drink, so it would be a pretty cheeky thing to attempt to get the gentle barkeeper to chalk it down."

By this time De Lormé had arrived at a point, which commanded a view of the interior of the saloon.

It was a small place but neatly fitted up, and a

red-faced, black-mustached, short-haired, bulldog-looking man was behind the bar.

"Looks, like the proprietor in person," the young man mused, "and as far as outward appearance goes he seems likely to be a tough customer to deal with.

"Really, it appears to me that this is going to be as tough a job as I have tackled lately.

"Business is apparently a little quiet with him, too, and that will not make him better humored; but the riffle must be made, so here goes!"

De Lormé strode into the saloon with as confident an air as though he had the Bank of California at his back.

The proprietor—the young man was right in his conjecture that the short-haired individual was the owner of the place—laid aside the newspaper he had been reading and rose to attend to him.

"Got any good champagne?" asked De Lormé, leaning upon the counter and nodding as familiarly to the man as though he had known him all his life.

At the time of which we write—in the old flush days of the Golden State when everybody made money easily and as easily spent it—champagne was "on draught" in every saloon that amounted to anything, and a glass of it cost no more than a mug of beer.

Beer and brandy, champagne and whisky, all sold for the same price over the counter—two bits a glass.

"Oh, yes; I keep as good brand of fiz as you kin scare up anywhere in the city—Moet and Chandon, Krug and The Widow," answered the other, with the alacrity of the experienced barkeeper.

"Well the best there is, is good enough for me, so give me a glass of Krug," replied De Lormé, in his easiest way.

The proprietor set the speaker down for a "thoroughbred," and made haste to fill out his wine-glass.

De Lormé watched the straw-colored liquid as it foamed into the tapering glass with a great deal of satisfaction. Its delicious perfume rising on the air was incense to the altar of Bacchus.

"Do me the honor of taking a glass with me," the young Bohemian said, with a courtly bow and as much deference as though he was one of the bonanza-kings before whose shrine all California was bowing.

"I reckon you will have to excuse me, for I seldom drink behind the bar," replied the proprietor, who however, felt flattered by the attention.

"'There are exceptions to all rules, you know," returned De Lormé, persuasively. "It is late, and a single glass of wine can't harm you, particularly such glorious nectar as this, for there isn't a headache to a basket."

"Right you are!" exclaimed the other, stimulated by the manner of the young man. "It is my favorite tipple when I drink anything, and, seeing that it is you, I don't mind if I do try a glass."

The beaker filled, De Lormé exclaimed:

"To our better acquaintance!"

They drained the glasses.

This ceremony performed, the Bohemian cast his half-dollar on the counter with the air of a man who was rolling in wealth.

"Have another with me!" cried the proprietor, inclined to be sociable, and before the young man could open his mouth either to accept or reject, the glasses were filled.

"Many happy returns of the day!" exclaimed the saloonist.

De Lormé made due salutation, and the sparkling

wine disappeared.

"Let me see, you have oysters here?" remarked the caller, looking around him with a reflective air.

"Yes, sir, tip-top ones—as good as you can find in the city."

"Is it too late to get a fry?"

"Oh, no; my order-cook is on duty all night. This shebang never closes, you know. We do an all-night trade. There is a lot of sporting-houses around the corner on the next street, and the sharps drop in at all hours to get a bite."

De Lormé was as well posted in regard to resorts of this class as any man in San Francisco, and remembered that a half a dozen of the largest gaming-houses in the city were in the near neighborhood.

"Aha, I have made a mistake," he mused to himself.

"I ought not have put this four-bit piece in here. I should have gone to the cheap house where they generally play a pretty square game and bought a couple of two-bit checks.

"I might have played a lucky game and come out fifty ahead, in fifteen or twenty minutes, but it is too late now, and I must play this gentleman for all he is worth."

"Would you care to try a few oysters?" asked the proprietor, noticing that the young man looked around him as if irresolute. "They are prime; I can recommend them."

"Well, I rather think I will try some. The fact is, I have a lady friend in this neighborhood whom I have just brought home from the theater, and I was just thinking that a few oysters and a bottle or two of champagne would be agreeable to her."

"You bet!" cried the proprietor, tersely. "I reckon that would be a regular surprise-party."

Albert W. Aiken

"The trouble is that that lay-out is rather an expensive one and I am not as flush as I might be," De Lormé remarked in a reflective sort of way. "But, I will tell you what I will do: I will throw the dice with you to see who pays for it."

The saloon-keeper leaned back and stared in amazement at the young man.

"Well, sport, you are a thoroughbred and no mistake!" he exclaimed. "Let me see, oysters a dollar—two bottles of pop—quarts I suppose?"

"Of course; what good is a small bottle to a thirsty man?"

"Champagne ten dollars; total eleven dollars; and you want me to chuck dice for a lay-out like that?"

"Certainly; what is the use of always playing a picayune game? Make the stake large enough to be interesting once in a while."

"Hang me if I haven't got the sand to go you!" cried the proprietor, abruptly, producing the dice.

"Will you take the first hack?"

"Oh, no; you lead out; age before beauty any day in the week."

"You're a rustler, and no mistake. Three throws?"

"Three," responded De Lormé.

"I'm the worst man to tackle with the dice you ever ran across," the other remarked, as he rattled the ivory cubes in the box.

And he made the boast good, too, by throwing forty-two.

"Aha! How is that for high?" the saloonkeeper exclaimed, in great glee, as the final throw was counted.

"That is pretty good," De Lormé replied. "I have seen diamond pins, and watches, and all sorts of valuable articles won by a no better throw."

"I believe you," the saloonist exclaimed, in exultation.

"A man would be safe in betting about two to one that you will not beat that figure."

"I'll take up that dare in tens, fifties or hundreds!" De Lormé exclaimed, promptly.

"No, you don't!" the other immediately replied.

"You have got me in pretty deep now, and I want you to understand that I don't propose to go into it by the wholesale. Enough is as good as a feast, but the dice are yours."

De Lormé tried his luck, and, to the amazement of the other, threw forty-four.

"The game is yours!" the saloonist exclaimed, and then immediately gave orders to prepare the oysters.

And when the lunch was ready, all arranged neatly in a basket, the host offered to send it; but De Lormé preferred to take it himself, for if its destination was known it might give rise to gossip.

So after another glass of champagne at the expense of the host, off he set.

But fate did not design that he should reach the presence of the beautiful woman who had fascinated him without accident.

As he proceeded down the street he encountered four young men, all a little the worse for liquor, who immediately called upon him to halt.

CHAPTER VIII.
AN UNEQUAL CONTEST.

"Hallo, sport! Come to anchor and give an account of yourself!" cried one of the four, the moment they came within hailing distance of De Lormé.

The Bohemian recognized the style of the newcomers immediately.

Four young men about town—would-be "bloods"— out on a spree, who considered it fine sport to take advantage of their numbers to have some fun with the stranger, particularly when they discovered that he carried a basket.

De Lormé was one of the quietest fellows in the world, and would gladly have avoided an encounter of this kind. But under the circumstances it was impossible for him to get out of the way, for coming abruptly around a corner, they were on him almost before he was aware.

The only way to avoid an encounter was to take to his heels and run—a proceeding not to be thought of for a moment.

"What have you got in that basket?" cried a second one of the young men, and the third, catching a glimpse of the protruding necks of the champagne bottles, called out:

" 'Fore Heaven, boys, this is the richest kind of a find! Gen'lemen, just cast your optics on those suspicious articles sticking out of the basket. If we haven't struck a bonanza then I am a Dutchman."

At this there was a yell of delight from all the young men.

To their befuddled wits it seemed to be the richest kind of a joke to relieve the stranger of the bottles.

De Lormé saw that he was in for a row, and that there was no way of avoiding it. So, in order to prevent himself from being surrounded, he placed his back against a dead wall and set the basket down at his feet.

"Gentlemen, if you do not go on and mind your own business you are liable to fetch up in a police court," he observed.

There was a howl of derision from the revelers at this warning.

"Police court!" exclaimed the one who had first spoken. "Why, I say, young feller, you don't know what you are talking about. We are the police."

"You bet! Detectives, every mother's son of us!" cried the second.

"I see you don't recognize me," added the third. "I am the chief of police, in person."

"You are a liar!" exclaimed the fourth, with scant ceremony. "I am Alex Kettleton, and you are a fraud!"

"It is my idea that you are all so drunk you don't know who you are, and if you will take my advice you will get home and to bed as soon as possible. All of you will have an attack of the big head in the morning."

"Oh, I will have to pull your nose so as to teach you manners!" the first blood exclaimed, shaking his fist in the face of De Lormé.

"You go in and pull his nose, Ed, and we'll go for the basket!" added the second.

"If you fellows don't clear out and mind your own business, I will whip all four of you!" the Bohemian threatened.

Again they laughed derisively, and then the young man who had acted as the leader of the party exclaimed:

"Now then, boys, we will close in on him altogether, and use him to wipe up the sidewalk.

Albert W. Aiken

"One, two, three, bounce!"

And, simultaneously, the four made a rush for De Lormé.

But their very numbers interfered with the success of their plans, for of course they got in each other's way, and the manner in which the Bohemian handled them was amusing.

A trained boxer—as good an amateur with his fists as all San Francisco could boast—his arms shot out with the regularity of the piston-rod of an engine.

Blood number one, who was in the advance, received a right-hander on the chin that seemed fairly to drive his jaw in, and over backward he tumbled.

Number two caught De Lormé's left fist between the eyes, and as he, too, sought a reclining position.

The other two, dismayed at the reception that their comrades had received, halted, but it was too late. They were within distance, and each one got a "facer," which sent them reeling back in some disorder.

The fallen men rose to their feet, all idea of trying any more conclusions at the game of fisticuffs with the man whom they had fancied would prove to be such an easy prey completely gone.

But the leader of the four was more game than his fellows, and, although he had received by far the severest punishment, yet he burned for revenge.

He thrust his hand into his pistol-pocket and drew a revolver, an ugly little weapon, carrying a heavy ball.

But De Lormé understood what he was up to, and was prepared. No sooner was the weapon drawn than he sprung forward, grasped the pistol with his left hand, while, with his right, he dealt the blood another terrible blow in the face which sent him reeling back like a drunken man, the weapon remaining in De Lormé's

49

grasp.

The moment this was accomplished, the other three took to their heels in affright, for to them there was a decided difference between attacking an unarmed man and one with a six-shooter in his hand.

As soon as he recovered from the effects of the blow, the young man from whom the revolver had been wrested, looked in disgust upon his fleeting comrades, and then glared in anger at the man who had vanquished him so easily.

"I am not myself to-night, I want you to understand!" he exclaimed, husky with rage.

"Well, I am glad to hear that," De Lormé responded. "If you want my honest opinion I think it would be as much as a hundred dollars in your pocket if you had never been born at all."

The effect of the introduction of this well-worn joke was only to increase the rage of the vanquished man.

"My senses are clouded with liquor or else you would never have been able to get the best of me in the way you have."

"You see you ought to have taken my advice," De Lormé replied; "I told you at the beginning that you ought to go home and to bed."

"I do not know who you are, or what you are, but I can tell you that this will not be the last of the affair."

"As far as you are concerned, I know that it will not be," the Bohemian replied.

"To-morrow your head will feel as big as a bushel basket; in fact, I don't think you will be in a presentable condition for a week at least, for I have an idea you are going to have an awful pair of black eyes; and, speaking of that, reminds me to advise you that a few raw oysters, or a piece of raw beefsteak, will take the swelling down as soon as anything I know of."

"Curse your advice!" cried the young man, in a rage. "Satisfaction is what I am after!"

"Well, if you are not satisfied now, you are the hardest man to satisfy I ever ran across. Even fools generally know when they have got enough and do not long for more."

"Enough of your insolence!" cried the other, hotly. "The advantage is on your side now, but the next time we meet it may not be."

"Well, if we don't happen to meet again I guess I can survive it," De Lormé remarked.

"Ah, but we will, for I shall take pains to hunt you out if you dare to give me your name."

"Suppose you oblige me with yours, first."

"Certainly, I am not ashamed of it. My name is Edward McMichael."

The moment the young man disclosed his identity, De Lormé recognized the name as that of a well-known personage—the son of one of the bonanza kings, and reputed to be one of the wildest young fellows in the city.

His father had but lately shuffled off this mortal coil, leaving all his vast wealth to his only son, and this young man was making away with it in all sorts of foolish ways as fast as possible.

The trouble was that neither the father nor son had been used to any money until, by a sudden turn of fortune's wheel, they found themselves millionaires.

And the abrupt rise to wealth had been too much for them, for it turned the heads of both, and led them into all sorts of folly.

"Ah, yes; your name is not unfamiliar to me; and now I suppose you would like to know mine."

"Yes; and as soon as I am in a condition to take the

field, my second will wait upon you."

"My name is Andrew De Lormé, and a message to the Alta California office will reach me."

"Ah! You are a newspaper man!"

"Yes, I'm one of those darned literary fellers."

"Very well; in a few days you may expect to hear from me, and I trust I shall be able to make you repent of this night's work."

Then the spoiled "darling of fortune" strode haughtily away.

"If he has sand enough to come up to the mark when the liquor is out of him, I'll have a duel on my hands," De Lormé soliloquized, as he picked up the basket and again went on his way.

"Well, variety is the spice of life! Champagne and oysters to-night and a leaden ball to-morrow. Such is existence."

CHAPTER IX.
THE LITTLE SUPPER.

When De Lormé reached the house he found that, agreeably to promise, La Belle Helene was on the look-out for him.

Through the blinds she had watched his approach and was ready to receive him at the door.

"You got the oysters without any difficulty?" she asked as she admitted him and piloted the way to the dining-room, where she had the table all in readiness for the feast.

"Oh, yes; no difficulty at all. Here are the oysters—don't they emit a perfume that appeals to you at once? And a couple of bottles of champagne to wash them down."

And as he spoke he drew from the basket the portly wine-bottles and placed them upon the table.

"Oh, you dear, good fellow!" she cried, clapping her hands in true girlish delight. "You are a treasure, and no mistake!"

And in her glee she caught him by the ears, and drawing his face down kissed him on both cheeks, and, in his turn, encouraged by this signal mark of favor, he pressed her close to his breast.

"There! You are my lover now, I guess," she murmured, submitting to the caress.

And then she glided from his arms, and, making a descent upon the basket, got out the oysters.

"I can't live on love, you know!" she exclaimed, laughing. "I am only a mortal, and require more substantial food.

"But the idea of bringing these two great bottles of

wine. You surely don't suppose that I could drink the contents of even one of those bottles?"

"Well, I don't know; they don't hold so very much. They are deceptive. Look at the big hollow there is in the bottom."

"Yes; it is a regular cheat, isn't it?"

"There is cheating in all trades but ours, you know. But, seriously, I believe I could get away with the two bottles myself without any very great trouble. I think I must have been born thirsty, for I always have a terrible appetite for drink."

"I don't suppose it is a nice confession for a girl to make, but I am fond of champagne, too," she said, with a charming smile, as she arranged the oysters upon the table. "In fact, I drank a couple of glasses at the theater to-night with Mr. Kettleton—the chief of police, you know."

"Oh, yes, I am well acquainted with the chief. He is the kind of fellow whom it is very useful to know, sometimes," De Lormé remarked, busying himself with extracting the cork from one of the wine-bottles with the aid of a patent folding corkscrew, which he carried in his pocket, like a true son of Bohemia.

This avowal on the part of La Belle Helene somewhat opened the eyes of De Lormé, and went far to explain the reason for the girl's peculiar actions.

He had noticed, before leaving the theater, that there seemed to be something odd in her manner, and was unable to account for it.

She was acting differently from what she had ever done since he had known her, and despite his careless, easy way—he would have been puzzled to describe in what particular way the girl was acting strangely. Yet he felt that there was something out of the common in her manner.

He murmured to himself as he bent over the bottle preparatory to extracting the cork:

"If a couple of glasses of champagne make her this affectionate toward me, what will be the result when she disposes of a half-bottle or so?

"Upon my word, I think we will be married in the morning!

"But will that suit me? Do I really wish to link my fate with this girl, who is charming beyond comparison, but of whom I know nothing?

"As the Mexicans say, who knows?"

Then, with a loud pop, the cork flew out, and De Lormé filled the glasses.

Side by side they stood and held the glasses on high while they watched the bubbles ascend and break.

"Kiss me before you drink!" she cried, abruptly, holding up her face, "and tell me which is the sweetest— my lips or the wine?"

He obeyed the injunction promptly, saying gallantly, after the caress was given and received:

"There cannot be any comparison, of course. One is nectar such as the gods drank in the brave old days, while the other is but a dull imitation contrived by man's cunning hand."

"Are you satisfied that you are my lover, now?" she exclaimed, archly, as she pushed him into a chair, and, bending over him, smoothed back the short curls, which clustered on his forehead.

Then she proceeded to fill his plate with oysters; and this done, she refilled the glasses and took her seat upon the opposite side of the table and began to help herself to the viands.

"These freely-bestowed caresses ought to be

convincing proof," he replied, smiling.

And yet, there was a feeling within his heart, which belied his words.

An idea had come up in his mind that the girl was not sincere in these demonstrations of affection, and that there was some deep purpose back of them.

The thought seemed to be a ridiculous one, and he had not the least proof to back it, but De Lormé was a man who believed in presentiments, and his instincts warned him that there was something false in the girl's demonstrations.

In his mind he reasoned against the idea, though, for he was not willing to receive it.

This girl was a strange, odd creature, and it was not right to judge her by the standard by which other young ladies could be measured. And then, too, possibly it was the wine that made her act differently from what she usually did.

For a few minutes neither spoke, both doing justice to the oysters, which were unusually fine. Then the glasses being drained, again the girl hastened to fill them.

"Don't spare the wine!" she exclaimed. "Isn't it delightful? I was afraid that it would go to my head but it doesn't seem to affect me in the least."

"Only to give your eyes a brighter sparkle!" he remarked.

"You men are always so full of compliments." And between the bites at the oysters and her sips of the wine, she added:

"Didn't I hear you and the chief of police enjoying a long talk in the wings to-night?"

The gentleman looked surprised.

"I suppose you wonder how I happened to know it, eh?" she continued.

"Yes, I do wonder a little at it, for I didn't notice that you were anywhere around."

"Why, I was right at your elbow, and I guess I heard nearly every word both of you said. That was a very private conversation, wasn't it?" as she laughed merrily, and took up the champagne glass to regard De Lormé over the edge of it with a quizzical glance.

"Well, I must admit you astonish me, although the interview was none of my seeking, and right at the beginning I told Kettleton that, behind the scenes of the Bella Union was no place to discuss a business matter. But I suppose you know enough of the man to understand that he is as obstinate as a mule, and he insisted upon talking about the affair there and then. As it really was no particular business of mine, I let him have his own way. Such men live longer if they are not crossed."

"Well, how I happened to overhear the conversation is just as simple as simple can be.

"You have been in my dressing-room of course?"

The gentleman nodded.

"You know what a little bit of a cubby-hole it is?"

"Yes, not room enough to swing a cat."

"No, nor a kitten, even. Well, I rebelled, and I told Mr. Macduff that if he didn't give me another room, or contrive to enlarge mine somehow, I would never sing another note in his mean old theater. He saw to-day that I was in earnest, and so the partition which separated my apartment from the small property-room right next to it, was taken down. That made my room just about twice as large as it was before, and against the end wall of the new part you and the chief leaned while you conversed.

"The wall is only of thin boards covered with paper, and as I happened to be seated at that end of the room reading, waiting for my 'turn' to come, I heard every word of the conversation just as plainly as though both of you had been in my apartment.

"I know it wasn't very lady-like to listen to a private conversation; but then on this occasion no harm was done, and I really became interested in the matter, although, of course, it doesn't concern me in the least."

"Oh, no, no particular harm, although I don't believe the chief would relish the fact if he knew it," De Lormé replied.

"Well, he mustn't know it. You will not betray me, will you?" and with her brilliant eyes she threw an earnest glance of entreaty at the young man.

"Certainly not," was his immediate reply.

"But he was a great idiot to discuss the matter in so public a place if he was anxious to keep the affair a profound secret from every one!" the girl exclaimed, her lip curling in contempt.

"Oh, come, you must not call the chief an idiot, you know," De Lormé expostulated. "He is one of your greatest admirers."

"That may be, but I don't admire him. He has altogether too good an opinion of himself. But about this matter I really became interested, for it seemed to me just like a romance."

"It is a rather remarkable affair."

"Five million of dollars! Oh, what a sum!" the girl exclaimed, with uplifted eyes. "What couldn't a woman do with, in her own right, such a sum of money as that?"

De Lormé laughed at her enthusiasm.

"Five million is a pretty sum," he assented.

04. "I can't live on love, you know!" she exclaimed, laughing. "I am only a mortal, and require more substantial food."

CHAPTER X.
THE STORY.

The secret was out now, and De Lormé understood why the girl had been so anxious for the "little supper," and why she had bestowed such marks of favor upon him.

She had employed the usual feminine weapons to get him into a good humor—to render him her slave, so that she might be able to learn what she wished to know.

The demonstrations of affection were not real, and did not come from the heart, as he had anticipated.

The story, which the chief of police by his foolish want of precaution had allowed to reach her ears, had fired her imagination. And though De Lormé could not conceive why she should take any interest in it, yet it was plain she did, and had resolved to question him upon the subject.

Again had his presentiments come true, and his instinct had not been at fault when it warned him that there was no true affection at the bottom of the girl's caresses.

"Pretty sum!" she exclaimed, repeating his expression. "Why, it is perfectly magnificent! Just think how long it will take you to count a million, then think of any one being worth five times that sum!

"But, Andrew, tell me all the particulars of the story over again," the girl continued. "I have hardly done anything but think of that five million ever since I heard of it."

"The story is simple enough: Years ago an Englishman by the name of Archibald Macarthy came to this country. It was in the time of the gold discoveries when vast fortunes on the Pacific Slope were made and lost in a day. The stranger was successful, and became one of the gold kings. Then he invested his money in wild lands in Southern California. In time there came reverses, as usually happens in such cases. The lawyers discovered a flaw in the title of the Southern California lands, and the matter got into the law courts.

"Macarthy took to drink and soon became a wreck. At last, by the aid of a society of Englishmen who took pity on him, he was sent home to die.

"In England, just before his death, he confided to his brother, who was a wealthy man and whose house sheltered him, his conviction that in time the Southern California property could be recovered. He further disclosed that he had a child in the Pacific State, whom he had deserted in San Francisco some twenty years before.

"He employed the brother to hasten to California, recover the child and fight for the property.

"That brother is now here. An act of Congress has cleared the title to the property, and the estate is now easily worth five million dollars, made so by the great rise in land value since the time of the first purchase. Land which could be bought then for about fifty cents an acre is now worth from fifty dollars to five hundred dollars."

"It is wonderful!" she exclaimed after long, hard-drawn breath. "It is like a tale of the Arabian Nights!"

"Yes, but while the property is just where it originally stood, waiting for the heir to come and claim it, yet the heir cannot be found."

"How comes it that the chief of police is so interested in this matter? What is it to him?" she asked. "That is a matter I do not understand."

"It is the old story of Ali Baba and the greased measure," De Lormé replied. "The envious brother, who lent the measure greased it so that some of whatever he might measure would stick, and when the utensil came back, lo! There was a piece of gold in the bottom.

"So, in this matter," De Lormé continued, "Kettleton wants to be the measure through which this five million must pass, and he will grease his palms and catch a good share of the money as it goes through."

"I see, I see; and a fine sum would fall to his share, no doubt. And as I gathered from your conversation, he is anxious for you to search for the heir."

"Yes; that is the part assigned to me. The chief does me the honor to believe that I am keen-witted, and he prefers to place the matter in my hands rather than dealing with any of the detectives, public or private."

"And I understood you to say that you would undertake the task?"

"Yes; I am to have a good fee if I succeed in getting on the track of the heir, even if I do not succeed in discovering the party."

"It is a difficult task," she observed, with a wise shake of the head.

"Oh, no; not at all. I shall wait upon the chief to-morrow afternoon and claim the fee."

"You will?" exclaimed La Belle Helene, in amazement.

It should be understood, that all through this conversation neither the oysters nor the champagne had been neglected. Both had eaten between the pauses in the conversation, and drank as well—La Belle Helene taking particular care to see that De Lormé's plate and glass were both replenished whenever the supply ran low.

Nor did the girl neglect herself, for she did full justice to the oysters, and drank champagne with the gentleman glass for glass. And, what was strange, the potent juice of the grape did not seem to have any more effect upon her than so much water.

And now, De Lormé, who was watching the girl closely, saw how wrong he had been when he surmised that the couple of glasses of champagne that she drank in the theater had gone to her head and influenced her actions.

"Yes, my dear Helene. To-morrow I shall call upon our esteemed friend, the chief of police, and take a hundred dollars out of him according to agreement. And I assure you the money will be welcome, for, in the parlance of miners, I am down to the bed-rock, flat broke. I am without a cent to bless myself with, if I contemplated doing anything so silly, which I don't."

"You are speaking in riddles; I do not understand," she said, with a shake of the head. "I fear I am very stupid, sometimes."

"Oh, not at all. You are not guilty of anything of the kind," he replied, gallantly.

"When I get through with this banquet I shall go home, take a quiet pipe for about an hour to settle my nerves and then go to bed. I shall get up about noon, take a lunch, and then wait upon the chief with the intelligence which I have secured."

"Yes, but when are you going to secure the intelligence? Will it come to you in a dream during your sleep?" she asked, laughing.

"Oh, no; if I dream at all, which I seldom do, it will be of a divine beauty called La Belle Helene!"

"I suppose you think that deserves a caress?" she said, with a charming pout. "But I have given you enough to-night, and I am not going to give you any more for fear of spoiling you."

"No fear of that, I assure you. But to explain the mystery: by one of those odd coincidences which more often happen in this world than most people are aware of, for the last week I have been looking into this lost-heir business."

"Is it possible?" she exclaimed.

"Yes, but you must be careful and not betray my secret, for the sapient chief of police would never be apt to forgive me if he discovered that I kept quiet and allowed him to tell me the story of the child, lost here in Frisco, when I was as well acquainted with all the particulars as he was himself."

"But I do not understand how such a thing can be," she persisted.

"The explanation is simple enough: when Maximilian Macarthy came to San Francisco in search of the lost child, his first move was to call upon the chief of police for information; but Kettleton, of course, had none to give. Saying that the matter was entirely out of his line, Kettleton advised him to apply to some of the private detectives.

"But the chief, being in possession of all the facts, had determined to have a finger in the pie, for he saw immediately how great an advantage the party who got possession of the heir would have.

"I suppose of course that you are not familiar with the pecuniary position of the renowned chief?"

"Of course not; how should I be? I presume, though, that he makes plenty of money for I have often heard it said that a man in his position has a great many opportunities to acquire wealth.

"He has made me some handsome presents, and said in an off-hand way that, when I made up my mind to marry him, I should enjoy all the luxuries the heart of a woman could possibly crave."

"'Talk is cheap, but it takes money to buy land,'"

remarked De Lormé, sententiously. "If you married the chief he would have you back on the stage before your honeymoon was over, and he would save you the trouble of going for your salary by drawing it himself; and indeed, the manager might regard himself as a lucky man if Kettleton didn't get all the money in advance before you had sung a note!

"The chief is always short of money. The trouble with him is, he thinks he can play poker and he can't. To use the vulgate, that is what breaks him all up. Now, I waste money on poker myself, but I know I'm no player and so I am not skinned alive."

CHAPTER XI.
DE LORMÉ'S DISCOVERIES.

The girl laughed outright at the candid confession and made haste to refill De Lormé's glass.

"An honest confession is good for the soul they say," she remarked, "and so you ought to fare well, for surely you are honest enough."

"Yes, I try to be honest with myself, and in regard to that point, there is where a great many men miss it. They palter with and attempt to deceive themselves.

"A man who has a weakness, and is sensible enough to know and acknowledge it, is far stronger than the man who has the weakness and refuses to admit it, even to himself.

"Now, Kettleton will never admit that it is his own stupid playing which causes him to lose night after night. He blames the cards—swears that no one ever saw such cursed luck—instead of putting the censure where it rightly belongs, on his own blundering folly."

"He is self-conceited. Any one cannot fail to see that who is in his company for any length of time," La Belle Helene remarked.

"Yes, he is about the poorest chief of police the city ever had, yet he acts as if everybody admitted that he was the best.

"Now, take this matter for instance, and see how he blundered," De Lormé continued.

"When the Englishman told the story of the lost heir he made up his mind to try and get a slice of the five millions for himself, and so cavalierly dismissed the stranger with the remark that it was impossible for him to do anything for him.

"He advised the other to employ private detectives, and the Englishman immediately set to work to do so. But the chief, a prey to procrastination as usual, never takes a step in the matter until he happens to encounter me. Then he puts the case in my hands, after losing valuable time.

"In the meanwhile the Englishman goes to a private detective firm and puts the matter into their hands.

"These men, though, think there isn't much chance of finding the child. All the material to go upon is the slender statement that twenty odd years ago an Englishman by the name of Archibald Macarthy abandoned a child somewhere here in Frisco. Not even the name, age or sex of the child is known. So, they gave the case into my hands.

"More out of charity, I guess, than anything else, for there was a fifty-dollar note in the job. Anyway, they probably concluded that fifty dollars never came amiss to such a spendthrift dog as I am—"

"A pretty character you are giving yourself!" she interposed, smilingly. "Do you suppose a girl of sense, as I claim to be, would marry any such man as you make yourself out to be?" and she shook her finger warningly at him.

Whereat he laughed.

"Well, you will never be able to accuse me of having deceived you," he replied.

"But to resume my story: the job was given to me, and the first thing I did was to hunt all over Frisco to find some men who were intimately acquainted with Archibald Macarthy when he lived here.

"It was not an easy task, but I had a clew which helped me. Macarthy was a hard drinker, and it was through the use of liquor that he became the wreck he was when sent to England to die by the Sons of Saint George, a society of which he had been a prominent member in his prosperous days.

"Now, a man who indulges freely in liquor must go to the saloons, and most men of that class have some favorite haunt where they are to be found oftener than anywhere else.

"But if anybody thinks it an easy job to go into every saloon in a city like San Francisco, take a drink and manage to engage the barkeeper in a sociable conversation to ascertain if one Archy Macarthy, an Englishman, was in the habit of favoring that particular saloon with his patronage years ago, I would like them to put in a day at it."

"I should think it would be dreadful," she observed.

"The first day was a blank. On the second, in a little shebang, away out by the sand-lots, I struck my man."

The interest of the girl was intense at this point, but, though De Lormé had his eyes upon her so that not a movement of her expressive face was lost upon him, he managed the matter so well the girl never suspected how close was the watch he kept.

"It was a little bit of a rum-shop, probably as poor a place as can be found in the city.

"The man who kept the place was an aged Irishman, all doubled up by the combined influence of rum and rheumatism.

"He had seen better days, as he took pains to assure me, when he served me with my drink and joined me in a social glass at my request.

"There was a time, as he assured me, when he had been the head barkeeper with an interest in the concern of one of the best saloons on Bush Street, twenty years back.

"Here was a veteran; the very kind of man I was looking for. And when I put the question—did he know one Archy Macarthy, twenty years ago? He immediately answered that he did; but he was no Englishman he assured me.

Macarthy was a good old Irish name, but as Archy hadn't a brogue, he denied his country and called himself an Englishman.

"Macarthy and me, boss, were like brothers," he declared.

"'Let me see,' I said, 'that was about the time that Macarthy got married, wasn't it?'"

"'It was, and by that token I remember this babby well, for I was in the saloon whin Macarthy brought the child in and axed my boss to find some good woman to take care of it for him.'

"'Where was the mother?' I asked.

"'Indade, that is more than I know,' he replied, and that was all the information I got out of him.

"But it was enough to give me a good clew, unless there was some mistake about the matter and this Archy Macarthy should chance to turn out not to be the man of whom I was in search.

"I got the name of the boss, and as he was a well-known man in the city I easily hunted him down."

"Ah, you found him!" the girl exclaimed, following the narrative so closely that she might be said to hang upon the lips of the speaker.

"I found him. And yet I did not find him," he continued. "To explain the contradiction, the man had been dead and buried for a couple of years.

"He was an old bachelor, by name Abraham Gwinnet, a well-known man about town, for he had kept a saloon in San Francisco ever since eighteen hundred and fifty.

"At the grave of Gwinnet, the clew stopped.

"He had no relatives, seemingly, in the world, for when he died, he was buried by strangers.

"In his later days, too, he had the misfortune to lose the gains of a lifetime, and as there was no property for the heirs to fight over, none made their appearance.

"It is only when the dead leave money behind them that heirs start up in all directions.

"Not a solitary thing could I learn in regard to the child, which the old Irishman asserted Archy Macarthy confided to Gwinnet's care.

"Gwinnet died in the public hospital, and when I visited the institution to see if he had left any effects behind him, I found that he had nothing when he entered the hospital but the suit of clothes he wore.

"I inquired for the clothes, for I thought there was just a chance that there might be some documents concealed in them, and was informed that the suit the man wore when he entered the hospital had been buried with him."

There was a convulsive movement of the lips of La Belle Helene at this moment, as though some startling idea had shot rapidly across her brain.

The movement did not escape the keen eyes of De Lormé, who saw everything while apparently seeing nothing.

"It certainly seems strange that such a man, as this old saloon-keeper must have been, did not have acquaintances who might have thrown some light upon his life," she remarked, musingly.

"That was exactly the idea that occurred to me, but you must remember that San Francisco was one of the most peculiar cities in the world in its early days," her companion answered.

"The majority of the men who flocked here, attracted by the gold discoveries, were young and unmarried. And of the men of family who came, not one in a hundred brought their families with them.

"A more cosmopolitan city than this in its early days—or, for that matter, even now—does not exist.

"The population was continually on the move. Men who were here on Monday had vanished before the week was out.

"The discovery of Gwinnet made me understand why Macarthy had not taken more pains to post his brother. Believing Gwinnet to be alive, he thought all his brother would have to do would be to find him and receive all the particulars."

"It is the strangest tale I have ever heard. And the idea that there are five millions of dollars waiting for this lost heir," the girl remarked, reflectively.

"Yes; the money is ready for the claimant who can prove a right to it."

"I have thought out a romance; let me tell it to you!" cried La Belle Helene abruptly, rising as she spoke.

CHAPTER XII.
LA BELLE HELENE'S STORY.

She came around the table, and drawing a chair close up to the one in which he sat, took a seat by his side.

Placing her arm caressingly upon his shoulder, she brought her beautiful face close to his.

"All trace of this heir then is lost?" she said in a reflective sort of way.

"Yes, that is the report which I shall make to Kettleton to-morrow, and by means of which I collar the hundred which he offered."

"You have earned the money honestly enough," she remarked, "for you furnish the information which he desires.

"That some one else has paid you for the same service is no business of his."

"Exactly; that is the view I take of the matter, and so I shall receive his money without any compunctions."

"What a strange story it is," she observed. "Do you know it has made a wonderful impression upon me, and I haven't done anything but speculate upon the matter ever since I heard about it?

"I think," she continued, "take it all in all, this is the most romantic tale I have ever heard."

"It is certainly strange enough."

"The idea that this magnificent fortune waits for an heir who cannot be found," mused the songstress.

"Five millions of dollars and no one to claim it.

"So odd, too, that this poor wretch of a—what was his name?"

"Macarthy," said De Lormé, "Archibald Macarthy," and as he answered the idea came to him, from something there was in the girl's manner, that her ignorance was assumed, and that she was as familiar with the name as he was.

"Oh, yes, Macarthy," she observed. "The idea that this poor wretch should die a miserable death in England, dependent upon the bounty of his brother, when if he had only had strength to struggle for a few months, this colossal fortune would have been in his grasp. Then he would have been able to have sought for health in any part of the world."

"Such is life," De Lormé remarked, philosophically. "Just as we are in sight of the goal—just as the race seems to be within our grasp—death steps in and strikes us down."

"There is not the slightest clew to the heir?" she remarked, reflectively.

"Not the slightest," De Lormé replied. "When I first heard the story there was a great deal of unbelief in my mind.

"I had a suspicion that the tale of the child lost in Frisco was but the delirium of a dying man, and that no heir had ever existed. But my discovery of the old Irishman, who had been Gwinnet's barkeeper, upset that idea.

"The Irishman knew what he was talking about and I haven't the least doubt that some twenty years ago, Archy Macarthy did entrust his child to the care of this Abraham Gwinnet, but what on earth the man did with the child is a mystery.

"Of course, in this case the old saying that it is 'the unexpected that always happens' may prove to be true. By accident a clew to the lost heir may be stumbled upon, but I do not think that it is at all probable."

"From what you have said it seems to me that this marriage of Macarthy's must have been a secret one," the girl observed.

"Oh, yes, there isn't much doubt about that, for none of the parties who knew Macarthy in the days when he flourished in San Francisco had any idea he was a married man, much less the father of a child."

"And the mother of the child—the wife—was probably dead at the time he entrusted the child to the care of his friend, for if she had been living it is safe to conclude she would not have allowed a child of such tender years to be taken away from her."

"That supposition seems to me to be correct, and from the first I have gone on the idea that the wife and mother was dead."

"All the proofs in regard to the identity of the child were evidently in the hands of this Gwinnet, for the dying man plainly believed that all his brother had to do was to come to this city, find Gwinnet, and then all would be easy."

"My dear Helene, you are tracing this matter out with a skill that would do credit to an acute attorney," De Lormé remarked, laughing.

"It is because I have become interested in the affair," she replied.

"It is a mystery, you know, and all mysteries appeal powerfully to all women.

"Besides I am only using common sense in the matter."

"That is exactly what most people don't use when they get hold of an affair of this sort," De Lormé observed.

"The mother was evidently dead at the time the child was given to Gwinnet, so there isn't any use of any one bothering their head about her," La Belle Helene remarked.

"That was the conclusion at which I arrived," De Lormé replied.

"Then, too, as there wasn't the slightest clew to the mother in the beginning, and none was developed in the search, it was an utter impossibility for me to proceed in that direction."

"Some very strange ideas have come into my head in regard to this matter!" the girl exclaimed, abruptly.

"You know I am an odd fish, anyway, and so no one ought to wonder at anything I may think or do."

And as she spoke she put her head down upon his shoulder and gazed smilingly up into his face.

To be so favored by such a beautiful girl was enough to make almost any man supremely happy, and with the majority of men, delight at being so honored would have rendered them incapable of feeling any other sentiment. But although De Lormé passed his arm around her slender waist, caressingly, and seemed to yield to the joy of the moment, yet his senses were not in the least affected by the situation.

He had been certain, almost from the very beginning, that the woman had some deep purpose in view, for the change in her manner seemed too abrupt to be honest, though she had always been very friendly with him, as was natural under the circumstances. He had been of service to her, yet she had never manifested any particular affection for him, and from what he had seen of her he had come to the conclusion that she was a girl who would never be apt to feel much love for any one.

And now that she was becoming so affectionate he was sure the revelation of the mystery was near at hand.

"You are the most fascinating girl in California, for dollars!" he exclaimed, gallantly.

"But you don't care anything for me if I am," she

replied with a half sigh, as though she deeply regretted the fact.

"Why, how can you say such a thing when I am just dying for love of you?"

"And what would you do to prove your love?" she demanded, with an earnest glance of her glorious eyes.

"Anything!" he replied, with all the ardor of an anxious lover.

"Suppose I should enter upon a difficult undertaking, would you aid me to the best of your ability?" she demanded.

"Most certainly," he replied.

The revelation was now at hand, he believed.

"If I reveal to you my secret, will you swear never to betray me?"

"I will, by the prettiest oath ever framed!"

"Oh, don't talk nonsense now!" she exclaimed, petulantly. "It is business, at present. Aid me to succeed, and then when you are my husband, you shall have as much love as ever woman gave to man in this world!"

"Command me and I will obey!"

"Listen, then," she said, impressively. "I have been in a sort of maze ever since I heard the story of this imperial fortune that waits for an heir.

"It seemed to me as if some ten years ago I knew a man called Archibald Macarthy. I was then a girl of fifteen, fresh from a convent school.

"My father was a speculator who, by the death of my mother, when I was a child of tender years, was burdened with my care.

"The convent school partially relieved him of that burden, but when I was fifteen, in a fit of desperation caused by a prolonged run of ill-luck, he committed suicide. I was then left friendless and alone to look out for myself.

"Thanks to my musical abilities, I could easily support myself as a teacher, but I had not been engaged in this miserable occupation but a few weeks when I chanced to meet with Archibald Macarthy. And, although he was old enough to be my father, I listened to his suit and became his wife. We had not been married a week, though, when the blow came that stripped him of the wealth for which alone I had sold myself. During that brief time, too, I discovered that my lord and master was a miserable drunkard who was not sober six hours of the twenty-four.

"He had promised me a life of luxury and when he was unable to fulfill that agreement, I considered I was released from mine. So I quitted him immediately, taking such measures that it was impossible for him to follow me.

"But, for all that, I was legally his wife. I never took the trouble to obtain a divorce, for I was so disgusted at my wretched mistake that I did not believe I should ever want to get married again. And on his part I am certain he never took any steps to have the marriage annulled, for the loss of his fortune turned him into a miserable wretch without either energy or ambition.

"Now, then, as the legal wife of Archibald Macarthy, can I not make good my claim to this five millions of dollars?"

CHAPTER XIII.
THE PROPOSAL.

De Lormé had listened to the story of La Belle Helene in utter astonishment, for the tale had taken him completely by surprise.

As we have said, he felt certain from the beginning that she had some deep purpose in view but he had not anticipated any such disclosure as this, and, with all his shrewdness, he did not know exactly what to make of it.

Was the story true or an ingeniously concocted falsehood, which the girl had hatched in her cunning brain after she had heard the tale of the vast inheritance waiting for a claimant?

But if it was not true, how did the girl expect to prove to the satisfaction of an incredulous world that she was the wife and heir of Archibald Macarthy?

Supposing the tale was correct, how came it that Macarthy, on his deathbed, spoke to his brother of his lost child and did not mention his second wife at all?

It was a mysterious affair altogether, and De Lormé did not know what to make of it.

"If you are the widow of Macarthy, and can prove that fact to the satisfaction of the courts, most certainly you will be entitled to a good slice of this five million," De Lormé remarked.

"Yes, and there is where the trouble lies," she observed with a dubious shake of the head. "It will not be an easy matter for me to prove my marriage.

"I always had an old head on young shoulders, and when Archibald Macarthy sought to win me, in my eagerness to secure for a husband a man who was supposed to be one of the richest in California, I took all possible measures to keep the matter secret.

"My father died with a cloud upon his name—a cloud so black that I was afraid if my lover heard of the circumstances he would never dream of marrying me. So, at my request, all the arrangements were strictly private.

"We were not married by a minister but by a magistrate—a justice of the peace, who lived in some obscure street on the outskirts of San Francisco.

"We were married in the afternoon, and took the boat immediately after the ceremony for Sacramento, where we put up at a large hotel, the name of which I have forgotten, but I could easily identify the building if it is still in existence.

"We remained in Sacramento about a week, and during the latter part of the week the news came of the disastrous ruling which made Macarthy a beggar.

"The few days I had spent in his company had completely disgusted me with him, for the brute became foolishly drunk before we had been an hour on the boat, and hardly drew a really sober breath all the time we were in Sacramento."

"A nice sort of man for a young and beautiful girl to pick up for a husband," De Lormé remarked.

"Yes, and the moment his wealth vanished I fled. There was a stormy scene between us, for in my indignation I did not conceal from him the opinion of him I had formed.

"And when he found I was determined to be free once again he became very much enraged," she continued, "and swore he would destroy all proofs of our marriage and would never acknowledge me as his wife.

"I retorted that he could not do me a greater service, and so we parted.

"I never expected to either see or hear from him again, and what did it matter to me whether he acknowledged me as his wife or not?

"Of course, I never dreamed there was any possibility that anything would ever be recovered from his financial wreck, or else I would not have been so foolish."

"He was as good as his word," De Lormé remarked. "For in England when he spoke to his brother of his lost heir, he never mentioned you. And yet, as his second wife, you must certainly have a claim to a share of the property."

"He was keeping to the oath he swore when we parted, but in spite of that I shall make a fight for my rights.

"If I can find the magistrate who married us, and he identifies me as the girl whom he married to Macarthy, will not that be strong evidence?" she asked.

"Most decidedly," De Lormé replied.

"I am certain I can find him, for I met him on California street only a few days ago, and I am certain from the way in which he looked at me that I have not faded entirely from his memory. And, when such a stake as five millions of dollars is hanging in the balance, it surely will not be a difficult matter to find this magistrate!" and as she spoke La Belle Helene looked in his face with a meaning smile.

The glance said as plainly as though she had put it into words:

"If the right man cannot be found, it will not be impossible to find some one who will be willing to swear to having performed the marriage ceremony, provided he is well paid for the service."

"Have you your marriage-certificate?" De Lormé asked after a moment's pause.

"No, I am afraid not," she answered.

"I did not set much value upon it, as you can probably imagine, now that you are acquainted with the circumstances under which I procured it. But I have some things in an old trunk up in the country, where I usually go for a few weeks in the summer, and it is possible that it may be in this trunk. I have not had occasion to examine the trunk for years, and I do not really know what is in it."

And again she looked in his face with a meaning smile.

And De Lormé translated the look to say, "When the magistrate is found who is willing to swear to having performed the ceremony, will it not be an easy matter to discover in this old trunk the little document which in affairs of this kind, legal gentlemen consider so important?"

It was apparent that La Belle Helene had given the matter much thought, and had endeavored to cover every point.

"The marriage-certificate would of course be strong evidence, provided it was brought forward in such a shape that no doubt could be thrown upon its genuineness," the gentleman remarked.

"Oh, trust me for that!" La Belle Helene exclaimed, confidently.

"I think I understand something about such matters, and I shall not endanger my case by presenting any evidence which can be easily disputed.

"And now come, tell me, will you be my ally in this matter? Will you fight my battle as if it was your own? And if you will, I can only say, secure the fortune which belongs rightfully to me, and then I am yours as soon as you care to claim me."

And, as if to seal the compact, she held up her ripe,

red lips for him to kiss.

De Lormé would have been more than mortal to resist such a temptation.

The salutation exchanged, she released herself from his embrace, rose quickly to her feet, and an exclamation of surprise escaped from her lips.

Her gaze had fallen upon the little clock, ticking upon the mantle-piece.

"Why, it is nearly three o'clock!" she exclaimed.

"Who would have believed that it could be so late?"

"No, you mistake! It is early!" he remarked.

"Late or early, it is time that you were gone," she replied.

"Here's a little wine left," and she filled the glasses as she spoke.

"Now then, a parting toast, success to our scheme!" she cried, as she held her glass high in the air.

"And may you soon win your share of the five millions!" he added.

"We will enjoy life like princes then, far from this miserable city!" she cried.

"And as I ride in my carriage, dressed as I know how to dress, how many will think as they look upon me that I was ever glad to sing for my bread upon the vile stage of the Bella Union Theater?"

Their glasses clinked, the wine was drank, and then De Lormé departed.

His head was feverish and hot as he gained the street, and he was grateful for the cool morning air.

La Belle Helene had plied him liberally with the champagne, and, thanks to the skill with which she had kept his glass constantly full, he had partaken of more than his share. But as he had a head of iron as far as liquor was concerned, it did not affect him as much as she had calculated it would.

On his homeward way he soliloquized with himself in regard to the astounding revelation that La Belle Helene had made.

"I knew that she was an odd, peculiar creature," he murmured, "but I hadn't any idea that she was anything like what she is.

"She is a beautiful woman, if there ever was one in this world, and a fascinating one, too. But for all that, I am not so deeply infatuated as to risk the State Prison for her sake.

"No, no; this scheme is too deep for me. I will go just so far, but not a step beyond.

"When she tries desperate devices she must find some other tool."

De Lormé had a room in a large building on Bush Street, which was divided into offices on the first floor above the street and furnished and unfurnished rooms above.

Entering the house, he gained the landing of the second floor on the way to his third story room, when the sound of a slight struggle came to his ears. De Lormé heard a low, suppressed voice cry hoarsely:

"Speak! Or I'll kill you on the spot!"

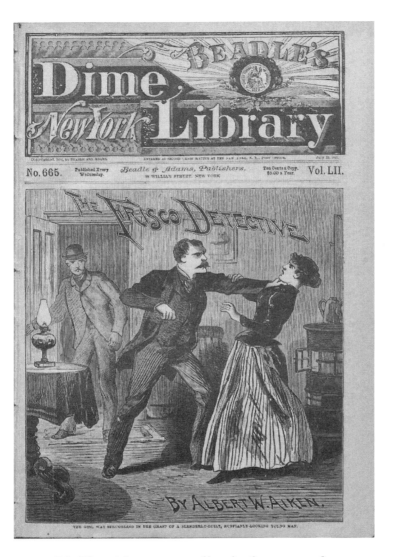

05. The girl was struggling in the grasp of a slenderly-built, ruffianly-looking young man.

CHAPTER XIV.
THE DRESSMAKER.

In such a case as this, De Lormé was not a man to hesitate for an instant.

The voice came through the door of a room upon his left hand, right at the head of the stairs, and the entry was in almost utter darkness, for the gas-light which was supposed to illuminate the hall, was turned down so low that it gave out little light.

But De Lormé was so well acquainted with the locality that he had no trouble in understanding where the voice came from.

The room from which the noise came was occupied by a young woman. She was rather tall, and rather good-looking, with regular features, dark eyes and hair, and with whom the young man had established a bowing acquaintanceship.

She was a dressmaker, so the little tin sign attached to her door announced, but as it did not give her name, and as he had never learned it from any other source, De Lormé was ignorant in regard to her appellation.

The dressmaker was evidently in danger.

There was a light streaming through the keyhole, showing that the room was not in darkness.

Guided by this light De Lormé's hand sought the handle of the door; turning the knob gently, so as not to make any noise—his idea being to surprise the parties within—the door opened without a sound, and De Lormé, peering into the room, beheld a strange sight.

The girl was struggling in the grasp of a slenderly-built, ruffianly-looking young man, who with his left hand grasped her by the throat, while with his right he brandished an ugly-looking bowie-knife.

The back of the fellow being toward the door he did not notice the entrance of the intruder, and therefore had not the slightest suspicion that a witness had come onto the scene.

Upon a round table by the wall stood a lighted lamp.

The table was set ready for a meal, plates being laid for two, and upon the little stove—cook and parlor stove combined—a coffeepot sent out its fragrant fumes.

The girl had evidently been pressed by work and had been hard at it all night, for a dress not quite completed was upon the floor, just where it had dropped from her hands when she was seized by the ruffian.

De Lormé entered the room and quietly brought the door to a close behind him.

He anticipated that there might be trouble between himself and the stranger, and did not want to alarm the house, as he felt perfectly satisfied in his own mind that he could settle the matter without any outside help.

As De Lormé got fairly in the room, the ruffian repeated the threat, which had convinced De Lormé of the necessity to look into the matter.

"Speak! Tell me where it is so I can get it, or I'll make an end of you with this knife with as little mercy as though you were only a rabbit!" the young ruffian said.

De Lormé waited to hear no more, but stealing up quietly behind the stranger he grasped the wrist of the hand that held the knife, and with a sudden jerk threw the steel clear across the room; at the same time he twisted his left hand in the coat collar of the other, and at the moment that he disarmed the stranger, with a powerful effort he dragged him from the girl and threw him into the corner of the room in the opposite direction from where the knife had gone.

Never was a man more astonished than the young ruffian when he was thrown into the corner and came in violent contact with the wall. He had not the least idea that any one had entered the room and he was taken completely by surprise.

The girl sank into a chair that stood near her, faint from the effects of the shock she had experienced.

The young ruffian was the first to speak. Recovering from his surprise, he assumed a blustering air.

"What in blazes do you mean by intruding into this apartment?" he cried. "And how dare you put your hands upon me? I've killed men for less than that!"

And he put his hand behind him as if to draw a pistol from his hip-pocket.

De Lormé's right hand was thrust into the pocket of the loose sack-coat, which he wore, and as the stranger made the threatening motion he raised the hand, still in the pocket, in a peculiar manner.

"Young man, don't attempt to draw a pistol on me," he said, "or I shall be obliged to plug you so quick that you will never know what hurt you."

The stranger hesitated and glanced in a suspicious way at the upturned skirt of De Lormé's coat.

"How can you do it?" he asked. "You haven't got any pistol."

"Don't you attempt to bet on that or you'll get salivated in the worst kind of a way," De Lormé retorted. "If you try to pull a pistol on me I will be obliged to go for you in a way you will despise.

"I've a derringer here in my pocket, a double-acting tool, carrying a ball of sixteen to the pound, and any man or beast that ever gets hit with one of those pills will not have any more use for this world. So, if you are wise, you will not try any funny business.

"And now you will not stand upon the order of your going, but 'git' at once."

"By what right do you order me out of this room?" demanded the other, withdrawing his hand from behind him, but still arrogant in his manner.

"Well, upon my life!" De Lormé exclaimed, "If you ain't the coolest hand I've seen for a dog's age I don't want a cent!

"Here I have just arrived in the nick of time to save you from murdering this young lady, and instead of either putting a bullet through you or handing you over to the police to be tried in a police court, I am willing to permit you to clear out.

"Since I see you have only frightened the lady, and you have the cool impudence to demand to know how dare I give orders in these premises, that's how it is! Young man, you take the cake, you do! Yes, I may say the whole bakery!"

"I was only joking with the girl!" the other growled, sulkily.

"Joking!" cried De Lormé, amazed at the excuse. "Well, all I have to say is, you have the queerest way of joking of any fellow I ever ran across."

"She's my sister," the young man explained.

"Your sister?"

"Yes; and I was only fooling with her; so now, Mister, you had better get out as soon as you can!" cried the rough, spitefully.

"You had better keep a civil tongue in your head!" De Lormé warned.

"I don't know about that!" replied the other, defiantly.

"You will be wise so to do, or it will be the worse for you. I don't take any stock in your yarn about it's being all a joke, and if you are the young lady's brother that fact doesn't give you the right to take her by the throat and threaten to put a knife into her."

"I didn't mean it—I wouldn't do her any harm and she knows it well enough," the young man answered.

By this time the girl had recovered from the choking which she had received, and was able to take part in the conversation.

"He is not my brother, sir, although he pretends that he is when he comes to me for assistance!" she exclaimed, indignantly.

"'Tis no such thing! She doesn't know what she is talking about!" the young ruffian declared.

"Yes, I do!" the girl replied, immediately. "I am an orphan and was brought up by this man's father, but there is not the least bit of relationship between us. Since I have lived here in San Francisco, this wretch has fairly persecuted me.

"When I first came to the city to follow my trade and happened by chance to meet him, I was glad of it, for I did not know then how greatly he had changed since I last saw him.

"And when I prospered and succeeded in establishing a good business, and he wanted to borrow little sums of money I was glad to accommodate him, until I found out that he considered all such loans as clear gain and never intended to repay them."

"No such thing!" sulkily growled the young ruffian. "I reckon to pay 'em one of these days when I make a big strike. The trouble with you is that you ain't got any patience. I have had a bad run of luck lately, but it won't last forever. And then, when I make that big strike, I wish I may die if I don't square the whole thing up!"

"You know you don't intend to pay me!" the girl

cried, indignantly. "But I don't care for the money. I told you that you were welcome to it, only I couldn't afford to let you have any more. But he has got the idea in his head that his father placed something in my charge which he ought to have and that was why he threatened to kill me unless I gave it up."

"So the old man did. I know that he gave you something that I ought to have, and I'm going to have it too," the young fellow cried, fiercely.

"Get out—no more talk! Get out, and if I ever catch you bothering this lady again I'll put you where the dogs won't get at you!" De Lormé exclaimed, sternly.

The fellow slunk through the door grumbling to himself but not daring to show his teeth openly.

"Oh, he's a bad fellow, sir!" exclaimed the girl. "I never expected to see Harry Gwinnet turn out so badly!"

CHAPTER XV.
A CLEW.

De Lormé had commenced to make his way toward the door, preparatory to taking his departure, when the announcement of the young man's name fell upon his ears.

"Excuse me, miss, what did you say his name was?" he asked.

"Gwinnet—Harry Gwinnet."

Then believing that accident had given him the clew which he had so vainly sought, he essayed a bold stroke and said:

"Gwinnet! Why that name is familiar to me. If I remember right a man named Abraham Gwinnet once kept a saloon here on Bush Street not very far from where we now stand."

"Yes, sir, he did," responded the girl, speaking as though she was well acquainted with all the particulars connected with Abraham Gwinnet.

"And is this young man the son of Abraham Gwinnet?" De Lormé questioned, hoping in his heart of hearts that it was not so, for if he was supposed to be Gwinnet's son, who according to all accounts was a bachelor, it would seem to indicate that it might be possible he was the heir to the five millions.

"Oh, no, not that scoundrel!" De Lormé muttered as the thought came to his mind. "No, no, La Belle Helene decidedly ought to have the money in preference to that young brute."

"Oh, no, sir, Abraham Gwinnet was his uncle," the girl replied.

"His father was named Thomas, a good old man

who was like a father to me.

"And when I think how good the father was, I am amazed that the son should be so bad."

And now De Lormé's thoughts went off on another track. Who was this girl, reared evidently by the Gwinnet family? Was it possible that, just by accident, he had met the lost child in the person of this girl?

"Come, now, this wouldn't be so bad," he murmured to himself as he surveyed the girl; ladylike, decidedly prepossessing and evidently a hard-working woman. She looked like she deserved a good turn of fortune's wheel if ever a mortal did.

He thought, "Yes, yes, between this girl and La Belle Helene I should think, decidedly, that this one ought to have the money."

"It is odd," he remarked aloud, replying to the girl's speech.

"But that is one of the strange things in this world. A good father often has a bad child and vice versa.

"This young rascal is evidently a bad egg and I regard it as being very fortunate that I happened to be passing through the entry and was able to interfere. Although, bad as the young scoundrel is, I hardly think he would have dared to carry out his threats."

"Well, sir, I don't really know," the girl observed, with a dubious shake of the head. "He was very much incensed against me to-night, and as he was slightly under the influence of liquor there is no telling what he would have done if you had not happened to come to my aid.

"I don't know how I shall ever be able to repay you for the service."

"Don't worry your head about that. Just wait, you know, until I send in the bill."

And then they both laughed as if they fancied the

conceit was a capital one.

"I always make a rule never to pay until the bill is sent in," he continued.

"And in fact," he added, with a grimace, "sometimes, if the bill amounts to anything, it has to be sent in half a dozen times before I am able to attend to it, and if you are no quicker in settling your debts than I am in regard to mine, it will be six months or a year before you need to trouble your head about the matter." And then again they laughed.

"But, by the way, I tell you what you can do for me," he said, as his eyes happened to fall upon the coffeepot sending up its aromatic steam on the stove.

"You can give me a cup of coffee, if you don't object to my occupying a corner of your room while I drink it."

"Certainly I don't object! I shall be delighted to oblige you!" the girl replied, immediately.

"We are not exactly strangers to each other, you know, for I have often had the pleasure of meeting you in the passageways, and I believe we have at times gone so far as to say good morning to each other."

The girl smilingly acknowledged that such was the fact.

"You see you are an early riser, while I am a late goer-to-bed, and as I come in to seek repose I meet you going out for the milk."

The girl laughed outright.

"Why do you smile?" he asked.

"At the funny mistake I made in regard to you," she replied.

"Meeting you every once in a while so early in the morning, coming in while I was going out. I of course came to the conclusion that you were returning from getting your breakfast, and I said to myself every now and then, in a joke, you know, that gentleman must have something on his mind or he would never get up so early. And now to find out that you were just coming in to go to bed—why, it's too funny for anything for me to make such a mistake." And then again both laughed heartily at the joke.

"You see, the profession I follow makes my habits of life very much different from the ordinary run of men. I am a journalist, and of course, in search of things to write about. And I am more likely to find my game when darkness covers the earth than when the sun shines."

This was partly the truth, as he did write for the press at odd intervals. Yet there was a certain amount of deception about it, and this girl seemed so pure that he hated to descend to deceit even when no harm was done or intended.

"Oh, if you are an author then you are a great man, and I feel highly honored at your accepting a cup of my poor coffee! I shall have to be careful how I behave, too, or you will be putting me in a story the first thing I know! I have read enough about such things to know that you authors are always on the lookout for subjects," she said, archly.

"Ah, yes, but I can hardly be called an author. I'm only a poor wretch of a penny-a-line writer, who does the amusements or police reports, or in fact any work to which I may be assigned. I seldom aspire to anything above a column sketch to be worked into a Sunday issue.

"But I forgot, I haven't introduced myself yet. My name is Andrew De Lormé, and I occupy a room on the third floor, back."

The lady made a curtsy in acknowledgment.

"And my name," she said, "is Lucille Gwinnet, dressmaker to command—although I do not presume that will interest you any, unless you chance to be married—"

At this point she paused abruptly and looked at him with inquisitiveness written in her bright eyes.

"Oh, no, I'm not married. The fact is—I will confide to you my secret—I never yet met a girl who would have me."

"Yes, yes, I've heard that said before; but for my part I do not believe that there is a man in the world who can't get a wife if he wants to, no matter how old, ugly, or cross he may be!" she exclaimed, decidedly.

"Ah, you relieve my mind; there is some chance for me then?"

"Oh, yes, there's a chance for every man, for there are plenty of girls who would seemingly rather submit to almost anything in the married state rather than try to live by themselves."

"But you are not one of that kind?"

"No, I am independent, and always was ever since I was big enough to look out for myself.

"I am an orphan, without father or mother, or a relative in the world, as far as I know.

"Just a friendless foundling, left dependent upon the charity of strangers; but since I have grown to girlhood I have managed to support myself.

"I came a perfect stranger to San Francisco, and although it was hard work at the beginning, yet I have built up a good trade. At present I really have more work than I can do.

"That is the reason why I have been up all night. I promised one of my best customers that she should have this dress," and she indicated the one which lay upon the floor, "by noon to-day, but when I came to get to work upon it I found I had promised more than I could perform unless I sat up all night. Rather than forfeit my word and disappoint a customer who was one of the first to employ me, and who introduced me to all her friends, I resolved to stick to my work until I finished it.

"Now it is so nearly done that a couple of hours more will complete it."

And she surveyed the dress with a triumphant air.

"What a contrast between this girl and the other," De Lormé murmured to himself. "And which of the two will win the great estate? Will it come to me to decide? I hope not, for I admire La Belle Helene despite the fact that I place no trust in her, and I should hate to be the instrument to bring to ruin her glorious castles in the air."

CHAPTER XVI.
THE TIN BOX.

"But now I will not talk shop anymore!" Lucille exclaimed, catching up the dress and spreading it upon the little sofa at the end of the apartment.

"I know that gentlemen don't take any interest in dresses and such things, and so I will not weary you with my chatter.

"Sit down and make yourself as comfortable as possible."

And she placed a chair for him.

"I am not very well prepared to entertain company, for I do not have any to speak of, with the exception of my customers.

"That unfortunate wretch Harry used to come and see me pretty often until I put a stop to it. I saw that he was really imposing upon my good nature and that the more I did for him the more I could do."

"I am much obliged for your hospitality, I am sure," De Lormé said, as he accepted the proffered chair and seated himself at the table.

"I haven't much of anything to offer you in the way of breakfast," she remarked, as she busied herself in pouring out the coffee.

"You see, meat is really so dear that I do not feel able to afford it more than once a day, so I breakfast on bread and coffee, have meat for my dinner, and bread and cake, with some kind of fruit and tea for my supper."

"No one ought to object to such a bill of fare."

"Oh, help yourself to bread and butter, now. Those are short-cakes I baked myself on top of the stove, you know, and some of my customers think they are just prime."

"They are splendid!" he exclaimed, as he buttered a piece of the short-cake and tasted it. "Do you know this is a great treat for me? It is a long time since any girl has turned out a cup of coffee for my humble self or pressed shortcakes upon me of her own baking, living as I do entirely in restaurants."

"But you have a mother or sisters somewhere, when you are at home, I mean?"

"No, I am all alone in the world. In fact I never knew any relative except my father. He wasn't much of a relative, although he was the only parent I have ever known. I grew up like a weed, almost totally uncared for. Had it not been for a singular old hermit miner who lived in the neighborhood, I should have grown to manhood as rough, rude and untaught as a young bear.

"But when I was only about five years old my father died.

"Drank too much at the village one night. In making his way home, he mistook the road, walked into the river, and although the water barely reached to his waist died amid the ripples of the Stanislaus."

"The Stanislaus!" exclaimed the girl, amazed.

"Yes, on the upper waters of the Stanislaus I was 'raised,' as the saying is."

"And so was I!"

"Is it possible? Why it is odd that we never encountered each other."

"Yes, it is strange, but then until I came to the city I was never two miles away from home in my life."

"Well, I didn't go round much myself. But to resume my story; when my father died the hermit miner took me in and brought me up as carefully as though I was his own son.

"He was an educated man, had traveled all over the world, and knew a little of almost everything, and so I enjoyed unusual advantages.

"A love disappointment had made the old man a recluse in early life, and though he avoided the society of his fellow-men yet he was to me the most generous of benefactors.

"If he had lived, perhaps my career in life would have been different, but death struck him down suddenly and I drifted here to San Francisco, and have lived an aimless, useless life ever since."

Strangely, De Lormé had asked the girl to give him a cup of coffee so that he might get an opportunity to question her regarding her history without exciting her suspicions and yet he had in some way drifted into telling his own story.

"Well, you had a father, but that is something I never possessed as far as I know," the girl remarked.

"There was some mystery about my birth, but just exactly what it was I never could find out.

"Mr. Gwinnet—Mr. Thomas Gwinnet, the one who reared me, although one of the nicest old men in the world, yet once in a while drank more liquor than was good for him. Then he would talk to me in the oddest fashion, so utterly incomprehensible that I could never make head nor tail of it.

"'You are now obscured by a dark cloud, Lucille, my dear,' he would say, 'but one of these days your star will burst forth in such brilliancy that all the world will be apt to bow down and worship at your shrine,' and a whole string of such nonsense.

"When he got over the effects of the liquor and I asked him what in the world he meant by talking so queerly, he would laugh and reply:

"'Oh, don't bother your head about such foolishness.'

"'When a man has got a certain amount of good whisky in him he is apt to say all sorts of foolish things,' and that was all the satisfaction I could ever get."

"He wanted to make you believe that there wasn't anything in it."

"Yes, but I knew there was. And this scamp of a Harry had some suspicion in regard to the matter, because, when I came to the city, bringing the news that his father was dead, almost the first question that he asked me was if the 'old man' had made a clean breast of it before he died in regard to me. When I said he hadn't he would not believe me.

"'Well, then, if he didn't speak he gave you something. He had some documents, and there is a good deal of money in them if they are rightly handled.' And that is what he referred to when you heard him say that if I did not speak he would kill me."

"I see. He has got an inkling that some valuable secret exists and is anxious to have a finger in the pie," De Lormé observed, thoughtfully.

He was thoroughly convinced that he was on the right track of the long-lost heir now.

Accident had triumphed where design had failed.

"He and I have not been on good terms for some time now," the girl continued, "for I grew tired of helping the worthless fellow when I discovered what a scamp he was. But he made his appearance about eleven o'clock last night, saying that he had no place to sleep and begged me to allow him to lie on the sofa until morning.

"I saw that he was under the influence of liquor, and as I was going to stay up all night, I consented. I was afraid that if I turned him out he would get into the hands of the police, but it was a cunning trick on his part to get a chance to threaten me at a time when he believed there wouldn't be any one near to assist me."

"And it is only fancy then in regard to this secret— but pardon me, I meant not to pry into your affairs," De Lormé added, hastily.

"Oh, I can reply," the girl answered, frankly.

"As far as I am concerned, I know of no secret that Mr. Gwinnet left behind."

De Lormé was baffled, for he thought he was on the right track.

"It is a strange affair," he remarked. "But speaking of that old mining region, do you know I would like to go back there again? I would like to stand once again on the old flats of the Stanislaus."

In amazement the girl jumped to her feet, astonishment written in every feature.

"What is that you say?" she cried. "Repeat that last sentence, please, so that I may be sure there isn't any mistake!"

"Mistake?" asked De Lormé, unable to comprehend the girl's meaning.

"Yes, for I must be careful to fulfill the trust confided to me."

"But I do not understand!"

"Repeat the sentence—or rather the last few words."

"I said I would like to stand once again on the old flats of the Stanislaus."

"The old flats of the Stanislaus," repeated the girl.

"That is correct, word for word, not one wrong."

"The box is yours."

"The box?"

"Yes, the little tin box confided to my care by Mr. Gwinnet on his death-bed, and he made me take a solemn oath on my bended knees that I would never speak of the box, nor give it to any one until a person should come to me and say, 'the old flats of the Stanislaus,' and then I was to deliver the box to him."

"Oh, but this is purely accidental on my part!" De Lormé exclaimed. "I know nothing of the box, and when I spoke I had no idea that I was giving you any signal."

"The instructions were as plain as plain can be: 'To the first person who says to you those words you must deliver the box!'" the girl exclaimed, positively.

CHAPTER XVII.
AN UNEXPECTED DISAPPEARANCE.

De Lormé was silent for a few moments canvassing the matter in his mind.

That the tin box, which had been entrusted to the girl's care, would be apt to contain some documents that would throw some light upon the dark mystery of the lost heir was almost certain.

And as the chapter of accidents had thrown the box into his hands, why should he not take advantage of the fact?

There wasn't much doubt in his mind that the girl was the lost heir to the five millions of dollars.

In this matter, as often happens, just by chance the discovery had been made.

"Well, I suppose I may as well examine the box; I don't see as it will do any particular hurt, although I am quite positive that it is not intended for me," he said at last.

"Be that as it may, I think I ought to obey my instructions to the letter, and I can only do so by giving you the box," the girl persisted.

"Nothing at all was said as to whether the party to whom I was to deliver it knew anything about the box or not.

"The command was:

"'To the person who says to you, 'On the old flats of the Stanislaus,' you must deliver the tin box which you will find concealed in a cavity in the floor right under the head of my bed. Upon examination you will find a small piece of the floor broken away. It looks like a rat-hole; put your fingers in it and lift; you will find that about a foot of the board will come up, and in that hole you will find the box.'"

"A novel hiding-place truly," De Lormé observed.

"Yes, and one which from its simplicity would not be apt to be discovered," the girl replied. "And since the box has come into my possession, I have been greatly troubled by the fear that some one would discover that I had it. They might jump to the conclusion, from its peculiar appearance, that it contained valuables."

"And you were afraid of being robbed of the treasure, eh?"

"Yes, sir, and I assure you it will take a weight from my mind to be enabled to surrender it to you."

Then, rising, she took a pair of scissors and ripped open the end of one of the sofa pillows. In the pillow, the box was concealed.

"Well, that is about as odd a hiding-place as any one could devise," De Lormé remarked.

"Yes, I did not believe that anyone would think of looking for valuables in such a place.

"Of course it was ridiculous, but ever since the box came into my possession I have been worried by the idea that somebody might suspect that I have it and endeavor to take it away from me."

"It certainly doesn't look as if it contained anything valuable," De Lormé observed, as he examined the box, which the girl had placed, in his hands.

It was a small tin affair, about five inches long by four wide and two deep.

Just about such a box as children use to carry their luncheon to school, but unlike them it was securely locked, as De Lormé discovered when, in a spirit of curiosity, he endeavored to open it.

"It is locked," he said.

"Yes, and I haven't the key."

"Oh, it doesn't make any particular difference," he replied. "The first locksmith that I come across will undoubtedly be able to open it.

"As far as I can make out it is nothing but a common kind of a lock, without anything complicated about it.

"Of course you understand I am going into this matter really under protest, for I don't think I am the party into whose hands it was intended the box should fall."

"Oh, that is all right," the girl answered, with a light laugh.

"Even if such is the case there will not be much harm done, and when you examine the contents of the box you will know about it."

"Neither gold nor silver in it judging by the weight," De Lormé remarked, as he balanced the box in his hand.

"No, probably papers.

"That rascal of a Harry got the idea into his head that his father had entrusted some valuable secret to me before he died, and he has tried in a dozen different ways to get me to reveal it to him.

"His idea though was that his father had some treasures stowed away, the secret hiding-place of which he had revealed to me on his death-bed. Of course I protested stoutly that I knew nothing about any such thing, and it was the truth, too."

"I will hunt up a locksmith the first thing in the morning, and then when the box is opened we will know about it."

By this time De Lormé had finished his coffee, which he had been leisurely sipping during the conversation, and rose to retire.

"I am very much obliged to you for the coffee, and now I will say good-night—or, good morning, rather.

"I will get a few hours' sleep, and then set to work to solve the mystery attached to that marvelous box."

"I must admit that I am very curious in regard to it, but then curiosity is one of my leading traits, you know."

"The moment I get a key fitted I will bring the box to you, and you shall have the satisfaction of opening it with your own hands."

"Oh, no, I mustn't do that, you know. That privilege belongs to you."

"Yes, but on this occasion I shall most certainly give it to you, and as I yielded to your request to take the box, you must oblige me in this matter."

"Very well, just as you say; it will not do any harm, anyway."

"Good-by, and again I thank you for your coffee," he said, with his hand on the door knob.

"Don't mention it, I beg," she replied. "It is I who should thank you for coming in so timely a manner to my assistance, and I don't really know how I will ever be able to pay you."

"Don't trouble your head about that matter; the debt that is never demanded will never have to be paid. Adieu."

And then he took his departure.

De Lormé proceeded straight up-stairs to his room, and as he made his way through the entry and up the stairs the thought came into his mind of what a wide difference there was in the two girls with whom he had the pleasure of partaking of refreshments that night.

"By Jove! I really believe I enjoyed the second repast, simple as it was, more than the first," he soliloquized, as he mounted the stairs.

"The fascination exercised by La Belle Helene is like the influence of a draught of strong liquor. It both exhilarates and intoxicates, and when the victim wakes in the morning his head feels as big as a bushel basket, and he is almost ready to swear that he will never expose himself to the temptation again, while this other girl's presence acts upon a man like a soothing potion. It both calms and refreshes.

"Oh, decidedly if there is war in regard to this matter—if the five millions of dollars lie between La Belle Helene and Lucille Gwinnet, it will be impossible for me to enter the lists as the champion of the Bella Union beauty even if I do not take up the cudgels openly for the other." By the time that the young man had come to this conclusion he had reached the door of his apartment.

His door had the usual lock, and also provision outside for a padlock, installed by some former tenant. Once inside, he turned the key and left it in the lock as usual.

"Now then a nap for about four hours will fix me all right and I will see what this mysterious tin box contains," he remarked, as he placed the box upon the table and regarded it with a curious look.

Then it suddenly occurred to him that he had a bunch of small keys, some one of which might chance to fit the lock.

The trial was made, but they all proved to be too large.

"Well, there isn't any hurry about the matter," he observed, as be sat down upon the edge of the bed and removed his coat and shoes.

"The box will not run away while I sleep, and five or six hours' time will not make any particular difference.

"It is hardly worth while to undress for so short a time, so I will lie down just as I am," he continued. And suiting the action to the word he extended himself upon the bed.

De Lormé was in a perfect state of health despite the rather irregular life that he led, and possessed the happy faculty of going to sleep almost immediately after extending his limbs upon the couch.

Within ten minutes from the time of lying down he was sound in slumber's chain.

Like most people to whom sleep comes easily his slumbers were light and a slight noise served to awaken him.

He had not slept more than thirty minutes when he awoke with a sudden start.

It seemed to him as though the door of his room had just closed, but this was not probable, for he had locked it after entering.

Naturally though he glanced toward the table to assure himself that the tin box was all right.

But the box had disappeared.

CHAPTER XVIII.
WHAT BECAME OF THE BOX.

The celerity with which De Lormé leaped from the bed to the floor when he discovered that the box had disappeared would have delighted the heart of a professional acrobat.

His eyes fell upon the clock as he bounded to the floor.

He had been asleep just thirty minutes.

"By Jove! It was no dream!" he cried, as he stood erect and gazed around the room.

"Some one has been in the room and taken the box, and it was the creaking of the door in closing roused me from my slumbers; but they have not had time to get far away and I stand a chance of overtaking them!"

He rushed to the door.

As he had anticipated it was unlocked, and yet he was certain he had turned the key after he entered.

It only took De Lormé a moment to put on his shoes, slip into his coat, and then he rushed to the door prepared to give chase.

But when he turned the knob, the door would not open, and, for a moment, De Lormé was perplexed.

The device by means of which the intruder had gained admittance to the room in spite of the locked door, was easily guessed by the young man, whose Bohemian life had made him acquainted with a great many queer things.

The door had been unlocked by means of a pair of pincers—the burglar's nippers—which seizing the end of the key, projecting through the lock on the outside, easily turned it in its wards and so shot back the bolt.

But how the door had been fastened without the aid of the key was for a moment a mystery, although the reason for the operation was plain enough.

The sneak-thief, who had stolen into the room and purloined the box, feared pursuit, so took measures to guard against it.

Then, all of a sudden, as he turned the knob and endeavored to open the door, which refused to budge, the idea of what device the intruder had used to delay pursuit flashed upon him.

Upon the outside of the portal were two "screw-eyes," one fastened in the door frame, the other in the door itself, and so arranged that when the door was shut the two came together, one just above the other.

Some fearful tenant who had occupied the apartment before De Lormé's time, had arranged the screw-eyes so as to slip a padlock through them whenever he went out.

The intruder had seen this feature and utilized the screw-eyes to check pursuit by slipping a wire or a stout cord through the two, a maneuver that only required a few seconds of time for its execution.

Grasping the door-knob, De Lormé applied all his strength.

Gradually the door yielded to the pressure, and when it was opened half an inch, by inserting his left hand in the crack the young man was able to bring his strength to bear in an effective manner; then, with a sudden jerk, he forced the door open.

A bit of copper wire had been passed through the screw-eyes, and if the intruder had not been in such a hurry to make his escape as to neglect twisting the ends of the wire, it would have been almost an impossibility for any one to open the door from the inside.

From the fact that the room had been entered by means of a pair of nippers and that the intruder had been provided with this piece of wire, it seemed to indicate to De Lormé's mind that some regular "professional" had seen fit to pay him a visit. But it appeared odd to the young man that the intruder had contented himself with the tin box without attempting to secure other plunder.

"Probably I stirred in my sleep, and so scared him away," De Lormé muttered, as he hurried to the stairs.

From the manner in which the stairs were arranged it was possible from any of the landings to see the stairs below, so De Lormé could command a view clear to the lower entry, but not a soul was in sight.

"The delay in forcing open the door has given him time to gain the street!" the young man exclaimed, as he hurried down the stairs, descending with astonishing rapidity.

After gaining the lower hallway he hurried out into the street.

The cold gray light of the morning had begun to chase away the dark and gloomy shadows of the night and all objects could be plainly distinguished.

Not a soul was in sight.

"To the right or left?" he cried, as he hesitated for a moment in the doorway.

"To the right!" he exclaimed, in answer to the question.

"Experience teaches that man involuntarily turns to the right if uncertain in what direction to proceed."

Acting upon this theory, De Lormé went to the right and hurried up the street.

Not a living soul was yet in sight, nor was there even the distant sound of footfalls to suggest that some fugitive was hurrying away.

"He must have turned this first corner if he went this way," De Lormé muttered, as he attempted to run along with noiseless steps so as not to alarm the intruder if he was within hearing.

It did not seem probable to De Lormé that the fugitive had time enough to get out of both sight and hearing.

Of course it was possible, De Lormé thought, that he had made a mistake in turning to the right, and that the fugitive had gone in the opposite direction.

But it was too late now to act on that belief.

De Lormé hurried around the corner of the street and, in his haste, pretty near pitched headlong over the form of a man extended at full length upon the sidewalk.

"Hallo, hallo! What the deuce is this?" he cried, as he knelt by the prostrate man. Hardly had the words left his lips when he recognized the other.

It was Harry Gwinnet, the fellow who had threatened the girl, and as he made the discovery a sudden idea flashed into De Lormé's head.

"The chances are a hundred to one that this is the rascal who went for the tin box!" the young man exclaimed.

"He listened outside of the door and either managed to overhear our conversation or else through the keyhole saw the girl hand me the box.

"But what on earth is the matter with him now?

"Seized with a fit, maybe, brought on by excitement.

"I'll 'go through' him and soon see whether my suspicions are true or not."

De Lormé knelt by the side of the insensible man and proceeded to examine his pockets.

The first articles he fished out of Gwinnet's pocket was a pair of burglar's "nippers," and a small spool of copper wire, similar to that which had been used to fasten the door on the outside.

This was pretty strong proof that he had been the intruder who had made away with the tin box, but the box itself did not come to light; a gold pen did, though, which had been on the table by the side of the box, which in his hurry De Lormé had not noticed to be missing.

"But what the deuce has the fellow done with the box?" the young man muttered.

"Is it possible that he had it in his hand and when he fell the shock forced it from his grip?"

And then De Lormé bent a searching gaze around, but no tin box could he see.

By this time Gwinnet began to recover his consciousness.

"Well, I've got him foul, anyway," De Lormé soliloquized, as he knelt by the side of the prostrate man and watched him gradually recover his senses.

"He either tells me what he has done with the tin box or else I will throw him into the calaboose!"

At this point Gwinnet's eyes opened.

They blinked vacantly for a few moments, and then, suddenly recognizing the other, shot forth a glance of hatred.

"Aha, you know me, I see, my boy!" De Lormé remarked.

Gwinnet rose slowly to a sitting posture.

"What do you want here, curse you?" he exclaimed in a feeble voice, evidently quite weak.

"Come to look after your health, of course," De Lormé responded. "You have no idea how much interest I take in a fellow about your size."

"Oh, stow that and clear out!" the other responded, angrily.

"No, no, I couldn't think of doing such a thing; but,

I say, what is the matter with you—how comes it that I find you stretched out here?"

"I have been assaulted."

"Assaulted?" cried De Lormé, in surprise.

"Yes, by a scoundrel with a sand-club, I presume.

"All I know is that just after I turned the corner a tall, ugly-looking fellow jumped out from that dark doorway there and gave me a lick with something that laid me out cold, and I reckon it must be a sand-club from the way it fetched me."

CHAPTER XIX.
THE SEARCH.

Here was an explanation of the mysterious disappearance of the tin box.

Gwinnet in his flight with the supposed treasure had run into the ambush of a night-hawk on the watch for prey—and had been sandbagged. The ruffian had secured the tin box and then been frightened away by the noise made by De Lormé in his approach before he could get any more booty.

"You mustn't blame the man; he had evidently never been introduced to you," De Lormé remarked.

"If he had been acquainted with you he would not have troubled you, of course, for dog won't eat dog, you know."

"Say, you had better keep a civil tongue in your head," the other retorted. "You needn't think because you got the bulge on me to-night that you can keep it up all the time, for you can't do it. My turn will come, and I will go for you in a way that you will despise."

"Brag is a good dog, but holdfast is a better," De Lormé remarked, sententiously.

"And when you come to talk about my having the bulge on you, I think I have got it now, and in the worst kind of way, too."

"How so?" demanded the other, evidently a little uneasy.

"What have you done with the tin box you took out of my room a little while ago?"

"A tin box!" and Gwinnet affected to be amazed at the charge.

"Yes, a tin box!" cried De Lormé, sternly. "It isn't of

the least use for you to attempt to get out of it, for I have got you dead to rights.

"Here's the pair of nippers with which you turned the key in the lock of my door from the outside, and so gained admission while I was asleep. Also, here is copper wire, some of which you used to fasten my door on the outside so as to keep me from pursuing you. And last, but not least, here is a gold pen which you took from my table at the same time that you collared the box."

"You can't prove it—it's all a lie!" the young rascal exclaimed.

"That is a question which the police magistrate will probably be able to settle," De Lormé retorted.

"Say, let up, can't you?" whined Gwinnet, changing his tone abruptly, apparently coming to the conclusion he was in a bad box and that the quicker he got out of it the better.

"What do you want to hit a fellow for when he is down?"

"You own up, then?"

"To what?" Gwinnet muttered.

"To what I said!" De Lormé cried, sharply. "Why do you try to quibble about the matter? Were you not in my room?"

"Well, s'pose I was?"

"You stole the pen and the box—you listened outside of the door of Miss Lucille's room, or else peeped through the keyhole and saw her give me the box."

"What business had she to give it to you, anyway?" he interrupted, indignantly. "I was the fellow who ought to have it."

"Never mind that question! There isn't the least use of wasting time in discussing it. The box was in my possession and you stole it!"

"Yes I did," Gwinnet acknowledged, sulking.

"And now what has become of it?"

"The cuss that sand-bagged me got it, of course.

"I had it in my hand inside of my coat, and I s'pose he thought he had struck a bonanza, but I reckon he will find out that he made a mistake before he gets through.

"I was disappointed about the thing myself, for I reckoned the box would pan out something handsome; some diamonds, mebbe, or something of that kind. But from the weight of it I reckon that there isn't anything but papers in it; they may be valuable, and then again they may not.

"I always reckoned the old man was more or less crazy during the last ten years of his life, and it would be just like what a lunatic would do to put up a lot of trash in a box of this kind and then go on to making out that it was worth a heap to somebody or other.

"But I say, old man, are you going to let up or not? I'll give you my word that I will not trouble you again in any way."

"If you are wise you will not," De Lormé remarked, in an extremely significant way, rising to his feet as he spoke.

The other was quick to follow his example.

"Oh, that is all right; you needn't try to scare me, for I ain't that kind of a hairpin," and with this remark Gwinnet retreated.

De Lormé returned to his room somewhat annoyed at his ill-success.

The tin box seemed to be something akin to the Irishman's lively flea; when you put your finger on it, it wasn't there.

Now it had fallen into the hands of one of the night-hawks, and whether it could be traced and reclaimed was a question.

One thing seemed pretty clear to De Lormé's mind though, and that was that young Gwinnet would not be apt to trouble his head about the matter.

De Lormé did not in the least doubt that he had heard the true story of the disappearance of the box.

Gwinnet had sought to get the article in his possession under the idea that it contained valuables.

The footpad who had waylaid and sand-bagged the young rascal undoubtedly would jump to the same conclusion when he saw the box so securely fastened.

But now the question arose, would the man who now held possession of the box have sense enough to know the value of the document, or documents, contained in the box, supposing that there were any such articles in the tin casket?

Of course, of his own knowledge, De Lormé was not sure that such was the case.

If the contents of the box seemed to be of value to the man who held it, most certainly he would preserve them carefully with the idea of selling them to somebody.

And after duly weighing the matter in his mind, De Lormé came to the conclusion that the likeliest method of getting on the track of the tin box would be by a carefully-worded advertisement in the newspapers, supplemented by a small handbill which could be thoroughly circulated in all the low saloons and dives of Frisco.

By this means the attention of the man who had captured the box might be secured.

With his experience of the undercurrent of life as it is in all big cities, De Lormé knew there wasn't much use in doing anything until about noon.

The evil spirits who prey only during the hours

when darkness covers the earth, seek their rest during the morning hours, and seldom stir from their lairs until the sun has passed its meridian.

So, about noon our hero put his scheme into operation.

The handbills were widely distributed, and each one of the afternoon papers contained an advertisement under the head of "Personals," referring to the lost box.

As young Gwinnet had said, his attacker was a tall fellow, and like a great spider he had skulked in the shelter of the dark doorway waiting for some unsuspecting wayfarer to make his appearance who looked as if he was worth robbing.

In his hand he brandished the weapon so dear to the heart of the Western ruffian, the sand-club, a tool borrowed from the villains of the East, and which is merely a long canvas sack filled with sand and looking more like a large sausage than anything else.

Around the corner came the prey.

The desperado, who was no other than the jovial Scotty Bilk, only waited long enough to assure himself that the newcomer was worth "going for" and then jumped out at him.

A single lick, which young Gwinnet vainly attempted to guard against by throwing up his hand, and down the victim went.

Out came the hand from beneath the coat, and the tin box was disclosed.

The appearance of the box caught the eyes of the night plunderer immediately.

"Aha!" he cried, in grim satisfaction, "this hyer looks like something w'ot will be worth picking up."

Then he thrust the box under his coat, after first

ascertaining that it was securely locked.

"Now, then, for to see w'ot this hyer galoot has got inter his pockets, for fear some mean cuss might come along and go through him, which would be a sin and a shame."

But as he stooped to make the examination his keen ears detected that footsteps were cautiously but rapidly approaching.

"The perlice, or I'm a sucker!" the footpad muttered.

And then springing to his feet, he retreated as rapidly and quietly as a nocturnal animal disturbed at his prey.

CHAPTER XX.
THE O'BALLYHOO.

The well-known Frisco blood, Edward McMichael, after his encounter with and defeat by the Bohemian, departed in a great rage, vowing vengeance.

And, to do the blood justice, he meant every word he said.

It was no idle boast.

He prided himself upon keeping his word in such matters, as many an unfortunate fellow had discovered to his cost.

McMichael was possessed of plenty of money and had but little to do except to kill time. The family wealth had been so carefully invested by his prudent father, the horny-handed old Scotsman who had originally acquired it, that about all the business McMichael had was to go to the bank and get his money when it came due.

And the estate was such a princely one that even with all his extravagant ways, the young man seldom overdrew his regular interest.

Further, the idea that he, a man rated as being second in wealth to no man on the "coast," should be ignominiously defeated by this scamp of an adventurer, a nobody who depended upon his wits for a living, was simply outrageous.

The shame and mortification he experienced in regard to the matter went far to sober him, although he, in company with his boon companions, had been indulging freely in liquor.

But McMichael inherited the hard head of his sire as well as a good share of his Scotch obstinacy, so it required a good deal of liquor to upset him. And when he suffered an affront, as in this case, he rested not until he took measures to avenge the insult.

In this emergency he had "no use " for the wild young blades that had been his companions in the drinking bout. Then too, he was enraged that they had not backed his quarrel more heartily.

But he knew a certain party to whom he could go with the assurance that he would receive the best of counsel.

At the time of which we write, there flourished in San Francisco an Irish gentleman of middle age who proudly termed himself the O'Ballyhoo.

Captain Dionysius O'Ballyhoo was his full title, and he was one of the noted men of the town.

The O'Ballyhoo was a man whose personal appearance would attract attention almost anywhere.

He stood fully six feet high, well-built and muscular, and looked like a man of forty, although he would never see fifty again. Yet, he always claimed to be "just turned forty, me b'ye!"

His features were prominent and decidedly Celtic in their cast, and his luxuriant side- whiskers, mustache, imperial and short, curly hair were as black as the raven's wing.

Incredulous and suspicious people declared the gallant captain wore a wig and that his hirsute appendages would be a tawny gray in color were it not for the barber's aid.

The captain's features always wore a smile, and he essayed to be a hail-fellow-well-met with everybody he encountered.

On the street he invariably carried a light switch cane which he swung with a semi-military air, and as a rule he always nodded in the most polite yet deferential manner to every well-dressed man he encountered, whether he enjoyed the pleasure of his acquaintance or not. This was so that a stranger, noticing the Irishman's bearing upon the promenade, would surely believe that he had the most extensive acquaintance of any man in the city.

The captain was a gentleman, for he toiled not, neither did he spin. When some inquisitive stranger inquired how the man contrived to live in the style in which he did, for he always had plenty of money, the explanation was given that the captain was a gentleman possessed of a vast landed estate in Ireland. He had been obliged to quit his native land on account of a little difficulty with the "hated Saxons," who with iron heel pressed so heavily upon Erin.

Indeed, there were rare occasions when the O'Ballyhoo allowed liquor to get the best of him. This was not often, for it was his boast that he was a "four bottle man," and had never been laid under the table in a fair drinking bout in his life. But it was on these occasions he was wont to declare that when the time was "ripe," at the head of an army of the "b'yes" he would descend upon Ireland, and drive the "murthering red-coats into the sea," as great St. Patrick did the snakes and other creeping reptiles in the days of yore.

There were a few men in San Francisco though who knew the captain as he truly was, and were not imposed upon by his arts. They knew him as the king of all adventurers—the cleverest man with the painted pasteboards that ever flipped a card on the Pacific coast, and a really wonderful billiard player.

The O'Ballyhoo was a man who could handle the billiard ivories so expertly as to be able to play a losing game without allowing any one to perceive that he was playing to lose instead of to win. The men who did not know the captain as he really was, thought of him only as a fifth-rate player, and great was the wonder when the Irishman succeeded in winning a game opposed by a first-class player, and for "big" money.

Men who watched the captain closely soon discovered these series of lucky "scratches" never occurred to the O'Ballyhoo except when there was a large sum of money pending upon the game.

The captain was also considered the authority of the town when it came to an "affair of honor."

He had been "out" a half-a-dozen times since his advent in Frisco, and on every occasion he had succeeded in "doing up" his man.

With pistol or sword he was equally skillful, but with the rifle he would not meddle, as he declared with many a round oath that it was no weapon for a gentleman.

To the young fellows about town who desired to perfect themselves in the gentlemanly art of killing obnoxious people as neatly and as quickly as possible, the captain condescended to give lessons. For this service he was careful to say he made no charge, "for I'm a gintleman and no thafe of a fencing-master." But if the pupil felt a desire to aid in the liberation of "dear ould Erin," fifty or a hundred dollars would be gladly accepted, for he was the treasurer of the secret order. As it looked mean to refuse a little favor of this kind, the captain managed to make a pretty good thing out of his lessons, while the pupils paid a big price for the "favor."

So, by the aid of these varied accomplishments, the O'Ballyhoo managed to live like a fighting-cock, as he would have expressed it.

It was this redoubtable personage that McMichael

sought after his skirmish with the Bohemian.

The hour was late, but the O'Ballyhoo was a night-bird, and seldom sought his couch until the gray light of the dawn began to line the eastern skies, for the pigeons best worth the plucking were generally to be found after the theaters were out.

These birds were generally young men lucky enough to have plenty of money in their pockets, and who were out for the purpose of having what is known to the gilded youths as a "red-hot time." They are apt to be more easily induced to put up their wealth in a game of chance as midnight approaches, and the drinks which they have taken begin to have due effect upon their brains.

O'Ballyhoo's favorite resort was a palatial saloon only about a rifle-shot from McGuire's Opera House, then the leading dramatic temple of the Pacific slope.

This saloon was fitted up in elegant style.

On the ground floor was an elaborate barroom, with a gambling apartment in the rear, to which the common herd had access.

Up-stairs was devoted to a "big game," and there only men of standing who were known to be heavy players were admitted.

It paid to keep the game select, although from the very founding of the city of San Francisco, gambling in all shapes has always been more open and aboveboard than in any other place in the world, with the exception of the gaming spas of the European continent.

On the third floor of the building were private rooms devoted to "short card" parties, such as poker, which were always well patronized. The man in search of amusement in the gambling line, who could not find what he sought in this building, must indeed be hard to please.

Straight to this popular resort young McMichael proceeded, after his encounter with De Lormé.

As he had expected, the captain was in the second-floor apartment, occupied when McMichael entered in paying his respects to a magnificent lunch. This was really a banquet, flanked by wines and liquors of all sorts—which was always set out promptly at the stroke of midnight.

CHAPTER XXI.
PLANNING THE ATTACK.

"Aha, is it there ye are?" exclaimed the captain, who spoke with a slight "brogue," not at all unpleasant to the ear, being the soft and melodious accent of the south of Ireland and not the more harsh burr of the North.

"Clement, ye divil, let Julius here"—and he nodded to the grinning chef, a mature man of African descent who presided over the feast—"give ye a taste of this venison—a foiner bit of deer I haven't tasted since I killed the big red buck in the Connemara hills, and that was the talk of the whole country-side, for it was, by all odds, the finest deer that had been shot in fifty years.

"And I can be afther recommending this champagne too; let Julius fill you out a glass of that.

"It's neither English gooseberry-juice, nor American cider, but the real stuff, and a sup of it puts new life in a man."

"You can give me a glass of the wine, Julius, but I'll pass on the venison for I've just had supper," McMichael said.

The wine was filled out, the captain allowed his glass to be replenished, and the two drank in silence.

"Can you spare me ten or fifteen minutes, captain?" the young man asked, after the glasses were emptied.

"Certainly, me b'ye, delighted to oblige ye in any way!" exclaimed the captain.

And this was true enough, for a man like the Irish adventurer is always delighted to do anything in his power for so generous a patron as McMichael was to those whom he favored. Many a ten-dollar gold-piece had the captain "borrowed" from the young man when in want of funds, generally from a run of ill-luck at the gaming-table, when the veteran allowed his gambler instincts to get the better of his judgment, and he played recklessly and without due caution.

But when he was in funds again and went to repay the loan the young man always waved the money aside with a careless air.

"I never keep account of these trifles," he would say. "Keep it and lend it to some good man who has gone broke, and needs the cash."

It is hardly necessary to remark that the captain never struck any better man than himself, or one who needed the money more.

McMichael led the way to a corner of the room remote from the banqueting-board and from the gamblers, busy around the green cloth, where he and the captain could speak without the likelihood of being overheard.

In such a resort as this every one generally attends strictly to their own business, and a private conversation can usually be carried on without danger of eavesdroppers playing the spy.

After they were seated the captain noticed the peculiar look upon the face of the young man, whose bruises were yet to appear. Being well acquainted with the moods of McMichael, he understood that something had occurred to ruffle him.

It was the captain's business to study the "human face divine," and in such matters he seldom made a mistake.

"Phwat is wrong wid ye? Has something happened to vex ye?"

"You have hit it exactly. I have been insulted in the grossest manner, and I want satisfaction."

"To be shure—of course, that is only natural: and

how did it happen, me buck?"

"Well, it was my own fault that I got into the scrape, but, you see, some of the boys and myself were out for a time and when we happened to run across a fellow with a basket it struck us that it would be a jolly good joke to have some fun with him."

"Certainly, to be shure, the most natural thing in the wourld! Many is the times that I've had jollification in that way myself," and the captain rubbed his hands in glee as he thought over old times.

"Well, as the thing turned out, we didn't have such a jolly time as we expected when we started in.

"The fellow was not disposed to submit to the joke. He was ugly, showed fight, and in brief he laid us all out in first-class style."

Then he related the particulars of the contest, and the Irishman listened in astonishment.

"Now don't be after taking offense at me question, but was ivery mother's son of ye drunk that this feller played tenpins with you?"

"Oh, no; we had all been drinking pretty freely, of course, but none of us were so much under the weather that we couldn't handle ourselves."

"Faith! This feller must be a boxer, for ye are not bad wid yer fists yerself."

"Oh, yes, there wasn't any mistake about that. He was a boxer, and a champion one too, as we found out after we had got into the row.

"But I am not satisfied, you know. I have never allowed anybody to take such liberties with me, and I don't intend to begin now.

"I told the fellow he would hear from me again, and I mean that he shall too!"

"Of course, certainly, no gintleman could be afther

standing such treatment."

"I don't intend to, and I want you to wait on the fellow to-morrow on my behalf and invite him to take a quiet little walk with me some pleasant morning, so as to give me an opportunity to drill a hole through him with a leaden ball, or stick the blade of a sword in among his ribs, whichever he may prefer."

"Certainly, me b'ye, I shall be delighted!" exclaimed the Irishman rubbing his hands together, briskly, in a professional sort of way.

"I have never been so angry over a thing in my life!" McMichael asserted. "And nothing but the blood of this fellow will satisfy me."

"Of course—the most natural feeling in the wourld. I can sympathize wid ye.

"It will be aisy for you to fix the blaggard. Thanks to the lessons you have taken from me, there are mighty few men in this town who are yer equal wid either sword or pistol.

"But give me the spalpeen's address; I will be afther waiting on him the first thing afther breakfast, and ax him to be kind enough for to app'int an hour whin he can come out and be killed like a gintleman."

"I guess you know the fellow, he is pretty well known around town."

"Mighty few men in Frisco who are around town that I do not know!" exclaimed the captain.

"His name is De Lormé—Andrew De Lormé."

A low whistle escaped from the lips of the Irishman, and a look of astonishment appeared upon his face.

"You know the fellow, I see."

"There's mighty few men in Frisco that don't!" O'Ballyhoo replied.

"In the name of all that is holy, couldn't ye find

somebody else for to pick a quarrel wid?"

"Wow, wow! He's the worst b'ye in the town, quiet as he looks!

"Me b'ye, that man is a divil! He smashed a feller right in the face wid a tumbler once—a man who was a dead shot—the cock of the walk, do ye mind, and both out pistol. But De Lormé was the quickest, or the other feller's pistol missed fire—I don't know which was the rights of it—and this divil killed him right in his tracks."

McMichael listened to the recital with a gloomy brow.

"But it doesn't follow that because he got the best of this encounter he will be able to dispose of me so easily."

"Me b'ye, the man is said to be the best shot on the Pacific slope. I have seen him make ten bull's eyes off hand at a hundred feet, one afther the other.

"I've seen him stand wid his back to the target, wheel and fire, apparently widout taking aim, and hit it every time.

"And wid the sword—wow, wow! I faced him once wid the foils for a friendly bout—he was taught by an old Frenchman, a feller who had served under Napoleon, and had more tricks wid the sword at his finger's end than any man I ever knew.

"Well, sir, I could do nothing wid him, and if we had been engaged in the real thing he would have spitted me inside of five minutes.

"He has a wrist like iron, and I couldn't parry his straight lunges, leave alone his tricks, to save me life.

"Youth and strength must be served, you know, and he broke through my guard every time.

"I wouldn't insure yer life for sixpence to stand ag'in' that feller with either sword or pistol, or rifle aither!"

"What is to be done, then? Am I to tamely submit to my defeat? My blood boils at the thought!" McMichael cried, in a fury.

"Whist!" said the captain, with a cautious glance around.

"Are ye particular whether ye get at him fair or foul?"

"Not in the least, so I wreak my vengeance upon him!" McMichael declared.

"It will cost ye a thousand dollars!"

"If it costs five I'll go it!"

The captain studied his patron, and said, "It's a bargain!"

The two shook hands.

CHAPTER XXII.
WHAT THE BOX CONTAINED.

According to his notion, the social outcast, who called himself Scotty Bilk, had "played in hard luck" on this eventful evening.

His funds were about down to the "bedrock," as he would have said, and it was absolutely necessary for him to make a raise in some way. Therefore, he was inclined to denounce the ill-luck which was evidently following him when the sound of the rapidly approaching footsteps scared him away from his prey before he had a chance to go through Gwinnet's pockets.

If he had been more than mortal and gifted with the power of knowing the unknown, he would not have wasted much time in lamenting this fact, for he would not have found enough valuables on the person of his victim to pay him for his trouble.

But he didn't know this, and as young Gwinnet was well dressed and looked like a "Blood," the footpad fancied that he would have "panned out" rich.

He was somewhat consoled, though, by the capture of the tin box.

In the course of his "professional" experience he had run across similar articles, although he had never seen one as small as this before.

But the fact that it was securely locked led him to believe that it was a cash-box containing valuables.

The block was a short one, and as he was a swift runner, being possessed of a long and muscular pair of legs, he managed to turn the corner of the next street and thus get out of sight before the man whose approach had alarmed him, came into sight.

After he turned the corner he slackened his pace to a walk for fear of meeting some inquisitive policeman who might take it into his head to inquire why he was in such a hurry.

From long experience in such matters he knew that he was tolerably safe from pursuit, and as there wasn't any one in sight he proceeded to examine the prize he had secured.

His keen eyes had detected that there was a keyhole in the box when he first wrested it from the hand of his victim, and this fact led him to believe that the package contained something valuable, although it was the smallest cash-box he had ever run across.

He weighed the box in his hand.

"Nary gold nor silver into it," he muttered, its light weight convincing him of this fact immediately.

Then he shook his head in a dubious sort of way.

"Hope I ain't a-going to be dished on this ere thing too," he muttered.

"Looks mighty fishy now, I tell yer! Mebbe though it's chuck-full of bills, and if they were no bigger than fives, I wouldn't complain."

Then he shook the box and fancied he could hear the rustling of paper within it.

"S'posen they was fifties or hundreds?' he murmured. "Gosh! What a haul that would be, but I don't reckon to run into any such streak of luck as that.

"I'll be willing to call it square if there's only one-dollar bills into it. That would run the plunder up to somewhar round fifty and that ain't doing badly in these hyer hard times."

Busy was the mind of the footpad until he reached his lair, which was in a low street on the outskirts of what is properly known as the Chinese quarter.

It was a vile den; a lodging-house and restaurant combined, and it was a well-known fact to the police that nine of every ten patrons of the place were men "on the cross," that is, fellows who lived by preying upon those more fortunate than themselves in regard to worldly goods.

And, strange as it may appear, this house of evil repute was run by a woman.

Kate O'Neal was her name, but she was seldom spoken of by any other title than "Irish Kate."

Irish Kate and her "Great Eastern Saloon" were as well known in Frisco at this time, as any place of public resort in the city.

Hardly a week passed without the name of the saloon or its Amazonian proprietor figuring in the police reports.

Irish Kate was a woman of forty or thereabouts, coarse-featured, tall, and muscular—strong as a horse, as the common saying is—possessing a most violent temper. She had been known, when provoked, to seize a bung-starter and clear her premises of a crowd of roughs—roughs so ugly, that no single policeman in the city would have dared to disturb them.

But this virago had one merit.

She was as true to her friends as she was bitter to her enemies.

Any "cracksman" in trouble could seek shelter at Irish Kate's and feel perfectly secure that there wasn't money enough in this world to induce her to give him away.

Among her especial favorites, the ruffian who now possessed the mysterious box stood high.

The usual rule at Irish Kate's was money down.

If a drink was wanted the cash must be put upon the

counter before the bottle was produced.

The same rule prevailed in regard to a meal or a bed.

The cash for the aforesaid must be forthcoming before either would be granted.

With such slippery customers as made up the bulk of the Great Eastern's patrons it was the only way to prevent them from "beating" the house at every possible opportunity.

Only a certain number were exempt from this rule, and these were men who had gained Irish Kate's favor, and whom she believed she could trust.

Scotty Bilk was one of these favorites, and he had been dependent upon Irish Kate's bounty for nearly a month. As a natural result, he owed quite a bill.

Being a talented rogue, Scotty had usually very little trouble in making a good living. But for a month now luck had seemed to run dead against him, as he expressed it, and he had not made enough to pay for his liquor to say nothing of his meals and lodging.

But, on this occasion, confident that at least he had secured a booty, which would atone for the bad luck that had so persistently haunted him, he hastened to his lair feeling quite cheerful.

Irish Kate's was one of the all-night saloons, and it did more business from ten o'clock in the evening to two or three in the morning than all the rest of the day put together.

When Scotty arrived at the saloon, the Amazonian owner had just finished counting up her cash and was about to retire, as all her customers had departed.

When the footpad entered the saloon, a significant wink from him to the woman conveyed the intelligence that he had not returned empty-handed from the night's excursion.

Calling the bartender to take her place behind the counter, Irish Kate led the way to a little, private room behind the bar. This was an apartment sacred to the mistress of the place and only shared with such customers as were considered by her to be extra valuable.

And if the walls of this dingy room could have betrayed the confidences reposed in them, strange stories they could have told, for some of the most atrocious crimes which had thrilled the city of San Francisco to its very center had been planned in that apartment.

Irish Kate shut the door carefully, while Scotty seated himself in a chair by a table in the middle of the room.

Then from a closet, which the Amazon unlocked, she produced a bottle of whisky and a couple of glasses.

"Help your self," she said, as she placed the bottle and glasses upon the table, and at the same time took a seat opposite to where the ruffian sat.

"From your wink I reckon you struck something to-night, me jewel," she observed.

The title of Irish Kate applied to this woman was a misnomer, for she spoke with only a very slight brogue, and in her appearance had but little of the Celt about her.

"Yes, I struck something; jest at the last minute, too, jest as I was beginning to think I would have to come home empty-handed," the man replied, helping himself to a liberal allowance of the whisky.

The woman followed his example.

"Here's to yer better luck!" said Irish Kate.

The other nodded, and at a swallow they drained their glasses.

"Did you strike it rich?" she asked.

"Durn me if I know."

"How is that?'

"Wal, hyer's the plunder."

And Scotty produced the tin box and placed it on the table.

"Heigh!" exclaimed Irish Kate, taking it up and examining it with a deal of curiosity.

"Don't weigh much," she observed.

"S'pose it's full of bills, fives or tens, eh?"

She shook her head.

Evidently she did not expect any such stroke of luck.

"Might be, you know; must be something valuable or else the box wouldn't be locked so carefully," he suggested.

"I don't take much stock in this thing, me darlint," she replied. "I'm afeard that it's dished ye are ag'in. But out wid yer knife and rip open the thing till we see phwat is inside of it."

Scotty produced his ugly-looking bowie-knife, and in a second the box was forced open.

06. Irish Kate was a woman of forty or thereabouts, coarse-featured, tall, and muscular—strong as a horse, as the common saying is—possessing a most violent temper. She had been known, when provoked, to seize a bung-starter and clear her premises of a crowd of roughs—roughs so ugly, that no single policeman in the city would have dared to disturb them.

CHAPTER XXIII.
THE DECISION.

A cry of disgust came from the lips of the woman, while the ruffian muttered an oath as they looked upon the contents of the box.

Good reason was there for their disappointment; for all that the box contained was a sheet of folded paper, which looked like a letter.

Scotty took the paper and unfolded it, and the inspection revealed that it was closely covered with writing in a bold, masculine hand on two sides.

"Wal, this beats me!" the ruffian exclaimed, as he held the sheet open between his thumb and finger and gazed disdainfully upon it. "Cuss the luck! I am euchred again! I made sure I was a-going to strike something rich when I run afoul of this box, and hyer all that thar is in it is a durned old letter.

"Now, I tell you what it is, Kate; this is enough to make a man clean disgusted with the hull business.

"If I had had any idee that thar wasn't some plunder worth having in this durned old box, I never would have taken the trouble to tote the cussed thing home.

"I'm sorry now that I didn't lay the galoot out for good! The idee of any feller lugging a thing of this kind round jest for the purpose of fooling men of business like myself! When a feller runs into a swag of this kind it is enough for to make him sw'ar for to turn honest and never for to try to work a decent trick ag'in."

As will be perceived by these words, the disgust of the footpad was great.

"It is a mighty queer riffle," the woman observed, thoughtfully. "What in the divil's name did the man want to go for to lock trash of this kind up as keerfully as though it was gold?"

"Yes, that is the question that knocks me," Scotty observed.

"When I struck the box I was sure I had a prize that would be worth having, and now for to have it turn out to be nothing but a measly old letter, cuss me! If it ain't enough for to make a man wish he was a yaller dog!"

"Phwat else did the spalpeen have on him?"

"I dunno! I didn't git time to examine him," the man replied. "I was hiding in a door and I laid this galoot out as he came round the corner, but before I could git a chance to go through him, some durned cuss came up the street and I had to light out jest as quick as my heels would let me.

"I didn't care so much 'bout that, you know," Scotty explained, "because I thought I had struck a rich lead when I got hold of this hyer box."

"Oho, me jewel, you are in a bad run of luck, entirely!"

"Wal, now, you kin bet your bottom dollar on that!" the man exclaimed, decidedly. "But it can't last forever, you know. I must pull out of it one of these days."

"Oh, yis, no doubt about that, at all, at all!" the woman exclaimed.

"But I say, mebbe the writing is of some value to somebody," she suggested, shrewdly. "If it is no good, why should anybody take the trouble to lock it up in the box as though it was as precious as gold?"

"Yes, that is true enuff!" the man exclaimed, struck by the force of the reasoning. "It does look as if it was valuable, don't it?"

"Of course; read it, me jewel, and see phwat it is about."

A peculiar look appeared on the face of the ruffian as he examined the paper, turning it inside out and upside down, as though unable to make head or tail of the matter.

And this was true enough, for the ruffian could neither read nor write. As far as his reading the document was concerned, it might as well have been written in Greek as in English.

"Oho, mebbe ye can't read!" the woman exclaimed, suddenly, the truth flashing upon her as she beheld the eccentric movements of the man.

"That's so! You hit the bull's-eye plum in the center that time," he admitted. "You read it."

And he passed the letter over the table to the woman.

Irish Kate took the paper and examined it carefully, but Scotty detected immediately from the way she handled the document that her education had been neglected as much as his own.

"Aha, I reckon the schoolmaster was out when you went to school too!" he remarked.

"It would take the divil himself to read sich a crooked fist as this wan!" she replied, contemptuously.

"If it was print now I'll go bail I could manage it, as foine as silk!"

"Oh, yes, you're a big scholar, you are!" Scotty declared sarcastically.

"In your mind," he added. "But when you come right down to the truth you can't read writing nor print, any more than a hog!"

"No more kin the likes of yees!" Irish Kate retorted.

"Oh, I admit it. I ain't a-boasting of my schooling at this hyer stage of the game," he said.

"But now the p'int afore the meeting is, who kin we

git to read this hyer letter, 'cos for all we know, it may be durned valuable and worth a heap of money to some one?"

The woman turned up her nose in contempt at the idea.

"This wee bit of paper worth money!" she exclaimed.

"Yes, that is my say-so," he replied. "It don't look as if it was valuable, I know, but in my time I have known a bit of paper like this hyer to fetch a thousand dollars in clean cash."

"Is that so now?" the woman exclaimed in wonder.

"Oh, yes, you kin bet all your stamps upon it."

"It don't seem to me if the document wasn't good for anything that it would be so keerfully locked up in this hyer box."

"True for yees," assented the woman.

"Now, the p'int is for us to git somebody to read this hyer letter who won't try for to play any roots on us, 'cos if thar is any value into it, we are the galoots who ought for to get it.

"Is there any of the boys that you think you kin trust?"

Irish Kate reflected for a moment and then shook her head.

"I should hate to have to try it on in a matter of this kind," she replied.

"If there was any money in it, the spalpeens would be shure for to try for to make a stake out of it and leave us in the lurch."

"That is so, thar ain't much doubt 'bout it."

"I have it!" the woman exclaimed, abruptly.

"There's a wee bit of a girl lives up the street. Her mother is a decent lady who takes in washing, and as the old woman is fond of a sup of whisky once in a while, the girl comes here for it.

"The girl kin read and write, for she wrote a letter for me the other day, and she's a quiet little thing. If she understood phwat the letter was about she wouldn't be apt to open her head if I told her not to."

"First rate! Couldn't be better!" Scotty exclaimed.

"I'll sind for her whin she comes home from school to-morrow, or to-day I mean, for it is to-morrow already."

"Wal, that's Irish, anyway," the other commented.

"Hould yer whist! Take another pull at the whisky and be off to bed wid yer."

Scotty obeyed the injunction, and in ten minutes was fast in the arms of "Murphy," as the owner of the Great Eastern Saloon would have expressed it.

Irish Kate returned the letter to the tin box and carried it to her room, where she deposited it beneath her pillow for safe keeping while she slept.

Going to bed at such an hour, it was only natural that neither of the two should make their appearance in the morning until it was well advanced, and it was nearly eleven before the pair awoke.

During the woman's sleep she had dreamed about the mysterious box and its contents — a wonderful dream, for she imagined that by means of the letter she had secured a perfect shower of gold.

Enough to make her one of the richest women on the coast, and she had given up the saloon, setting up in a palace on the "hill" that was finer than anything else in Frisco.

The pair took their breakfast together, and Irish Kate, who was extremely superstitious and placed a great deal of faith in omens, related to the ruffian what she had dreamed during the night.

Scotty Bilk shook his head.

There wasn't a bit of superstition about him, and he didn't take any stock in dreams.

"I never dream, 'cept when I've eaten a big supper, and then I ain't apt to dream 'bout pleasant things," he remarked.

"Ah, yes; but this was a morning dream," she replied.

"W'ot of that?" said the doubter.

"Morning dreams allers come true, me jewel," she exclaimed, triumphantly.

"Do they?"

"Oh, yes; no doubt about it."

"Wal, if that's so, it's bad for me, for I have dreamed of being strung up by the Vigilantes a dozen times at least, and as I never go to bed until morning, all my dreams are morning dreams."

Irish Kate shook her head.

This reasoning did not shake her belief at all.

CHAPTER XXIV.
THE SCHEME.

After they had finished their breakfast the two repaired to the saloon.

The woman had removed the paper from the tin box and placed it in her bosom for safe keeping, storing the box away in a secret receptacle in the floor of her room under the head of her bed.

She understood how necessary it was to preserve the box as proof if it should turn out that the contents of the package were valuable.

When the two entered the saloon their attention was attracted to a small handbill tacked up on the wall.

"Where did this come from?" asked Kate.

"One of the detectives was in and stuck it up there," the bartender answered.

"W'ot is it about, anyway?" asked the footpad, who had a suspicion of all such things. He had previously been laid by the heels, in a way that he despised, a half-a-dozen times by means of such documents. Handbills and broadsides had warned the community at large that an individual about his size was wanted by the officers of the law.

"It's a reward offered for the recovery of a tin box lost last night," said the barkeeper, leaning over the counter and glancing at the placard which was tacked on the wall about a foot from the head of the bar.

Despite the self-possession of the two, which was the result of years of experience, it was as much as they could do to refrain from giving a start of surprise as this intelligence fell upon their ears.

"A reward for a tin box," repeated the woman,

slowly.

"That's a kinder queer idee," observed Scotty. "W'ot was in the box—does it say?"

And as he put the question he seated himself on the opposite side of the room with a careless air, as though he had only put the question for the sake of saying something and without really taking any interest in the subject.

"No, it kinder beats about the bush; says the contents of the box are of no value to anybody but the owner, but offers a reward for the recovery just the same."

"Kinder odd," Scotty observed.

"Yes, so it 'pears so to me. Jest listen to the yarn, anyway," said the other.

And then he read the handbill aloud, and it ran as follows:

"$100 Dollars Reward, for the recovery of a small tin box lost early on the morning of the 10th of May near the corner of Bush and Blank streets.

"The contents of the box are of no value to anybody but the owner, and the above-named reward will be paid for the delivery of the box, in good order, to the office of the Alta-California, or a suitable amount will be given for any information leading to the recovery of the box, and the informer can rely that no trouble will come to him in regard to the matter."

"Wal, that is a mighty queer kind of a yarn," Scotty observed when the bartender had finished the reading of the placard.

"Yes, and the detective give it to me on the dead square that there would be fifty in the thing for any man w'ot would put this Alta-California chap on the lay of the box."

"It looks to me as if the contints of the box were of considerable value to the owner, even if they ain't of no account to anybody else, or else the party wouldn't be afther taking all this trouble to git the box," the woman remarked, shrewdly.

"Oh, yes, thar ain't the least doubt about that," the barkeeper answered with the air of an oracle.

"I kin tell you w'ot it is," he continued, "if I knew the party w'ot had nipped that box—'cos I s'pose from the reading of this hyer bill that it has been nipped by somebody—they wouldn't git it out of me for no hundred dollars, for it's worth more money than that."

"Phwat makes ye think so?" Kate demanded.

"Why, it stands to reason that if the box war only worth a hundred that they wouldn't go to all this trouble.

"Thar's an advertisement in the morning paper too, just the same as this hyer hand-bill.

"Oh, I tell ye, I reckon thar's more inter this thing than you kin see on the surface, and I would be willing to bet big money on it too."

Irish Kate and the ruffian exchanged glances at this declaration.

Both of them had great confidence in the judgment of the bartender, for, to use the vernacular, he was "as smart a rooster as juggled a tumbler anywhere in Frisco!"

"Yes, sir-ee, I reckon you are right about it," Scotty observed.

"And if I was the cove that had got away with the box I would just go to this Alta-California chap and say, 'See hyer, my friend, you ain't a-bidding high enough for that box.'

"'If you want it so durned bad it ain't ary bit of use for you to offer a hundred chucks, for it ain't enough. You want to say four or five thousand and then, mebbe I will talk to you.'

"That is the lay-out I would give them, you bet!"

This speech of the ruffian was only a shrewd attempt to draw out the opinion of the bartender, for he was anxious to ascertain his thoughts in regard to the matter, yet did not want to manifest such interest in the affair as to ask outright.

"Well, axing yer pardon, pardner, that wouldn't be the game I would play at all," the other replied, with an air of great deliberation, leaning his arms on the counter and assuming the appearance of a prophet.

"No, sir, hoss-fly, that wouldn't be the game I would give them at all.

"In the first place I wouldn't let on that I had the box at all, or knew anything about it."

"Why not?" demanded Scotty, who was a rather bull-headed ruffian and not used to playing such fine points.

"'Cos I wouldn't give the detectives a chance to get at me.

"This hyer bill says lost, but was the box lost, or is that only a perlite way of saying nipped?

"'Early this morning,'" continued the bartender, quoting from the bill.

"Now don't that look as if some crib had been cracked and the box stolen? That is the way it looks to me.

"And if it was only a box lost in the ordinary way, w'ot would be the use of gitting out these handbills and sticking of 'em up in places like this by the detectives, so as to be sure to meet the eyes of the coves who are on the cross?"

"That is so, me jewel!" Irish Kate exclaimed. "There is something crooked about the matther."

"In course! You kin bet yer stamps on it, every

time!" cried the other, with an air of conviction.

"So I say. If I war the cove w'ot had nipped the box, or knew anything about it, I wouldn't go and let on that I did, for by trying that lay I would be giving the fly-cops a chance at me.

"It will be their game to clap the feller in quod who lets on that he knows anything about the thing and keep him there until he squeals."

Both the others nodded assent, for this seemed to them to be sound reasoning.

"A cove who has been on the cross allers has some old jobs hanging over him that he can be brought up on, so as to git him in trouble, if the detectives are anxious to make it warm for him."

Scotty made a grimace at this point, for it fitted his case exactly.

There were a couple of ugly charges against him, but thanks to certain political influence, which he had been able to command, they had been "pigeon-holed."

If the detectives though saw fit so to do they could make him answer for his deeds, and by bringing these old matters up throw him into jail and keep him there.

"No, the game I would play would be for to go to this hyer chap w'ot advertises, and say to him:

"'I know a heap of coves who are on the cross and if you can make it worth my while, I will take up this hyer matter. And if any of the cross coves in this hyer town have got the box, the odds are big that I kin git it. But it ain't any use for to talk a hundred, you know, 'cos the cross cove will have to have his whack afore he will give up the box, and in course I can't afford to give you my time for nothing.'

"You see, that wouldn't give the fly-cops no chance to git a hold on me, and you kin bet that the safe game is the one to play every time."

Both the others agreed to this, and then some customers came in and engaged the barkeeper's attention, so they took advantage of the fact to hold a conference.

"He has laid out the game, me jewel," the woman said, "and ye must play it."

"All right," nodded the footpad.

"Go to the Alta-California office and have a talk with the man, so that whin I get hold of the girl and have the letter read I'll know how the land lays."

Five minutes later Scotty was on his way.

CHAPTER XXV.
THE CHIEF OF POLICE DELIBERATES.

Obviously, De Lormé did not let the grass grow under his feet in regard to the tin box.

And, after having the handbills printed and setting the detectives at work, he called upon the chief of police.

Kettleton greeted him warmly and eagerly inquired:

"Well, what news?"

"Nothing to speak of."

"You have not succeeded in striking a trail?"

"Oh, yes."

"Aha! And the result?"

"Like the old story of the trail that ran into the woods and then up a tree and there ended."

The face of the chief plainly expressed the disappointment he experienced at hearing this statement.

"That's bad!" he exclaimed.

"Yes, it is not very encouraging."

"I was in hope that you would get at some information of value. You generally succeed pretty well in these difficult matters.

"In fact in such a case as this I would rather have you work the trick than any of my regular men.

"They are good enough at thief-catching, but when it comes to a job of this kind they are always sure to blunder."

"I am much obliged to you for the good opinion you have of my abilities," De Lormé responded.

"But you must remember that in a case of this kind it is ten times, if not a hundred times, more difficult in a city like San Francisco than one of the old settled towns.

"For the last twenty years—or in fact I may say ever

since the settlement of San Francisco—the people here are always on the move. They do not settle down for life, as men are apt to do when they strike a city and succeed in making a stake.

"I don't believe I would be making a rash statement when I say it is possible that not over ten men out of a hundred who dwelt in San Francisco twenty years ago can be found here to-day."

"That statement is within bounds, I think," the chief observed. "From my own knowledge of the city, acquired during the last ten years, I think you have not stated the case too strongly.

"Men come here to make money, and if they succeed they clear out and take up their residence elsewhere to spend it, and if they don't make the riffle and can't make a fortune here, they levant to try for better luck elsewhere."

"Yes, and that is why it is so difficult to ascertain anything about an obscure case like this which dates back to twenty years ago," De Lormé remarked.

"All of Macarthy's associates are either dead, or have sought fresh fields and pastures new. I made an exhaustive search and could only discover one man who knew anything about Macarthy."

And then he recited to Kettleton the story of his search, just as he had told it to La Belle Helene.

"Well, as you say, the trail does seem to run up a tree," the chief of police remarked, reflectively, when De Lormé ended his recital.

"Yes, nothing more to go on in that line."

"I have been thinking over the matter," Kettleton observed, after a few moments of silence, "and the idea has occurred to me that, if we could not strike anything here in San Francisco, it might not be a bad plan to try

Southern California."

"Southern California?" said De Lormé, in a tone of question.

"Yes, where this big estate is situated; somewhere down around Santa Barbara," the chief explained.

"I have kinder been laying myself out on the case, and it has occurred to me that it is mighty strange that Macarthy's wife hasn't appeared in the proceeding.

"There must have been a wife, or else there wouldn't be any child, you know."

"Oh, yes, no doubt about that, but I jumped to the conclusion, not hearing anything of the wife, that she was dead."

"Yes, that is what I thought at first. But when I came to put on my thinking-cap and go for the matter, red-hot, I kinder sorter got an idea that the woman might not be dead. There's a heap of mystery about the thing, you know."

"Not the least doubt about that."

"I began right at the beginning and asked myself some questions," continued Kettleton. "Who did Macarthy marry? Where did he get hitched? Where was the child born? And if the mother was dead, where did she die and where was she buried, and what was the reason why Macarthy kept this marriage a secret from every one, as he evidently did?

"You see, these are mighty difficult questions for a man to answer who don't know anything about the game and can't get a look at the cards nohow."

"Oh, yes; you can bet on that, chief."

"Well, I jest went to work to think out answers to the whole b'iling.

"I reckon, De Lormé, I ought to join you newspaper fellers, for I've got a mighty powerful imagination."

"Don't you do it; you will make a heap more money in the police line," counseled the other.

"Mebbe so; but it is a shame for a man who has got the intellect into him for to hide his light under a bushel, you know."

"Yes; but if it don't pay he had better," De Lormé rejoined.

"Well, sir, this hyer thing would pay if it was looked up, for it's jest like a novel, as I think you will admit when you hear the points. Now, jest listen."

And as he spoke the chief checked the "points" off on his fingers.

"Number one, whom did Macarthy marry? Some gal, who, for some reason he was ashamed of, and that was the reason why he never let on to any one that he was married.

"He was a big man, if you remember, at that time and held his head away up. If he had become fascinated by some poor gal, or some gal with a taint upon her name—although sich little things as this didn't go for much in California twenty years ago, for society wasn't screwed up quite so high-toned as it is to-day. But, as I say, if there was anything out of the way with the gal, he would be apt to keep the matter dark, for, as far as I can learn, he was a bullheaded Englishman, stuck-up and as arrogant as thunder when he had things his own way.

"That explains point number one all right.

"Number two—where did he get married?

"Not in Frisco, that is pretty sure, for at that time all his interests were to the south'ard, and until the break in his fortunes he spent the most of his time out of the city.

"Then, too, he came to Frisco bringing the child with him, which seems to me conclusive proof that neither the child nor its mother were in the city."

"Not much doubt about it," De Lormé assented, following the argument of the chief with the greatest attention.

"Point number three: where was the child born? That one is answered the same as number two. In the country, decidedly."

De Lormé nodded.

"Number four: if the mother is dead, where did she die and where was she buried?

"Now, why should we assume that she is dead? There is not the slightest proof of it — nothing to indicate such a thing except the fact that Macarthy brought the child to Frisco, and nowhere in the yarn do we hear anything of the mother."

"Yes, and that could be accounted for in another way than supposing her dead," De Lormé observed.

"Exactly, and I do account for it, for I don't believe she is dead.

"Point number five: why did Macarthy keep his marriage a secret? That I have already answered."

Again De Lormé nodded.

"Now I will put the story together as I have hatched it.

"Macarthy—a mighty big man at the time as far as money goes—fell in love with a gal who wasn't jest what he would like to show to the world as his wife, but he married her all the same, and a child was born.

"When the child was about a year old there was a row between him and his wife, and he scooted off to Frisco here and hid the child away so that the wife couldn't get hold of it, for if there wasn't some reason like this for his hiding the child, why did he get rid of it in sich a durned mysterious manner?"

"Very true—very true," De Lormé remarked.

156

"Now how do we know that the wife didn't follow him and get the child again, unknown to him, of course."

"That might be so," the other admitted.

"I have an idea I have hit off the truth, and so take yourself off to Southern California as soon as possible.

"Here's the cash I promised, and if you strike a trail I'll come down handsomely. Anyway you can have fifty a week for your trouble."

"All right! I'll be off to-morrow!"

And then De Lormé departed, but there was much to be done before he could leave the city.

CHAPTER XXVI.
THE CHALLENGE.

Andrew De Lormé was in possession of some information in regard to the Macarthy mystery, which he did not reveal to the chief of police.

As matters now stood, circumstances seemed to strongly point to the young girl, whose acquaintance he had made in so strange a manner, as the lost child of Archibald Macarthy.

And if this was true, the chief's theory that the mother had secured the child had nothing in it at all.

Still, he believed there was a deal of wisdom in the chief's advice to seek for information in Southern California, but he had no idea of going as far south as Santa Barbara.

His idea was to look for information more to the east, along the flats of the Stanislaus, in the neighborhood of the spot where Lucille Gwinnet formerly dwelt.

Macarthy at one time possessed mining interests in that quarter, and it was more than likely that in his prosperous days he spent considerable of his time there.

Then, too, De Lormé was in hopes that the tin box might be recovered, for it was possible that contained within it were some documents that would give a clew to the mystery.

Of course, there was the chance that it didn't hold anything of the kind, and the papers within it might refer to some matters entirely foreign to the Macarthy mystery.

But from the fact that the box had been entrusted by old Gwinnet to the care of the girl, and that to this Gwinnet's brother the last child of Macarthy had been given, the circumstantial evidence seemed strong that she was the child.

And the password, "On the flats of the Stanislaus," was to introduce her to some agent of her father, who was to be sent for her, it having been arranged that at some time Macarthy should reclaim his child.

But the sudden deaths of Macarthy in London, Abraham Gwinnet in San Francisco, and Thomas Gwinnet in the mining region of the Stanislaus, all occurring at about the same time, contributed to deepen the mystery and make it almost impossible for the girl to learn the truth in regard to her parentage.

De Lormé went straight to his office, a little hall room on the second floor of a building in the near neighborhood of the Alta-California office.

He had arranged with the newspaper people to send any applicants who might seek him in answer to his advertisement directly to his office.

That the footpad who had obtained possession of the tin box by sand-bagging young Gwinnet would be glad to give it up and take a hundred dollars reward, he nothing doubted.

The only danger was that there might be something in the papers contained in the box to indicate that more money could be made by holding on to them, and in that case the fellow who had possession of the documents undoubtedly would do his best to get every penny he could.

After reaching his office, De Lormé sat down to his desk and began to work on some "local sketches" which he was furnishing to the Alta-California.

He had hardly got fairly to work before he was disturbed by the entrance of a visitor.

But it was not a member of any of the well-known gangs that at this time infested San Francisco.

No "cross cove" whose warning cry of "hands up" rings out in the wild west and on the Pacific slope with startling earnestness.

On the contrary, it was a gentleman who was far more apt to fall a prey to such footpads than to do any business in that line on his own account, however expert he might be as a robber in a somewhat different manner.

The new-comer was the Irishman, Captain O'Ballyhoo.

The captain, being one of the notable men about town, was no stranger to the young man, and knowing him to be crooked all the way through, De Lormé immediately jumped to the conclusion that he had been sent as a negotiator by the outlaw who had secured the tin box.

On this point, though, he was quickly undeceived.

"If I mistake not, I am afther having the pleasure of addressing Mr. Andrew De Lormé?" the Irishman said, with an elaborate bow.

"Yes, sir."

"I think I have been afther meeting yees before," remarked O'Ballyhoo, with another bow.

"You are right, sir."

"I have come to see you, sor, upon a most important matther. Permit me to offer you me card."

And the captain tendered the pasteboard with all the ease and grace for which he was celebrated.

De Lormé took the card, laid it upon his desk, and then pushed a chair over to the captain.

He was sure now that he had come in reference to the tin box.

"Be seated, sir," he said.

"Thank you, sor."

And the captain dropped gracefully into the chair.

"As I said before, I come upon a most important

matter, and now I will add that I fear it will prove to be an unpleasant one."

De Lormé looked slightly surprised, for this was not what he expected to hear, but he simply nodded his head as a signal for his visitor to go on.

"But, as a man of the wourld, you will understand that whin these duties devolve upon us we are forced to attind to them."

Again De Lormé nodded, although for the life of him he couldn't imagine what the man was driving at.

"Mr. De Lormé, I take it that ye are a gintleman," the Irishman continued.

"If you were to assume that I was not, and dared to publicly express the opinion in my presence, I should be obliged to adopt harsh measures to convince you to the contrary," the young man replied.

"Oho! Don't for the wourld belave for a moment that I would be afther doing anything of the kind!" O'Bally-hoo hastened to exclaim, for he understood well enough that De Lormé was a dangerous man to trifle with.

"No, sir, you are a gintleman—a perfect gintleman, I feel shure of that, and I, as a gintleman, come to you on behalf of another gintleman!" the captain exclaimed with a flourish of his hand in the air.

De Lormé was puzzled, for his chance encounter with McMichael had entirely passed from his mind.

"I am at your service, sir, although I must confess I don't exactly understand what you want of me."

"I come to you on behalf of a gintleman who labors under the impression that he has been insulted by you in the grossest manner."

"Is that so?" De Lormé remarked.

"Yis, sor, it is a disagreeable duty to perform, but as the fri'nd of Mr. Clement McMichael I have waited upon you to demand the satisfaction which under such circumstances is due one gintleman from another gintleman."

"Oh, yes, yes!" exclaimed the other, a sudden light breaking in upon him.

"I remember now, but I declare the circumstance had entirely escaped me. I had clean forgotten all about it. Well, isn't he satisfied with what he got last night? Does he hanker after more?"

"As a gintleman he cannot rest satisfied until he has avenged the insult that you put upon him, sor.

"Of course an ample apology on your part—"

"Apologize to that drunken fool?" cried De Lormé, his brows contracting. "Don't talk about such a thing, sir, or you and I will be apt to quarrel."

"Certainly not, my dear sor, I am only acting strictly in the line of my duty you know."

"If McMichael is hankering after satisfaction he shall have it. No man ever yet had cause to complain of me on that score."

"You accept Mr. McMichael's challenge to mortal combat then?"

"Yes, and since he is anxious for it I will do my best to drill a hole in him, and perform the task with all the pleasure in life."

"As the challenged party you have the choice of weapons, but I thought, maybe, as yees are expert with all, you would be afther waiving the privilege in this case," the Irishman remarked, insinuatingly.

"Not by a jugful!" De Lormé replied. "Oh, no, I never yield a point in such a game. Jack Batcliff of the Bella Union Theater will act for me and you can see him to-night."

The Irishman stood, bowed, and then departed.

07. An issue of the Daily Alta California newspaper
from 1870, as mentioned in
The Frisco Detective.

CHAPTER XXVII.
THE AGREEMENT.

After the departure of the Irishman, De Lormé settled himself again to work.

He received the challenge to mortal combat with the same coolness as he would an invitation to dinner; in fact, he scarcely allowed his mind to dwell on the matter, merely observing to himself as he took up his pen:

"I suppose I shall be obliged to wing the fellow so as to give him a lesson. He mustn't imagine because he happens to have a little money that he can ride rough-shod over all the rest of mankind who haven't the luck to be so fortunately situated.

"I must own that I am a little astonished at the fellow's pluck in taking this mode to revenge his defeat. I remember, now, that he threatened to have satisfaction, but what a man says at midnight when his brain is heated with liquor and what he does in the morning when he is sober and comes coolly to reflect upon the matter are, generally, two entirely different things. But, in this case, reflection has evidently not cooled the young man's ardor, and since he is so anxious for a lesson I suppose I ought to be accommodating enough to give him one."

And De Lormé laughed quietly to himself as he reflected upon the adroit suggestion of the Irishman that he should waive the choice of weapons to which, according to the laws of the duello, as the challenged party, he was entitled.

"I didn't really think O'Ballyhoo would be donkey enough to believe me to be such a greenhorn as to throw away any of the advantages to which I am entitled in such games as this," he remarked.

"I take things so easily, though, as a general rule, that it is only natural a sharper of the O'Ballyhoo stamp should believe he was smart enough to fool me once in a while. But no one of them as yet has succeeded in making the trick work, though of course every new man thinks he is smarter than the rest of his fellows and so tries it on.

"This will delay my departure for the Stanislaus a little, but as there isn't any particular hurry, it doesn't matter.

"Now then let me bring this sketch to an end, so as to get it off my mind."

But he was not fated to proceed in his work without interruption, for he had hardly a half a page written when he was again interrupted.

And this time the intruder was the lanky ruffian whose acquaintance he had made up in the Feather River country, Scotty Bilk.

"Wal, durn my cats!" exclaimed the outlaw in amazement after he had entered the room and recognized its occupant.

"Hallo! What brings you here?" De Lormé inquired.

"Reckon I ain't made any mistake 'bout the matter," Scotty said in a dubious sort of way as though he did not feel particularly positive on this point.

"Any mistake about what?" De Lormé asked, and then it suddenly occurred to him that the other might have come in answer to the advertisement so widely circulated through the town of Frisco.

"Were you sent here from the Alta-California office?"

"Right you are," Scotty responded, with a grin.

"Well, you are at the right shop then. I am the man you want to see."

"Durn me if I expected to meet an old pard though," the other remarked, as he helped himself to a chair.

"This is a mighty uncertain world, and we can never tell what is going to happen," De Lormé responded.

"You are the cuss w'ot had the handbills sent round?"

"Yes, sir."

"Mighty cute dodge!"

"It was about the thing to do under the circumstances, and so you are the man who got the tin box!"

"I didn't say so," replied Scotty, with another grin.

"I am aware of that, but I guess there isn't much doubt about it. You did the job up in first-class style; as a sand-bagger you are a success."

"Say, pard, is this thing all right and regular?" Scotty inquired, abruptly.

"What do you mean? I don't think I exactly understand you."

"No gum-game about it, is thar—no trap fer to ketch a feller and git him into trouble?" questioned the ruffian, suspiciously.

"Oh, no, nothing of the kind!"

"Honest Injun?"

"You can depend upon it. You know me of old, and you ought not be afraid to do business with me."

"Of course not! You are jest the kind of critter I like to tackle; but I ain't acting fer myself in this hyer matter, you know. I'm jest attending to it for a friend."

"Oh, yes, I understand; that is the old dodge."

"Wish I may die if it ain't the honest truth."

"No, no, I know better," De Lormé retorted. "Why do you try to fool me with any such stale old yarn. You were the man who did the sand-bagging. There isn't the least doubt about it. Why, I met you earlier on the same night, and you were on the lookout for prey then."

"That don't go for to show I did this job though," the ruffian retorted. But I say, pard, was the galoot that got left a friend of yours?"

"Oh, yes, of course; but now, to come down to business. Have you come to collar the hundred dollars?"

"Wal, pard, I reckon I'm kinder squinting that way."

"Have you brought the box with you?"

"No."

"Why didn't you bring it, if you came to talk business?" De Lormé demanded.

"Wal, pard, to tell you the honest truth, I jest come to spy out how the land lay," and Scotty indulged in another enormous grin.

"You see, my pardner, who happened to find this hyer box, jest by accident, has kinder got an idea inter his head that the thing is worth more than a hundred chucks, and he wanted me fer to see the party w'ot sent the handbills 'round and ax him if he couldn't do a leetle better than that."

"Aha, you have opened the box then?"

"Wal, yes, I s'pose so; my friend has, maybe."

"And upon examination you think the contents are worth more than a hundred?"

"That is the way it strikes my pard."

"Well, now, Scotty, to use your own saying, I'm going to tell you the honest truth. I don't really know what the contents of the box are worth, and when I offered to give a hundred for the return of the property I was putting up a stake on a hand of whose value I was ignorant.

"I was just anteing up a hundred on the chance that the box was worth that amount, but when you come to strike me for a higher figure, all I can say is that I must have a look at the cards before I chip in again."

"Oh!" and the ruffian looked surprised, "You don't know w'ot is inter the box?"

"Nary time!"

"Wal, that's queer!"

"Good many queer things in this world," De Lormé rejoined. "But I can tell you one thing, Scotty, if the contents of the box are valuable I will pay as much for them as any other man that you can strike in California. But before I make another bid I must have a look at the stuff, so as to know what I am bidding on, for I am not going it blind as much as I was."

The other reflected upon the proposition for a moment.

It certainly seemed fair enough.

Then, too, Scotty had a deal of confidence in the young man.

De Lormé had helped him out of a pretty bad scrape when he was being tried for horse-stealing in the Feather River region. And then on the previous evening, when he was in a tight place, De Lormé had let him out. He felt pretty certain that if the papers were worth any more than a hundred, De Lormé would do as well for him as anybody else he could strike.

So, upon reflection, he came to the conclusion he would "trade" with De Lormé, for if he sought any one else, the chances were that it would be a detective, and in that case he knew that the "professional" would certainly try to get nine-tenths of the value of the papers for himself.

"Pard, it is a go!" Scotty exclaimed, abruptly. "But the way that things are fixed we can't do anything until about five this afternoon for the party I am waiting for won't be in town until then."

His idea in using that story to put off the examination

until the afternoon, was to give a chance for Irish Kate to find out by means of the little girl all about the letter contained in the tin box. Then they would be able to get some idea as to the actual value of the article. Scotty was of a grasping disposition and although De Lormé had once saved his life, yet he intended to "bleed" him in this case as much as possible.

"Meet me in front of the Bella Union at five and I will take you straight to my pard," the ruffian said.

"All right, I will be there."

"We'll do the right thing for you," and with this assurance the footpad departed.

CHAPTER XXVIII.
AN UNEXPECTED EVENT.

"I shall be able to make a bargain with this scoundrel," De Lormé remarked as he took up his pen to resume his work.

He was a shrewd guesser and De Lormé fancied he fathomed the reason why Scotty was not prepared to push the matter to a conclusion at once.

"Either he has not examined the box and doesn't know what it contains, or he is bothered in regard to the actual value of the papers and will make some inquiries before he comes to bargain for their disposal."

And then a sudden idea occurred to our hero.

"By Jove! The odds are ten to one that the fellow can't read and so is ignorant of the value of the prize he has secured. He is waiting to hunt up some pard he can trust in order to find out the value of the prize!

"The documents in the box may be of value and then again they may not be.

"I feel certain that this rascal is doubtful in regard to this point or else he would not have hesitated at all in the matter.

"If he had come to the conclusion that the papers were worthless he would have jumped eagerly at my offer of a hundred for them. On the contrary, if he had formed the impression that they were worth a great deal more money he would not have hesitated for a moment in saying so, for fellows of his kidney are not apt to hide their light under a bushel.

"Decidedly, the scoundrel is as ignorant as I am of the true value of the papers contained in the box."

And after having come to this conclusion the

young man addressed himself again to his article for the Alta-California.

Promptly at five o'clock however, Scotty Bilk was on hand, looking somewhat the worse for wear.

The ruffian had been in difficulties.

After leaving De Lormé he had started to return to Irish Kate's but had stopped in a sporting saloon on the way. This for the purpose of refreshing the inner man with a drink, and also to learn what news was stirring.

In the saloon he encountered some old-time pards from the upper mining regions. As they were flush, while Scotty was down to the bed-rock as far as funds were concerned, he thought he would improve the opportunity to relieve the strangers of a little of their surplus wealth, so the party went to gambling.

And as luck favored Scotty he kept at it, unconscious of the flight of time.

We say that luck favored the footpad, but perhaps it would be more accurate to say that the marvelous skill he possessed of getting favorable cards up his sleeve, dealing from the bottom of the pack, instead of the top, when by so doing his chances would be improved, and "turning Jack," when the services of that gentleman were most desired, had more to do with his winning than the fickle goddess of fortune.

Anyhow he got about five hundred dollars ahead and then he tried to draw out.

In the first place, he wanted to consult Irish Kate and prepare for the visitor, and then, being a firm believer in the adage that it is always better to "let well enough alone," he wanted to quit playing so as to have no chance to lose the gains he had made.

His associates, the losers, wouldn't have it though. That was no way to play, they declared, to win their money and then sneak off without giving them a chance for revenge.

And they were so earnest in their demands that Scotty kept on playing and the result was that by four o'clock he had lost half of the five hundred. The tide of luck too seemed to be setting so strongly against him that all his skill could not land him a winner.

His opponents by this time also had become suspicious of the wonderful bits of "luck" that he had once in a while, especially when in tight places, and watched him so closely that he had little chance to aid fortune by means of a dexterous pair of fingers.

At this point he made up his mind to stop playing and retreat with his spoils, so as to have a chance to see Irish Kate and arrange for the reception of De Lormé.

But the others were just as determined that he should keep on playing until they got their money back as he was to stop.

A quarrel arose—all of them were pretty well primed with liquor—and the rest fell upon Scotty. They were proceeding to thrash him in the most scientific manner when one of his assailants, not feeling sufficient confidence in his fists, took recourse to his revolver. A blow from the butt of the pistol stretched Scotty out on the floor, apparently as dead as a door nail.

In alarm at this unexpected result, the assailants took to their heels immediately.

The barkeeper came to the assistance of the senseless man.

He had not fallen into the error of believing that a little crack on the head could finish a tough nut like Scotty Bilk.

The first thing he did though was to go through the fallen man and relieve him of his plunder.

If he was dead he didn't need it. If he recovered, he would swear that the fugitives had despoiled him.

It took nearly an hour to make Scotty feel like himself again, and his rage was great when he discovered that he had been robbed.

Of course he believed that his associates had stolen the money, and he swore that he would make San Francisco too hot to hold them. But as he had barely time to keep his appointment with De Lormé, he was reluctantly compelled to give up all idea of going after them at present.

"What is the matter with you?" De Lormé inquired, as the other approached. "You look as if you had been in a skirmish."

"Yes, I have been. I was double-banked by a gang; but I'll git squar' with them afore long, or I ain't the man I think I am," responded the ruffian, savagely.

"But come along and let us attend to biz. I want to get hold of some cash so I kin go fer these galoots and show 'em that when they tackled me they got hold of the wrong customer."

Scotty had made up his mind to take De Lormé directly to Kate.

He hadn't the least doubt that by this time she had ascertained all about the letter from the tin box. He knew the woman well enough to understand she wouldn't wait for him before proceeding to investigate, when she found he didn't come to time.

Straight to Kate's saloon he conducted De Lormé, and as the two approached they saw there was quite a crowd of people in front of the door.

"Something's up," Scotty remarked.

"Yes, looks like it," De Lormé replied.

"W'ot's the matter down the street, sonny?" asked

the ruffian of a boy approaching, who had made one of the crowd.

"A man killed, I heerd," was the reply.

"Blazes! They are kicking up a heap of a row about a little thing like that," Scotty remarked, facetiously.

Then they came up to the crowd, and De Lormé asked a man, "Anybody killed?"

"I reckon not; but mighty near it," the man who was addressed replied.

"Oh, no; not killed, for she has been carried off to the hospital," added another one of the crowd.

"She? It was a woman, then?" De Lormé said.

"Yes, a woman."

"And nary man," observed the speaker.

"How did it happen?" De Lormé asked.

"Oh, a couple of fellers with too much bug-juice into 'em took it into their heads that it would be a big lot of fun to clean out the shebang, but she wouldn't have it."

"She!" cried Scotty, aghast, for a dreadful suspicion had taken possession of him.

"Yes; she plugged both of 'em with her popgun, but one of 'em managed to lay her out with a bottle, and I heerd say that her skull is fractured. Anyway, the perlice took her off to the hospital, and if she wasn't a dead woman she looked mightily like one when they carried her away.

"Irish Kate?" persisted the ruffian.

"Yes; the boss of the shebang."

"And she was the woman who was hurt?"

"Now you are shouting, pard."

Scotty turned to De Lormé and whispered to him.

"Our cake is all dough; Irish Kate is the pard I was a-talking to you about."

"The deuce you say!" De Lormé exclaimed. "And was the tin box in her possession?"

"You bet!"

"Let us go into the saloon and make sure that it was Irish Kate who was hurt."

The two forced their way through the crowd into the saloon.

The man's story was correct, though.

Irish Kate at last had met her match, and in attempting to eject two drunken men, disposed to kick up a row, had been badly injured.

"In fact," the barkeeper said, in conclusion, "one of the doctors told me that he reckoned Kate would have a narrow squeeze for her life this time, for she had got an awful lick."

"Was she at all conscious after receiving her injury?" De Lormé asked.

"Oh, no; the fellow hit her in the head with a bottle, and it laid her out quicker'n a wink. As I reckon, she never knowed what hurt her.

"I was in the other room, and got to the door jest in time to see her git the lick. Oh! It was an awful one, I tell you!"

"Did she give you a tin box—a box which belonged to me?" asked Scotty, anxiously.

"Nary box," replied the barkeeper, turning away to attend to a customer at the other end of the counter.

"This is an ugly bit of business," De Lormé remarked.

"Yes, it seems to me that I'm in for an awful run of bad luck. She put the letter in her bosom, but I didn't know but what she might have taken it out again and put it in the box."

De Lormé's interest was immediately aroused at this.

CHAPTER XXIX.
AN EAGER SEARCH.

"Wasn't there anything but a letter in the box?" the young man asked.

The ruffian was immediately recalled to himself and put upon his guard by the question.

"Look-a-hyer! I reckon I am kinder shooting my mouth off a heap sight too much!" he exclaimed.

"What can you gain by attempting to conceal any of the particulars from me now?" De Lormé asked.

"Already you have allowed me to become possessed of the fact that there was a letter in the box, and as you didn't speak of anything else, it is only natural that I should come to the conclusion that it was all the box contained.

"I fancy that you are in a hole here anyway, for if there was only a letter in the tin box it cannot be of much value," De Lormé continued.

"My idea was that there was some valuable legal documents in the box, or else I never should have been willing to give so large a sum as a hundred dollars for the recovery of the package and its contents. This is reasonable, isn't it?"

"I s'pose so," growled the other, annoyed at the prospect.

"Now you might as well make a clean breast of the whole thing. Let me know all that you know about the matter and if there is any money in it, you shall have a fair reward."

"You won't go back on me?" Scotty demanded, suspiciously.

"Oh, no, that isn't the kind of man I am, and you

ought to be satisfied in regard to that. The past ought to be a guarantee for the future."

"Durned if I don't go it!" the ruffian exclaimed, abruptly.

"Mebbe I am going to git skinned in this hyer matter too, for I'm running in sich bad luck jist now that thar don't seem to be no chance for me, nohow."

"Luck is liable to change at any moment," De Lormé remarked.

"Wal, it ought to change pretty soon with me now, for I've had a heap of misfortune lately."

"Go ahead with your yarn."

The two had withdrawn to a corner of the saloon during this conversation. As all others within the room, or who entered, naturally remained in the neighborhood of the bar, the pair were secure from eavesdropping.

"Kate is an old pard of mine and allers grubstakes me when I'm busted!" Scotty began. "So, when I struck this hyer tin box I let her inter the riffle at once.

"I ripped the box open, thinking mebbe I would strike a pile of five or ten-dollar bills, but all thar was inter the box was a letter."

"To whom was it addressed and who was the writer?"

"Wal, now, pard, you've got me foul, and that is jist whar the hull trouble in this matter has been. You see, neither Kate nor me kin read, and so when we struck this letter we were knocked all in a heap.

"We both on us reckoned though that the thing must be worth ducats or else it wouldn't have been locked up in the box so durned keer'fully.

"And then, it was an old-looking letter, too, the paper kinder yellow, you know, and both on us thought thar was some money into it.

"Kate had a head on her shoulders, you bet, and she hatched a plan to git a little gal who lives somewhar around hyer to come and read the letter for her, so she would know how much it was worth to anybody.

"The gal was to come this afternoon, but whether she did or not of course I don't know, for I got mixed up in that scrape which wound up in my being laid out, and so I didn't put in an appearance.

"Now, you've got the hull thing."

De Lormé had listened attentively, and even while the man was speaking had decided what was best to be done.

"Kate in all probability has the paper in her bosom now exactly where she placed it for safekeeping, and at the hospital it will be taken from her when she is searched, and locked up with the rest of her valuables. By applying to the proper authorities I can get at the document."

"But s'pose it wasn't on her—s'pose she went and hid it somewhar in the house arter she got the kid to read it to her, 'cos I reckon there wasn't much doubt that she did git the gal to spell it out.

"Irish Kate wasn't the kind of heifer to wait fer me, you know, when she found that I didn't turn up at the right time."

"In that case we might hunt up the girl and find out from her what the letter was about.

"I am assuming of course that Kate is so badly injured that she will not be able to communicate what she knows to any one for some time."

"That's a good idee!" Scotty exclaimed, struck with the wisdom of the suggestion.

"Yes, it ought not to be a difficult matter to find out if any little girl was in the house during the afternoon."

"She's the gal of some woman who lives 'round hyer somewhar and does washing for a living."

"Interview the barkeeper and see if he knows anything about it."

Scotty did as he was bid, but the attempt was not productive of any results.

The barkeeper explained that if any girl had come to see the mistress of the saloon during the afternoon she would undoubtedly have entered by the rear gate, and he could not possibly have seen her or known that she was in the house.

He added the information, however, that during all the early part of the afternoon the woman had been absent from the saloon and that, in his opinion, it was likely she was entertaining a caller.

Prompted by De Lormé, Scotty inquired if he knew of any little girl in the neighborhood, the daughter of a washerwoman, who was in the habit of calling upon Irish Kate.

The barkeeper replied graphically:

"The woods are full of 'em!"

And he rattled off the names of half a dozen women in the neighborhood all of whom took in washing and possessed daughters.

"One to six of 'em apiece," he added.

And nearly all the little girls were big enough came to the saloon to get beer or stronger liquor for their mothers, but whether any of them were in the habit of calling upon Irish Kate in the privacy of her own apartments was more than he could say.

"Our first inquiry must be made at the hospital," De Lormé remarked to his companion.

To the institution the pair at once proceeded. The doctor was summoned and then the fortunate discovery was made that the Bohemian was well acquainted with the chief medical man at the hospital to which the injured woman had been conveyed. The visitors' quest explained to him.

"Of course I can't give up the letter, if the woman had such a thing on her person when she was brought in, without being authorized so to do in a legal way, but I can give you a look at it so you can master the contents, and that is all you want," the doctor remarked.

"That will answer, of course," De Lormé replied, "and I will be very much obliged."

"Don't mention it; delighted to accommodate you."

The attendant who had charge of the patient, a middle-aged woman, was summoned, but upon being questioned she replied that no letter, or, in fact, paper of any kind had been found on the person of the injured woman.

All of her clothing had been removed, too, for in her struggle with the first ruffian, who had clinched with her, her wearing apparel had been almost torn from her body.

Disappointed, the searchers withdrew.

Scotty was rather inclined to believe that the matron had found the letter, discovered that it was valuable and concealed it, for he was such a rascal himself that he was inclined to think every one else was as bad.

"Impossible," rejoined De Lormé. "There are always two or three present, and if the woman had wished to do such a thing the others would have prevented her by being there."

Then, too, there was another unfortunate thing about the case.

In the opinion of the doctor, Irish Kate would not be able to communicate any information for a week or so. In fact, he said he had grave doubts if she would ever wake to consciousness again, so great was the injury she had received

"The only thing for us to do now is to hunt up the girl," De Lormé observed to Scotty, as they headed again for the saloon.

"If she read the letter for Kate and we can find her we will be all right."

Scotty shook his head. He did not feel sanguine in regard to this.

His forebodings were correct.

Washerwoman after washerwoman, and child after child were questioned, but no clew was gained.

At last in despair the two were obliged to give up the search.

The footpad was disgusted.

"Hyer am I, broke in Frisco, and my grubstake gal in the hospital with a broken head! W'ot am I going to do?" he exclaimed.

"Here's a ten for you," De Lormé replied, giving him a gold-piece. "I give it to you for your good-will in this matter although it about cleans me out."

And so the two parted.

CHAPTER XXX.
ARRANGING THE DUEL.

This eager search had taken up considerable time, and it was between seven and eight in the evening when De Lormé left the lanky Scotty Bilk.

"Now I must get a bite of supper and then go down to the Bella Union to post Batcliff in regard to this hostile meeting," De Lormé observed, as he proceeded up the street.

"It may be, though, that when this blood finds that I decline to give him the choice of weapons, and he discovers that in this matter he will not be allowed to have everything his own way, his ardor will cool and he will not be so anxious to meet me.

"Time will tell, though, and I must make all necessary preparations for the event."

He proceeded straight to the neighborhood of the Bella Union Theater, entered a saloon and partook of a light supper, and then made his way behind the scenes of the popular place of amusement.

He found the stage-manager seated in his "den," as he was wont jocosely to call it, smoking a cigar.

The old actor was an odd, eccentric character. Batcliff was an Englishman, and report said that he came of an excellent family and had received a splendid education, being designed by his father for one of the learned professions. But from early manhood he had developed a passion for strong drink, and this had wrecked his life.

Then, too, just after leaving college—he had graduated at Oxford with high honors despite his irregular life—he had chosen to fall in love with a young actress whose pretty face and charming form had caught his fancy.

Batcliff had quarreled with his family on her account, and then in a fit of desperation, married the girl and came to America with her. There, forced by dire necessity, he had adopted the actor's life, and undoubtedly he would have made his mark on the boards if he had been content to let liquor alone. But the demon of drink ruined him as it has many other sons of genius.

Death had robbed him of his wife, for whose sake he turned his back upon a career in which undoubtedly he would have won honors. An outcast now, from home and friends, a strolling player and regarded as a vagabond by two-thirds of the people he met, Batcliff lived only for the present without any regard for the future.

Still a heavy drinker, yet he did not allow the liquor to so completely overcome him as in his younger days, and so took better care of himself.

Despite his present position and despite his early excesses, the old actor was a gentleman in every respect. From the time of their first meeting he and De Lormé had been fast friends.

It would be hard to find a better-posted man in regard to the "code" which regulates hostile meetings between gentlemen. At one time in his youth, Batcliff had studied for a year in one of the German universities and had been one of the champions of the "cut and thrust" school.

De Lormé accepted both the chair and the cigar which the old actor offered and proceeded to relate the particulars of the challenge which he had received, winding up with the request that he would like the other to act as his second.

"Certainly—delighted, me boy!" exclaimed Batcliff, rubbing his hands together as if delighted with the request.

"By my Halidame, I will go with you 'cheek by jowl!'" he exclaimed.

"Let me see, this McMichael is the young blood who is worth so much money?"

"Yes, the same."

"By Jove! The idea of a man worth two or three million being so anxious to risk his life just because he was fool enough to get drunk and then make an ass of himself."

"He evidently feels very sore over his discomfiture at my hands and is in a hurry to get square with me."

"What is the fellow's reputation in the duelist line?"

"Not particularly noted as far as I know. I never heard of his taking to the field of honor before, although I have encountered him once in a while at the shooting-galleries and in the fencing-schools."

"Ever had a bout with him?"

"No, I have faced his principal teacher though: you know him, this Irish captain, O'Ballyhoo."

"Oh, yes, smart fellow, that Irishman; lives like a fighting-cock on the best of the land, thanks to these young idiots who swallow his yarns and allow him to win their money."

"Yes, the captain manages to pull along pretty well. Parasites of his kind always flourish," De Lormé remarked.

"But you didn't tell me how you came off in your bouts with the captain."

"He is a good man both with sword and pistol, but he is old, lacks strength and quickness; youth must be served you know, and in nothing more than in athletic sports does that saying hold true.

"It was with the sword that I encountered the

Irishman and I came off an easy winner."

"I have seen him practice with the pistol, although I never happened to shoot against him. Though he is a tolerable good shot, yet he is very slow, dwells on his aim, and opposed to a man who was both quick and skillful wouldn't stand any chance at all. He would be winged before he got ready to fire."

"Yes, yes; I have seen just such men. But does a stream rise superior to its spring?" exclaimed the old actor, in his theatrical way. "Is the pupil greater than the master?"

"Sometimes it is that way, you know," De Lormé replied. "I remember in my own case that before I parted with the old Frenchman who taught me what I know of the sword, he acknowledged that I was his master.

"His superior skill did not equalize my superior strength."

"Undoubtedly; it is the course of nature."

"But I have stood among the spectators and seen this fellow exhibit his skill—show off, you know—in regular fool-like fashion, and I know that with neither sword nor pistol is he a match for me.

"I think the Irishman knows it, too, for in his wheedling way he tried to get me to waive my right of choice of weapons, which, as the challenged party, of course belongs to me.

"He had some deep game at the back of it, of course, for he is not the man to waste his breath without there is an advantage to be gained.

"What do you think he was up to?" Batcliff inquired.

"It struck me that it was possible that the blood has been practicing secretly with some out-of-the-way weapon, a broadsword or a saber or something of that sort, and he hoped getting the choice of weapons to take me at a disadvantage by naming some odd tool of this kind which he might be reasonably certain I was not skilled in the use of, and so he would be able to come off the conqueror."

"I see, I see; a deep game!"

"Yes; and one which a man of O'Ballyhoo's stamp would be apt to play."

"But it won't work, eh?" The old actor indulged in a hearty chuckle.

"Not much."

"What weapons will you select?"

"Rifles."

"Aha! You will be apt to catch him foul there, for the chances are a hundred to one that he is not an expert rifle-shot."

"While I am, for I have been used to handling a rifle ever since I was big enough to hold one. Then, too, brought up as I was in a wild region, I got used to shooting at all sorts of marks and at all sorts of distances. So I became, as a natural result, much more expert than one who practiced in a gallery at a target."

"Of course, of course; that goes without saying, as the French have it."

"So, when the captain comes, advise him that we will fight with repeating rifles, commencing at a thousand yards distance, and after the word is given either party to be at liberty to advance and fire when he so pleases."

"And the spot?"

"I was going to ask your advice about that."

"There is a quiet little spot about an hour's drive from the city to the southward," observed Batcliff, after a moment's thought.

"And by setting the meeting for an early hour in the

187

morning, say five o'clock, just after daybreak, there will be very little danger of any one being in the neighborhood to disturb the picnic."

"Very well, that will do, and the quicker the affair comes off the better; to-morrow morning will suit me as well as any time," De Lormé remarked, rising.

"That is rather too quick, De Lormé, I think. We must give them time for preparation."

"Yes, time for this fellow to go to some shooting-gallery and get his hand in a bit."

"In the old time such a thing would be considered a decidedly ungentlemanly thing to do," the actor remarked.

"Such an idea would never occur to this bullheaded Scotchman, but insist upon the day after to-morrow and no later."

"Just as you say," Batcliff replied.

CHAPTER XXXI.
LA BELLE HELENE AGAIN.

At this moment La Belle Helene passed by the open doorway and glanced into the apartment.

Perceiving De Lormé, she smiled and bowed and then beckoned for him to come.

De Lormé returned the bow, and then turning to the old actor said, "Don't yield an inch; you know this quarrel is none of my seeking, and since the fellow forced it on me I think that it is only right I should give him a lesson.

"I would like to be able to convince him that though he is worth a million or two he cannot have everything his own way in this world.

"It is my intention to use him so that for some time in the future he will have something to remind him of what a donkey he made of himself in this matter, and I have arranged it so that there isn't much chance of his being able to damage me."

"Oh, don't you be alarmed. I will take care that this Irishman with all his smartness does not get any the best of me.

"I haven't lived in this world and led a deuce of a life of fifty years for nothing. I will talk to the Celt like a Dutch uncle."

De Lormé laughed at the expression and then withdrew from the apartment to join the lady, who had passed down the stage to the first wing.

Hardly had he disappeared behind the sceneries when one of the boys attached to the theater brought the captain's card to the stage-manager.

"The gentleman is at the back door and would like

to see you, sir, on particular business," said the boy.

At a regular theater it is not an easy matter for any stranger to gain admittance behind the scenes no matter how particular his business may be, but in the class of variety theater to which the Bella Union belonged, the rules are anything but strict. So the captain was immediately escorted to the stage-manager's presence.

Batcliff and the Irishman were no strangers to each other.

On one occasion when some festive soul had insisted on all within the sound of his voice in the saloon of the Bella Union taking a drink with him, the actor and the adventurer had touched elbows as they stood side by side at the bar. Such a ceremony as this is equal to a formal introduction in the "glorious climate of California."

For the nonce, Batcliff suppressed the jolly Bohemianism so common to him and assumed that grand bearing, which on the mimic stage used to win him the approbation of the audience when he faced the footlights in the character of a fine old English gentleman.

He rose with the utmost politeness when his visitor was ushered into the apartment, bowed with elaborate dignity and commanded the boy to place a chair for the gentleman.

The lad did so and then retreated, full of wonder, for the change in the stage-manager's manner astounded him.

As a rule Batcliff generally received his visitors with a hearty slap on the back or a friendly poke in the ribs, followed by the offer of a drink.

After the departure of the boy the stage-manager carefully closed the door behind him, then took a chair himself opposite to where the captain was seated.

"Batcliff, sor, I regret to be afther having to say that

I have come upon a mighty disagreeable errand," the Irishman began.

"We must take the bitter with the sweet in this world, you know," the other replied.

"'In joining contrasts, lieth love's delights,' as the old dramatist beautifully remarks," observed Batcliff, assuming the manner which used to bring down the house when, as the wandering adventurer, Julian St. Pierre, he made his appearance and declared:

"Here take I my seat upon the palace steps, although they hang me from the portico!"

"An unpleasant business, sor," the captain repeated. "I come as the representative of me fri'nd, Clement Mc-Michael, Esquire, do ye mind."

"I have heard of him—a goodly gentleman of fair proportions, who carries within his purse much coin of the realm," returned Batcliff, with the utmost gravity.

The Irishman stared a little, but went on:

"Me fri'nd, sor, has been grossly insulted by Mr. Andrew De Lormé, and upon my applying to him for the satisfaction due from one gintleman to another, I have been referred to you."

"Sir, you have knocked at the right door, and now I throw open the portal and bid you enter."

"Phwat the divil do yees mane by this rigmarole?" exclaimed the captain, testily, suddenly coming to the conclusion that the other was making fun of him.

"Patience, gentle sir, let not your angry passions rise. You come here demanding satisfaction for your principal?"

"Yes, sor, I do!"

"You shall have it. Mr. De Lormé has done me the honor to request me to act as his second, and I will endeavor to do justice to his cause.

"Now, then, what do you require?"

"An apology or a fight!" cried the captain.

"The first demand is ridiculous, and we refuse it with lofty scorn," pronounced Batcliff. "The second hits us where we live, and that is the kind of hair-pins we are."

"Of course, as the challenged party," the captain allowed, "you have the right to name the time, place, and weapons."

"We know our right, and knowing, dare maintain!" cried the old actor, with lofty dignity.

"For weapons we name repeating-rifles, the distance one thousand yards, at the word the contending parties to be at liberty to advance and fire until either one or both on the surface of the cold earth is laid. The time; to-morrow morning at five o'clock, or the morning after at the same hour; we will give you your option in regard to that. The place, an open plain one hour's drive from the city, where, at an early hour, there will not be the least danger of any one interfering with the settlement of the business."

"Faix! It's a heathenish way to fight," the captain grumbled. "Repeating-rifles at a thousand yards! Do you call that the way for gintlemen to fight?"

"Oh, we don't do things in this great and glorious country after the stupid fashion common to the effete and rotten communities of the old world.

"The thing is as fair for your principal as it is for mine.

"Of course the chances are about a thousand to one that my principal will plug your man at the first crack, but that is what we go out for.

"Your principal is anxious for satisfaction, and if he ain't satisfied after being put into a suitable hole six feet in the ground, then he must be a hard man to please."

"Hadn't you better be saving your brags until the fight is over?" questioned the Irishman, sarcastically, as he rose to his feet.

"Mebbe yer man will not have such a shure thing of it as you are afther imagining.

"The conditions are accepted; the morning afther to-morrow will suit us best; but how will we be afther finding the place?"

"I will send directions the first thing in the morning to any place you say."

"Me head-quarters are at the Occidental Saloon."

"Very well; I will send there. Will you bring a doctor in your coach, or shall we?"

"Jest as ye please; but I know a foine gintleman, who will be delighted to officiate."

"Bring him along; that will suit us."

"Thin, sor, I have the honor to wish you a good-evening," said the Irishman, advancing to the door and bowing ceremoniously.

"Good-evening, sir."

And the actor hastened to open the door so that his visitor might depart.

"Permit me to escort you to the portal," Batcliff added, perceiving that the captain, bewildered by the novelty of the situation, was about to go in the wrong direction.

Then the stage-manager piloted the Irishman to the back door and saw him safely outside of it.

While this conversation had been going on, De Lormé had joined La Belle Helene in the "prompt wing."

"Are you going to see me home to-night, as usual?" she asked, bestowing one of her sweetest smiles upon him.

"Certainly—why do you ask?"

"Only to satisfy an idle curiosity," she replied, laughing.

"That was a splendid lunch you gave me last night. I do not remember that I ever enjoyed anything of the kind more in my life."

"I am glad to hear that."

"I am going to return the compliment tonight. I am going to give you a lunch; all the preparations are made, and that is why I wished to know if you were going home with me."

"You can depend upon me, lunch or no lunch. Your charming society is attraction enough!"

"Oh, you flatterer! I've something awful important to say to you, but that's my music!"

08. The applause, which greeted her appearance, was tumultuous.

CHAPTER XXXII.
A WOMAN'S STRATEGY.

A moment later the girl stood bowing before the footlights.

The applause, which greeted her appearance, was tumultuous.

As the astute manager of the Bella Union, the renowned Billy Macduff, observed to the young Bohemian who happened to be near him when the girl made her entrance upon the stage:

"Two hundred chucks a week is a mighty big sal for a shebang of this kind running at popular prices to stand, but you chaps with yer big notices and the gillies in front with their yells go for to make the gal think she is worth a heap sight more money than she draws, and thar ain't any wine-room biz to be got out of her, either.

"Now, if she would only go into the wine-room and pick me up an extra fifty a week, which she could do jest as easy as not, I wouldn't grumble in the least."

"Oh, be content, man," De Lormé counseled. "Here you are picking up five or six hundred a week out of the place and yet growling about the salaries you pay the artists who put the money in your pocket."

"Yes, that is all right, but I don't see why I should pay people more than they are worth," the manager replied.

"More than they are worth!" exclaimed De Lormé. "Well, come now, I like that! There is a brashness about that declaration that is really refreshing."

"It's the truth! Don't you s'pose I know how to run a show? Cuss me if they don't all of 'em get more than they are worth.

"Jest think of this gal—two hundred chucks a week jest for about ten minutes' work."

"If you don't like her price why don't you give her notice to quit? I don't doubt that she could find some one else who would be glad to have her at that figure."

This suggestion alarmed the proprietor of the Bella Union, for he had opposition, and the rival shows hurt his business more than he cared to own.

"Oh, that is all right, there are always lots of fools in this world who are ready to throw money away, but I run a theater to make ducats, not to pay out all that comes in on duffers w'ot ain't no good."

And then in order to put an end to the discussion in which he felt he was getting the worst of it, Macduff stalked gloomily away.

It was the first night of a new programme and La Belle Helene's "turn," to use the stage term by which the performance of each artist is designated, came early.

She went on at half-past nine and as her songs only occupied ten or fifteen minutes, the length of time depending upon the caprice of the audience, and whether they would be satisfied with a couple of songs or greedily demand four or five as was generally the case.

So on this particular evening of which we write La Belle Helene was through her performance and all dressed for the street by ten o'clock.

De Lormé was in waiting at the back door and the two left the theater together.

"I was just thinking of the changes that a few short weeks sometimes make in this life," she remarked as they walked down the street together.

"It was only a little while ago that I came to San Francisco almost penniless and wandered through the streets of this city seeking a position where I might earn my bread by the use of my musical abilities.

"I did not aspire to a public life then, but would have been perfectly contented to have procured an humble situation as a teacher.

"But day followed day and there seemed to be no place for me, then happening to sing one night for the amusement of Mrs. Briggs and her boy, the little fellow suggested that I ought to go on the stage.

"He managed to get money enough to patronize the Bella Union once a week on the average, and thinking he was a judge in such matters, he declared I was a far better singer than any lady he had ever heard on the stage.

"And from that chance observation of the boy I was led to make the venture which has resulted so happily."

"Let me see, didn't one of the old poets say something about 'from lightest trifles come deepest consequences?'" De Lormé said.

"Oh, I don't know. Don't talk literature to me, for I am an awful blockhead in that line.

"I never cared much for reading, any way, not even novels that most girls are wild about."

"Possibly that fact would be considered to be to your credit by most people."

"I do not trouble my head much in regard to what anybody says or thinks about me," she replied in a tone of indifference. "The world at large never did anything for me when I needed help, and I have a thorough contempt for its opinion."

"There's the old saying, you know, 'to Him that hath shall be given—'"

"Yes, and it is true too, every word of it!" interrupted the girl, quickly.

"Now that I am independent and don't need friends I have plenty who profess their willingness to do anything in the world to oblige me. And although I suppose a great deal of it is mere lip service and cannot be depended upon, yet some of the men are honest enough and I feel certain would be glad to favor me in any way."

"And among those reliable men please count your humble servant to command," remarked De Lormé.

La Belle Helene looked askance at him for a moment before she made reply.

"Well, I hope so," she finally observed, slowly.

"You speak as if you doubted. "

"No, but I am terribly suspicious by nature, and when I like any one, I am always worried by the fear that my liking is not returned."

"Such doubts do not do justice to your own charms," he replied.

"You do like me, don't you?" she asked abruptly, gazing searchingly into his face with her large, lustrous eyes.

"Oh, yes, there isn't the least doubt about that."

"As well as that English girl for whom you wrote the burlesque?" she inquired.

"You see, some kind friends," and her lips curled in disdain, "have been taking the trouble to enlighten me in regard to your past life."

"Oh, such a thing as that is always to be expected," he remarked, lightly, seemingly not in the least troubled by the circumstance.

"But you haven't answered my question," she said.

"That isn't the worst of it, my Belle," he rejoined.

"Oh! I suppose I know what you mean. You don't intend to answer it."

"You are not dull of comprehension, that is evident!" he exclaimed, laughing.

"As bright as you are beautiful, and that is saying a

great deal, as your mirror will surely inform you the next time you consult it."

"You are treating me like a child!" she exclaimed, apparently slightly vexed.

"Oh, no; not at all! How can you possibly say such a thing?"

"But you are! I have asked you a question and you ought to answer it."

"A question in regard to my past life—in regard to a matter which does not concern you at all.

"If the lady was living there might be some reason in it; but she is dead and in her grave, and there let her rest," he observed, his tone grave now.

"Oh, I know you don't love me half as well as you did her!" she protested.

"Now, if you care anything for me it will make you a great deal happier to think just the contrary," he declared.

"Wasn't it for her sake that you killed the man who ill-treated her?"

"Now, my dear girl, you mustn't rake up these old matters, for it is decidedly unpleasant for me.

"Let the dead past bury its dead, and say no more about it."

By this time the two had reached the house where La Belle Helene dwelt, and the girl conducted her companion into the dining-room, where a dainty repast was spread. The little feast consisting chiefly of cold broiled quail, flanked by a brace of portly champagne bottles.

"I cooked these birds myself this afternoon," she declared, as she took his hat and then removed her own outward coverings.

"Yes, sir; I wanted to show you that I could be useful as well as ornamental."

De Lormé surveyed the lunch, which looked exceedingly tempting, and gave an approving nod.

"Capital! I do not remember to have ever seen a more inviting spread on a small scale," he remarked.

"Now sit down, and let me do the honors this time," she said, as she placed a chair for him.

"I will carve the birds, but I think I will have to trouble you to open the wine."

"No trouble at all," he replied, producing his corkscrew and proceeding to operate on one of the champagne bottles.

"Mighty few men of sense will you encounter in this world who will call it trouble to open a bottle of good wine," he remarked.

And then with a loud pop the cork flew out and the creamy fluid came bubbling up.

De Lormé filled the glasses while La Belle Helene carved the birds.

"Will you have some of the salad?' she asked. "It is an oyster-salad and I made it myself expressly in your honor."

"Certainly. An emperor would be proud to be served by such fair hands," De Lormé exclaimed gallantly.

"Ah, it is not I who can serve you now, but you can serve me greatly if you only will do so," she replied. "But come, drink my health and then try some of the lunch before we descend to dry business."

De Lormé obeyed willingly.

CHAPTER XXXIII.
THE BOHEMIAN SPEAKS PLAINLY.

For ten minutes the two did full justice to the lunch; La Belle Helene observing that, "I am so terribly hungry! I never eat much of anything for my supper for fear that it will interfere with my singing."

"And as for me, I am like the man on a long journey, prepared to eat whenever I get the chance," De Lormé remarked.

The birds being eaten, the pair settled themselves to enjoy the wine and the plate of macaroons, which formed the dessert.

"By the way, I didn't make these," she said, as she passed the dish to the gentleman.

"I am honest with you; pray be sure to take notice of that," she added.

"Oh, I am full of confidence," he replied.

"But this sort of thing is awful extravagant," she observed.

"You see, I am a little inclined to be stingy, and, until I got up this lunch to-night, I really had no idea of how expensive such things are."

"I could have given you full information in regard to that," he observed, sipping his wine leisurely. "I have been there quite a number of times, much to the damage of my pocketbook."

"Altogether it cost me nearly fifteen dollars!"

And she shook her head gravely, as much as to bemoan such sad waste.

"Well, now, you managed it very well, indeed. That was getting off pretty cheap.

"If I had ordered such a spread at any first-class

restaurant it would have cost at least ten dollars a head."

"But if I had that five millions of dollars that we were talking about last night, such a picnic as this wouldn't be anything to the feasts that we might enjoy."

De Lormé had been expecting a speech of this kind for some time, for he understood that La Belle Helene had not gone to the trouble of getting up this lunch without an object.

"Yes, a person with five millions of dollars can manage to rub along pretty comfortably nowadays," he remarked.

La Belle Helene fixed her brilliant eyes upon him as though she hoped to read his very soul, but a better mask than the frank and open countenance of the Bohemian could not be found.

"Have you reflected in regard to that matter upon which we spoke last night?" she asked,

"Oh, yes."

"And come to a decision in regard to it?"

"Certainly. That is what you wanted me to do, you know, and I am always pleased to be able to oblige a lady."

These words sounded meaningless to the girl, for she craved a stronger statement.

"Oh, don't talk to me in that way!" she exclaimed. "We are not exchanging empty compliments now, but are contemplating an entrance into a struggle which will be colossal in its extent, and one which will surely tax all our energies."

The speech was full of fire, and De Lormé's face became grave as he listened.

"I have trusted my secret to you, the only living soul to whom I ever revealed it, and I did so because I had faith that you could be trusted.

"Then, too, since we have come together there has grown up in my heart a feeling for you akin to love, if it is not true love itself.

"I will say to you, frankly, I am a woman of such peculiar nature that I do not believe it is possible for me to feel the passion which is common to the most of womankind.

"It is not in my nature. I could not resolve myself into a weak, love-sick girl. It is not possible. But if you are the man I take you to be, I can learn to love you with a passion that will leave you no cause to complain.

"But first, you must prove that you are worthy of my affection by aiding me to seize my share of this rich estate, and in return for the service I will give you myself and all the wealth that your efforts secure."

She had hurried impetuously on in the speech, and De Lormé listened patiently, not attempting to interrupt her with any comments.

When she had finished he reached over and refilled her glass, which was empty, and then filled his own again.

"Oh, I don't want the wine!" she exclaimed, impetuously. "I am not burning up with thirst but with impatience. It is your answer for which I hunger!"

"Helene, you have been frank and honest with me, and I will endeavor to be the same with you," De Lormé remarked, slowly.

"I have thought this matter over and given due reflection to it.

"I have endeavored to sit in judgment upon your case and see that it received full justice.

"In the beginning I assumed that your story was correct in every respect, and I said to myself: 'Now then, what are the weak points where it will be difficult to prove to the satisfaction of the doubters that she is the legal widow of Archibald Macarthy?'"

"I see, I see; that was right!" La Belle Helene exclaimed, listening with the utmost attention to his words. "And it is so difficult in such a matter to free ourselves from the blindness which leads us to look at the thing in a personal light; our judgment is swayed by our wishes, and we wonder how any one can be so stupid as not to see the matter exactly as it appears to us."

"You have stated the case admirably," De Lormé remarked.

"From the beginning I have endeavored to divest myself of any personal interest in the matter, and have tried to look at it with unprejudiced eyes.

"Now then, you were married to Macarthy by a justice of the peace?"

"Yes."

"And you do not remember his name nor where his office was situated?"

"No."

"There were witnesses of course?"

"Yes, the official's clerk and some friend of his who were in the office at the time," she replied.

"There are three witnesses then who can prove the marriage—if they can be found, and if they remember the circumstance sufficiently well to be able to identify—not only you, but Macarthy also, for the important thing to be proved is that it was Archibald Macarthy whom you married.

"To prove that you were married in the office of the justice of the peace without being able to identify Macarthy as the bridegroom wouldn't help your case in the least."

"Yes, yes, I know that!" she exclaimed, impatiently. "I have thought of all these things and counted the chances as well as you; you must not take me for an id-iot!"

It was plain to De Lormé from this display that La Belle Helene had a temper of her own.

"The fact that you visited Sacramento on your wedding trip counts for nothing," he remarked.

"If you were able to bring forward undoubted proof that you were introduced there as his wife it would strengthen your case. But, under the circumstances, I don't see how it can be done, for after this lapse of time it would be almost impossible for the people of the hotel to identify Macarthy so that a court of law would be satisfied that he was the man who accompanied you.

"You see when you come to look at all these things you certainly must see that you have a weak case," he said in conclusion.

"If you commence by assuming that there isn't the least chance for me, it stands to reason you will be apt to make it is so!" exclaimed the woman.

The manner of La Belle Helene was petulant and her eyes flashed angrily.

It was clear that she was annoyed by the plain speech of her companion.

De Lormé did not appear to take any notice of her irritation.

"I see you have fallen into the error that most people make when they come to look at a matter of this kind in which they take a deep personal interest," he remarked. "You are not willing to examine the matter fairly. You are biased in favor of your own side of the case.

"That is not the way to get at the truth at all, and that is why so many people rush into lawsuits that are absolutely hopeless from the beginning. The truth is apparent though to every one but themselves and the legal sharks they employ; the legal sharks who are generally blind when fees are in the prospective.

"If you could produce the man who married you to Macarthy and the witnesses to the ceremony, and if they could surely swear that Archibald Macarthy was the man to whom you were married, then you would stand some chance…"

"It can be done!" La Belle Helene cried decidedly, interrupting De Lormé.

"Do you not remember that I told you I saw the man who married me to Macarthy in California Street the other day?"

And looking De Lormé squarely in the face in a manner that had a deal of defiance in it, she continued, "I hope you do not doubt my word in this matter? I hope you believe that I tell the truth about it? The man can be found, and the witnesses also, and money judiciously applied will be apt to stimulate their memories. Now the question is, can I depend upon your aid?"

"I will answer the question, my dear girl, as bluntly as you have asked it. You must not count me in this game, for—"

"Never mind your reasons!" cried La Belle Helene, springing to her feet in anger.

"I don't care for them; your friendship—your love for me, is a fraud, and henceforth we will be as strangers to each other!"

"Be it so," remarked De Lormé, rising, without betraying the least emotion.

"Good-by!" and then he departed, leaving the woman a prey to the most violent rage.

CHAPTER XXXIV.
ON THE ROAD.

De Lormé laughed quietly to himself after he had gained the street, as he reflected upon the peculiar conclusion of the interview.

"She is willfully and recklessly blind in regard to the matter, and is determined to go ahead," he remarked, communing with himself as he proceeded down the street.

"She is determined to get a slice of Macarthy's five millions either by hook or crook. And I think I can guess her game, although she has been careful not to expose her hand even when trying to get me to become her partner.

"I think she was telling me a falsehood when she said she had lately encountered the man who years ago married her to Macarthy.

"She is not sure that either the official who performed the ceremony, or the men who witnessed it, are in the land of the living. Or, if they live, that they are on the Pacific slope so that she can get at them to testify in her behalf.

"But as she must have witnesses who will swear to the fact of the marriage, she has determined, if she cannot find the real men who were present, to procure false ones.

"And as she thinks she cannot manage a matter of that kind very well by herself, that was why she was so anxious to enlist me in her cause.

"It was a cunning trick!"

De Lormé laughed contemptuously as he reflected upon the circumstance.

"She intended that I should find these false witnesses, and then, if by any accident the bottom should tumble out of the affair and the fraud be exposed, she could pretend that I had deceived her—swear she knew nothing of the trick, and so leave me to bear the blame.

"But I am far too old a bird to be caught in such a clumsy snare.

"La Belle Helene will have to find some man of duller wits than I possess to act as her cat's-paw, for, decidedly, I shall not burn my fingers in endeavoring to pull her chestnuts out of the fire."

The Bohemian proceeded straight home and went to bed, contrary to his usual custom, for he generally made the rounds of the all-night places before retiring to rest.

But for all his usual recklessness, De Lormé realized that he would only be acting prudently to get himself in good trim for the approaching contest. Though he did not have a particularly good opinion of young McMichael's abilities in the shooting line, yet he was too old a hand to commit the mistake of undervaluing his antagonist.

About noon on the next day the veteran actor made his appearance at De Lormé's office.

"It is all settled, my boy," he announced. "The opposite party agrees to the terms, although the Irishman kicked like a steer about the rifles, but I was firm as a rock, and finally he came to his milk."

"He was a donkey to suppose he was going to have everything his own way," De Lormé remarked.

"What kind of hair-pins did he take us for, anyway?"

"It was his game, of course, to secure all the advantage he could, but I wouldn't give an iota, and so perforce he was obliged to be content," the veteran remarked.

"We'll have to start about four to-morrow morning, I suppose?"

209

"Yes; I have furnished the other party with all the particulars, so that they will not have any difficulty in finding the battle-ground.

"I intended to write to the Irishman, but when I came to think the matter over, I came to the conclusion I had better go and see him in person so that there wouldn't be any mistake about the matter."

"Oh, yes, that was wise. A personal interview is always the most desirable."

"Everything is understood, and there isn't any reason why the performance should not be a success," Batcliff remarked, rubbing his hands in a professional sort of way.

"I did have an idea at one time that the 'blood' wouldn't come to time unless he succeeded in having everything his own way, and the Irishman intimated as much, and thereupon I told him promptly that my principal was not hungering to shed his man's gore, and that as you had managed to thrash him in the most handsome manner, you were perfectly satisfied with the way things had gone and were not at all disposed to complain."

De Lormé laughed.

"That must have worried him."

"Immensely! He squirmed like an eel undergoing the skinning process," the old actor replied, with a chuckle.

"And I told him too, right plainly, that in my opinion his man was disposed to funk, and that, after having mustered up sufficient courage to send a challenge, upon finding it promptly accepted, his courage had oozed out of his finger-ends and he was now anxious to find some excuse to get out of the scrape."

"That insinuation must have nettled him," De Lormé observed.

"Oh, it did. But he was sharp enough to see that he had got himself into a false position and so he made haste to get out of it as easily as possible."

"Everything is all arranged then?"

"Yes, I have ordered the hack to be at the corner above the Bella Union at four sharp tomorrow morning.

"There are always a lot of night-hawk hacks prowling around in that vicinity, and I thought for us to take it in that neighborhood would not excite any attention.

"It will not be apt to attract any notice."

"Take care of yourself until then."

"Trust me for that."

And then the stage-manager of the Bella Union departed.

Old Father Time went on in his flight and the hours came and vanished.

The night came and then departed, warned by the gray light of jocund day that his brief reign was at an end.

For the first time in a long while the Bohemian had not honored the Bella Union with his presence.

La Belle Helene noticed his absence and her lip curled contemptuously.

The indifference of De Lormé irritated her.

"Ah, I did not know this man!" she exclaimed communing with herself.

"I believed I had secured a hold upon him. Heaven knows, I tried all my woman's arts to attach him to me, and now I am obliged to confess that I failed most dismally.

"But I never felt certain of success. There was always something about the man that puzzled me.

"It was as if he wares a mask—as if he never allowed me to see him in his true colors, but I never even

211

dreamed that he would take a dismissal so coolly and retire without attempting to make up with me.

"It only shows though how slight was the hold I had upon him.

"I almost made a fool of myself on his account too, for he is the only man I have encountered in this world toward whom I ever felt the least bit of the sentiment which is called love.

"It isn't in my nature to love anybody much, I am satisfied, but I have got used to him and now that he is gone I feel as if there was a gap in my life.

"I don't love him—I know that I can never love anybody. But, slight as the strength of the feeling is that I have for him, yet if he had been in trouble or needed aid, I would have spent my last dollar for him or even risked my life in his behalf. But he, man-like, takes me at my word, and, because in a foolish moment, in my disappointment and anger, I treated him unjustly he goes from me as though there had never been any friendship between us."

It was noticed that she did not sing as well as usual that night, and despite her strong powers of self-control she allowed it to be seen that she was out of sorts. When the absence of De Lormé was noticed it gave rise to a deal of ill-natured gossip, for of all people in the world those who follow the stage for a living are most apt to indulge in that sort of thing.

But, to use the common expression, De Lormé had other fish to fry.

He had no time to waste loitering in and around the Bella Union, for such a course would naturally involve the acceptance of more or less liquor from jovial and thirsty friends who would not be content to take "No," for an answer.

Understanding this he abstained from visiting his usual haunts, and instead of showing up at the variety theater, spent a quiet evening with the dressmaker, the spirited Lucille Gwinnet. He entertained her with an account of the search after the tin box and the mysterious document contained within it.

"The thing is like a will-o'-the-wisp," she remarked when he had concluded.

"Yes, and where on earth it has got to is a mystery. It is probable that Irish Kate hid it away in some safe place before she received her hurt, and when she recovers sufficiently to be able to speak, the truth will come out. Or possibly it fell from her person during the skirmish, and was lost, or picked up by someone."

De Lormé spent a very pleasant evening, taking his departure, however, at nine o'clock, and going straight to bed, so as to secure a good night's sleep.

He set the alarm of his clock for half-past three, and promptly to the minute he was up.

He made his toilet and hastened to the meeting place.

Batcliff was in waiting. The two entered the hack and away they went.

CHAPTER XXXV.
THE CAPTAIN'S COUNCIL.

Very little conversation passed between the two on their road to the place appointed for the hostile meeting.

Batcliff had staid up as late as usual attending to his duties. The veteran actor had not sought his couch until after twelve. In fact, it was nearly one before he had got to sleep. And not being accustomed to rising at such an early hour, it was only natural that he should feel sleepy and out-of-sorts.

For three-quarters of an hour then after starting, Batcliff dozed in his corner of the coach. But at the end of that time, happening to wake up enough to glance out of the window, he saw that they had got beyond the confines of the city and were in the open country.

"Aha, we are nearly there!" he exclaimed, the discovery banishing all desire for sleep.

"That is good," his companion remarked.

"Yes, I am deuced glad of it, for it is almost impossible for me to keep awake. The easy motion of this vehicle induces sleep, and it is as much as I can do to keep my eyes open. Have you been enjoying a visit to the Land of Nod?"

"No, I do not feel inclined that way at all," the Bohemian replied.

"I went to bed at an early hour last night, and got a good five hours' sleep, and so I feel as fresh as a daisy this morning, although I got up at just about the hour that I usually go to bed."

"You acted prudently," the actor remarked.

"There's nothing like getting yourself in a good condition for an affair of this kind, and that is just where the average man makes a mistake," the Bohemian allowed. "When he gets mixed up in one of these affairs of honor, instead of taking all possible care of himself, he becomes, if anything, a little more reckless in regard to his habits than usual. Yet, the prize-fighter, who doesn't usually risk his life, considers it absolutely necessary to go into the strictest kind of training for a month or more."

"Oh, I suppose the idea is that a majority of men become involved in an affair of this kind almost before they know it, and they really do not comprehend the gravity of the situation until they come to face their opponent upon the field. But you act like an old hand at the bellows. "

"It is my first regular duel, though."

"You surprise me!"

"It is a fact. I have been unlucky enough to be mixed up in three or four encounters where the situation was so strained that I had either to fight or run, but I have never figured in an actual encounter on the field of honor."

"How do you feel—anyway nervous?" the stage-manager asked, with a professional air.

"Not in the least; why should I?"

"Well, I don't know," the other replied, reflectively. "I should think—under the circumstances—that a slight degree of nervousness would be experienced, it being your first appearance in such a line."

"No, I am rather phlegmatic by nature, and being so situated that I haven't anything particular to live for, the danger of risking my life doesn't appear to me so great as it would to a man with lots of things to make life desirable.

"I must die some time, you know, and what does it matter whether the end comes sooner or later?"

"Well, I suppose that is the right way to look at it, but

there's deuced few men gifted with philosophy enough to do that. But, I say: what do you think about this matter? Are you going to lay your man out if you can?"

"I most assuredly shall endeavor to teach him a lesson which will last him for some time," De Lormé replied. "There are too many bullies of this kind in the world, going about seeking whom they may devour, and it is only right for a man to 'down' such rascals on all possible opportunities.

"I don't wish to kill the fellow. I haven't any desire that his death shall be laid at my door, but I do intend to disable him, if I can, so that he will be laid up for some time. Then he will have leisure to reflect upon the matter, and it is possible that he will be able to see just what a donkey he has made of himself."

"I'm afraid that you will have to give him a pretty severe lesson to be able to effect a cure," the veteran actor remarked, with a shake of the head.

"The fellow has been carrying matters with a pretty high hand for the last few years; in fact, ever since his father's death.

"The old man kept a check on him, and he didn't dare to go it in the rapid style he now puts on.

"I tell you! It is one of the worst things in the world for a young fellow to be put in control of so much money, for he thinks, because he has a few millions, he can do as he likes."

"You are right, and that has been amply proved by the career of this McMichael," De Lormé observed.

"Since he came into his fortune and found himself his own master, he has been mixed up in some pretty bad scrapes, and in every instance a liberal use of money has enabled him to get out of the difficulty."

"But in this case his money will not do him much

good, eh?" exclaimed the veteran actor, with a chuckle.

"No, not all the money in the world will be of any avail to save him from the bullet of my rifle, when once I draw a 'bead' on him," the Bohemian replied.

At this point the coach came to a halt, and Batcliff, looking out of the window, cried:

"Here we are."

The two alighted from the hack, which had drawn up in the shelter of a little grove so as to escape observation.

The Jehu in charge of the vehicle was a prudent and discreet fellow who could be trusted to mind his own business.

Of course, in a case of this kind it was necessary to allow the hack-driver to have some idea of what was going on. It would be impossible to take a hack at such an hour for such a trip, and board the vehicle with an ominous-looking cased rifle, without arousing the driver's suspicions. And if he had not been forewarned and so prepared for such a thing, there was a chance that he might think it his duty to speak to the first police officer he encountered and so upset the whole business.

The hackman made haste to tie his horses to one of the trees, while his passengers were getting out, and then, approaching them, he said:

"I s'pose thar won't be any objections to a cove of about my size taking a squint at the picnic?"

"Oh, no, none at all," Batcliff answered. "Besides, we don't own the premises; this is a free country, and we couldn't hinder any one who happened to be in the neighborhood from taking a look at the show, even if we wanted so to do."

The hackman grinned.

"Of course I don't know either one of you two gents

from a side of sole-leather if any accidents happen," he remarked. "So you needn't be afeard to have me take a look at the fandango."

The others nodded and walked on, the actor carrying the rifle in the hollow of his arm.

The spot, which Batcliff had selected for the duel, was well suited for such a purpose, being an open sandy plain, about a mile square.

There were no houses in sight, the plain being in a hollow, and a better spot for an affair of this kind could not have been found within a hundred miles of the city.

There was a small clump of stunted trees at one end of the plain and this was the spot, which had been selected as the rendezvous.

"We are first in the field," Batcliff remarked, as they approached the little grove and he could see no human forms.

"So much the better; there isn't anything like promptness in this world. And then, too, if they delay their coming for ten minutes or so, it will give me time to get over the numbness of the carriage ride, and in the mean time we can enjoy a cigar, so we'll stroll up and down and enjoy the morning air."

De Lormé produced a couple of cigars, a match was applied, and soon the fragrant smoke of the choice weeds ascended on the air.

It was fully fifteen minutes before the hack containing McMichael's party arrived on the scene, so De Lormé and Batcliff found a patch free of dew on which to sit.

The McMichael party had been late in starting, for the young man, in spite of the sagacious counsel of the wily Irishman, had spent his evening after his usual fashion, and had not retired to bed until about one. It had been a difficult matter for his valet to get him up at such an unseemly hour in the morning.

The doctor, who was a medical gentleman of a sporting turn of mind, had been Mr. McMichael's companion and it was much trouble to get him up too, for both of them drank pretty freely during the evening.

"Begob! It's a foine condition he is in entirely to meet a man like that bold backer, De Lormé!" the Irishman exclaimed to himself as he saw the nervous state of his principal, the result of his night's debauch.

And in order to straighten his man out as much as possible the Irishman advised the use of some very strong coffee, which was duly partaken of by all of the party.

Then the captain seized upon an opportunity to take the young man aside.

"Upon me wourd! Ye would be committing suicide for yees to meet that divil of a De Lormé in this state with yer nerves all unstrung if I hadn't a finger in the pie, but as it is, ye'r' all right!

"One caution: Fire the minute ye get the word, it don't matter whether ye have got him 'covered' or not. Fire anyhow before he does or it's a hundred to one he peppers ye!"

CHAPTER XXXVI.
THE CONFLICT.

When the hack containing the opposing party halted and the three within it descended to the ground, De Lormé and Batcliff threw away their cigars and rose to receive the new-comers.

All bowed ceremoniously; the doctor was introduced. Then the principals withdrew a little from the others and the seconds proceeded to arrange the details of the fight.

"A thousand yards apart, or say a thousand paces; that will be near enough," the veteran actor observed.

The Irishman bowed in token of assent.

"That will suit us, sor, if it will be afther suiting you."

"The rifles to be repeating ones. You understood that, didn't you?"

"Yis, sor."

And then the captain removed the rifle, which he had brought from the case that covered it, and Batcliff followed his example.

Both the rifles were Spencers and as alike as two peas, excepting that the one the captain brought had evidently not seen as much service as the other.

"A foine pair of weapons," the Irishman remarked, critically, "although I must remark, Mr. Batcliff, to me mind it savors of barbarianism for two gintlemen to fight a duel wid such tools that are only fit for sodgers to kill one another."

"In the glorious climate of California everything goes," the veteran actor remarked. "And I reckon that if your principal is lucky enough to drill a hole in my man with a bullet from one of these, he will feel just as well satisfied as though he had accomplished the trick with any other weapon you can pick out."

"Yis, I presume so."

"After the signal is given each man is at liberty to advance and fire as often as he likes until the fight is ended."

"Upon me wourd, Mr. Batcliff, this is, I think, the most blood thirsty arrangement I ever heard of wid all my experience in matthers of this kind."

"Ah, yes, maybe so, but you can't judge us in this country by the rule that holds good abroad. We don't believe in any foolishness, and when we go in for blood, we mean business every time!" Batcliff exclaimed.

"Phwat will the signal be?"

"A revolver-shot; you can give it or I; it is not material; or we can toss up a coin to decide the matter."

"That will be the betther way."

The trial was made and the captain won.

A smile of satisfaction illuminated his face. "That is the first blow for our side!" he observed.

"One swallow don't make a summer, and there's an old saying that a bad beginning makes a good ending," retorted the other.

Then the two fell to loading the rifles, taking particular care to accomplish the job in a workmanlike manner.

The task completed, Batcliff suggested that the captain should pace off the distance, as his legs were the longest, and the Irishman, after a moment of pretended reluctance, gladly agreed to do the measuring, for this exactly suited the wily scheme that he had laid to compass the death of Andrew De Lormé.

The distance was paced off and the antagonists placed in position, rifle in hand.

De Lormé was within a hundred feet of the woodland, which, on the southern side, fringed the plain, while McMichael was out in the center of the opening, his dark figure clearly outlined against the sky.

To Batcliff's notion the Irishman had selected the worst position of the two for his man, but, as he appeared to be satisfied with it, the actor said nothing.

"I rather think this loud-mouthed Celt doesn't know as much about dueling as he pretends," was Batcliff's muttered comment.

There was certainly no doubt that it was easier to hit the man whose dark figure was so clearly outlined against the sky, than to damage his opponent with the woodland at his back.

De Lormé had noticed this seeming blunder on the part of O'Ballyhoo, and he was rather troubled by it, for he had a better opinion of the Irishman than to believe he could be capable of making such an error.

There was some reason for it he felt certain, but, with all his shrewdness, he was unable to guess the Irishman's game.

"I must be on the lookout," he murmured, as he grasped his rifle firmly and fixed his gaze upon his foe. "There is some cunning trick in this I am sure, and I must be on my guard to meet it."

"Are you all ready?" asked Batcliff of the captain after the antagonists were in position.

"All ready; are yees?"

"Yes, sir. Go ahead as soon as you like."

The captain drew his revolver, cocked it, and then pointed it in the air.

"One—two—three!" he counted, in a loud tone, and then there was a quick flash, and the sharp report of the revolver rung out on the air.

McMichael was nervous now that he found himself opposed to the man whose life he sought, for this was his first affair of honor, but he had steeled himself to meet the ordeal, and his nervousness was not perceptible.

O'Ballyhoo's admonition had full weight, and he had raised the hammer of his rifle so as to be in readiness to fire the moment the word was given, although for the life of him, he could not see what harm he could do his antagonist if he fired without taking the trouble to get an accurate aim.

But, for all that, he had made up his mind to obey the injunction.

And so the moment the signal-shot sounded on the air, up came his rifle to his shoulder, and, though he tried to draw a bead on his antagonist, yet he did not allow himself to dwell on his aim but discharged the piece immediately.

And almost at the same moment, only a second behind it, so as to enable one to perceive that there were two reports, came the sound of a loud explosion from amid the bushes about three hundred feet from where De Lormé stood.

The Bohemian understood the game now.

The captain had some confederate concealed in the shrubbery, either to attempt his life or by the discharging of the gun to attract his attention and so give his opponent an advantage.

If the man had been placed there to assassinate him the design had failed, for no bullet had whistled near enough for him to detect that such a thing had passed.

And if to distract his aim, it could not be done.

He never moved when the sound of the unexpected shot reached his ears, for just at the moment he had "covered" his adversary, and before the echoes of the two reports had died away his rifle spoke.

As he had told the veteran actor, he did not seek the life of the man who had forced this quarrel upon him, but he did wish to give him a lesson, which would be a warning for him not to attempt anything of the kind in the future.

So he fired to wound, not to kill, although, splendid shot as he was, it would have been fully as easy for him to do one as the other.

He had aimed to put a ball in the fleshy part of the leg, just above the knee, and he succeeded, although from a slight error in his calculations the ball struck the limb some two inches lower down than he intended.

With a groan of pain McMichael fell forward upon his face, and then, with the bulldog-like pluck of his old Scotch race, essayed to rise to his feet so as to be able to renew the battle.

The effort cost him dear, for the moment he attempted to support himself upon his injured leg it gave way beneath him, and with a groan of pain he sank fainting to the ground.

The doctor seized his case of instruments and immediately hastened to the aid of the stricken man; for all of the spectators understood that the duel was ended. It was clearly impossible for McMichael to longer keep the field.

O'Ballyhoo followed the doctor, seemingly anxious to aid his friend, while Batcliff, with drawn revolver, rushed to the spot in the bushes which the tiny white smoke, still curling upward on the air, betrayed as the lair of the unknown firer of the unexpected shot.

De Lormé followed at his heels.

As they approached the timber groans saluted their ears.

Quickening their pace they entered the fringe of bushes that encircled the trees.

And there in a little open space they found a rough-looking fellow writhing in dreadful agony.

The fragments of the shattered gun were strewn upon the ground and plainly revealed to the new-comers what had occurred.

In truth it did not require the eye of a prophet to understand why the man was lurking in the bushes.

He had come there for the express purpose of assassinating De Lormé.

The plot had been cunningly contrived too. The fellow had evidently been instructed to fire at the very same moment that McMichael discharged his weapon, so that the two reports would sound like one, and if the concealed marksman succeeded in hitting his man, as there was hardly a doubt he would do at such a short range, all would believe that De Lormé had been struck by the bullet from McMichael's rifle.

But Heaven had set at naught the murderous plan. The assassin's rifle had first hung fire and then exploded, carrying death to the villain who had attempted for gold to take a human life.

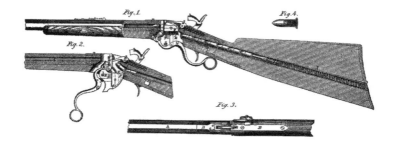

09. Spencer Repeating Rifle, design of 1862. Lever action with cartridges stored in a spring-loaded shaft in the stock. Around 200,000 Spencer rifles in several variations were issued to Union Cavalry and other forces during the American Civil War, although most infantry troops were still equipped with single shot muzzle-loading rifles.

CHAPTER XXXVII.
THE TRUST.

Now it was plain to both Batcliff and De Lormé why the Irishman had been willing to have his man placed in what was undoubtedly the worst position of the two, for by placing McMichael out on the plain his antagonist was naturally assigned to a position near the shrubbery and so brought within easy range of the concealed assassin.

"It is the work of that scoundrel of a captain!" Batcliff exclaimed, as he hastened toward the writhing man.

"No doubt about it!" De Lormé answered. "He had a misgiving in regard to his principal's being able to cope with me and so arranged this trap."

"To make 'assurance doubly sure and take a bond of fate,'" quoted the old actor.

"But this little game will end the captain's career in Frisco."

"Yes, if we can prove he had a hand in it, and that may not be easy," De Lormé answered.

"This fellow is badly hurt, perhaps mortally wounded," Batcliff remarked as he bent over the wounded man, the two having reached his side at this point.

"And it is possible that seeing death staring him in the face, he may be inclined to make a clean breast of it. His dying statement that the Irishman was the man who set him on will be apt to fix the guilt upon him so firmly that he will not be able to get rid of the stain, struggle as he may."

"On, no, friend Batcliff, you don't know this scheming captain yet," the Bohemian exclaimed.

"He never acted in this matter himself—never

227

appeared in his own proper person—but used some tool so that if the scheme miscarried he could not possibly be called to an account through the squealing of the ruffian employed to do the work."

As the two knelt by the side of the wounded man it was apparent to both that his sands of life were running fast to an end.

He had been fearfully mangled by the bursting gun, but yet retained his consciousness and had strength enough to speak, although growing weaker and weaker each moment.

"Pard, I tried fer to do fer you," he gasped, recognizing De Lormé, as the young man knelt by his side, "but I ax yer not fer to bear any malice, fer my jig is up, and I am booked fer to take the leap inter the dark, and whar I'll land is w'ot I'm fearful of."

"Who put you up to the job?" Batcliff asked.

"Some galoot w'ot staid in the background and didn't let on who he was," the man answered. "I was to git five hundred dollars fer the trick, and as I ain't been running in good luck lately, I jumped at the chance—all in the way of business, you know," he explained. "No malice 'bout it, strictly business, every time."

Then his strength failed him, and for a few moments it looked as if the end had come.

But with a great effort he rallied, and unclosing his eyes, looked up into Batcliff's face.

"I know you," he said, "you are one of the Bella Union gang. I've see'd you make things howl many a time, fer when I'm flush I hang round the Bella Union at night.

"You're a squar' man, ain't ye?"

"Well, I have always tried to be," the veteran actor replied.

"Say, I've got a little kid," the ruffian continued.

"His mother was a good gal and worked herself to death to support the boy when I was sent to the stone jug on a five years sentence.

"The kid is at Oakland, a-boarding with an aunt of his'n w'ot has been like a mother to him since his own hopped the twig.

"Mary Ann Maguire, right near the ferry. Any one thar will tell you whar the house is.

"I sent a lot of stuff to the kid yesterday, done up in a little trunk fer him to keep my clothes in.

"Jest you go fer that trunk. I fixed a false bottom to it, and thar you'll find some things w'ot ought to bring my kid some stamps one of these days.

"No crooked business, you know; but all right and straight. If you handle it right you kin make a pile out of it. I'll trust you, fer you've got a good face, and I don't believe you would play any roots on a poor little kid with neither pappy nor mammy."

Tears fairly came in the eyes of the veteran actor, old, time-worn man of the world as he was, as he listened to the plaintive appeal.

"I accept the trust, and as surely as there is a Creator above, I will see that your boy profits by the inheritance which you entrust to my care.

"But I will need some authority from you, or the trunk will not be given to me," Batcliff hastened to add as the thought came into his mind.

"There's an order all made out in my pocket," the wretched man gasped.

"Oh, I'm a prudent sort of a cuss, I am," he continued. "I thought, mebbe, that I might run across the right party at some time and I writ the order so as to be prepared, but I never reckoned when I got inter this scrape that I was going to be wiped out so soon."

At this point the wounded man's strength began to fail him.

He had made a great effort to reveal his secret so as to provide for his "kid," for, ruffian though he was he had at least the instinct of the beast to provide for his young, and the attempt carried him into the jaws of death.

He gasped, writhed in agony for a few moments, and then all was over.

"Poor devil!" exclaimed the veteran actor. "'Nothing in his life became him like the leaving of it,'" he quoted.

"And now for the order, since I am to be his executor," Batcliff continued.

A search of the dead man's person soon produced the document, which was contained in an old-fashioned leather wallet that the ruffian carried in an inner pocket of his rough "pea- jacket."

"I suppose in my official capacity I ought to take charge of the plunder," Batcliff remarked, upon making the discovery that the dead man had a common leather wallet in another pocket.

"Most certainly," De Lormé replied.

The money and a single revolver were all the valuables that were to be found, and Batcliff took possession of them.

While the actor had been searching the dead man's person, De Lormé had risen to his feet and taking out his pocket-knife proceeded to cut a stout switch, about as big as a man's thumb, from one of the bushes in the neighborhood.

Batcliff didn't pay any attention to what his companion was doing until he rose to his feet, and then he surveyed the switch in utter amazement.

De Lormé was flourishing it in the air, cutting "figure eights," as if to test its strength and pliability.

"Hallo! What are you going to do with that?" Batcliff asked.

"Well, I intend to call the Irishman to an account for this little business, and unless he gives me satisfaction I will cane him within an inch of his life."

"Good!" cried the veteran actor, rubbing his hands gleefully together. "That is a little scheme which to see worked would delight my soul."

"You will speedily be gratified," De Lormé replied.

The two then proceeded again to the open plain.

While this conversation with the wounded ruffian, which we have detailed, had been going on, the Irishman and the doctor had been engaged in examining McMichael's hurt.

He had fainted and the doctor proceeded to bandage the wound, after having declared that it was a serious one and might cost the young man his leg.

By the doctor's orders the hack in which they had come was summoned, and while the doctor and the hackman proceeded to place the wounded man in the vehicle, the captain advanced to speak to the victor and his second, now just emerging from the bushes.

"The affair is over, gintlemen," said the Irishman. "Me principal is so badly wounded that he is not able to stand upon his legs."

"I wonder that you have the audacity to look me in the face, you cowardly assassin," exclaimed De Lormé, sternly.

"Eh? Phwat is that? Phwat do you mane?" cried the Irishman, blusteringly.

"You unprincipled cut-throat, you hired a knave to kill me so that your patron might escape unhurt from this duel."

"It's a lie!" the Irishman roared, thrusting his hand behind him as if with intent to draw a pistol.

"You cowardly cur! Don't you dare to pull a weapon on me!"

And with the words De Lormé cut the captain across the face with the switch so violently that the stroke drew blood.

"I'll murder yees for that!" the captain howled as he plucked out his pistol.

But De Lormé was on the watch for just such a movement and with a dexterous blow of the stick he struck the pistol from the Irishman's hand and then rained such a shower of blows upon him that the captain was blinded and bewildered.

And though in his desperation he endeavored to close with his assailant, De Lormé easily evaded him, and in about a minute O'Ballyhoo was about as thoroughly thrashed as a man could well be.

Unable at last to stand the punishment he took to his heels and ran.

De Lormé pursued him for a few steps, dusting his jacket well for him with the switch and permitted him to escape.

And so the affair ended.

McMichael never troubled De Lormé again, and the Irishman bore his caning in patience for he dared not face the man whom he knew to be his master.

CHAPTER XXXVIII.
LA BELLE HELENE SEEKS ANOTHER ALLY.

And now, having settled this matter, De Lormé was free to set out on his mission to the Stanislaus region, and being a man who was not disposed to allow the grass to grow under his feet, he started that very afternoon.

It was not like going to a strange section for all his boyhood had been spent in that region. And after leaving Stockton he found himself amid familiar objects, although years of absence had wrought many changes.

Maximilian Macarthy, the Englishman who had crossed the broad ocean and journeyed all the way to the Pacific slope for the purpose of finding the lost heir of his brother, was still in search of his heir.

He had acted on the advice of the chief of police, and engaged the best detectives he could find in San Francisco, but all his efforts had been fruitless.

Not the slightest trace of the missing heir could he find.

The detective firm to whose care he entrusted the business were shrewd fellows and disposed to be honest with their customer.

So after the search had failed, they told the Englishman that, in their opinion, there wasn't any use of his wasting more time or money in the matter.

The chances were a thousand to one that the child was dead long ago, and his best course would be to employ a first-class legal firm and lay claim to the property as the next of kin to Archibald Macarthy.

This struck the Englishman as being extremely good advice, and he acted upon it immediately.

The detectives gave him the address of a prominent legal firm, and he lost no time in seeing them in regard to the matter.

After he had stated his business, the lawyers expressed their opinion that he had an extremely good case, and they agreed with the detectives that the odds were great that the lost heir of Archibald Macarthy had paid the debt of nature long ago.

Gladly they undertook the management of the affair, and the Englishman still further won their good opinion by planking down a good round sum as a retaining fee.

The Briton was both a cautious and a crafty man.

Although wealthy, he believed in holding on to his money as though he needed every penny. But when it came to a matter of this kind he knew that there was true economy in securing the best talent that could be had, and that there wasn't any greater incentive to spur legal gentlemen to action and to quicken their brains than a good large "retainer."

As Macarthy descended from the lawyer's office he encountered the chief of police Kettleton.

The two shook hands, and the chief invited the Englishman to come into a nearby saloon and have a drink, it being the idea of the official to "pump" Macarthy in regard to the lost heir affair.

Kettleton had not been able to get a single clew in the matter, and he had a natural curiosity to discover if the stranger had been more fortunate.

"I suppose you have found your child by this time?" the chief remarked.

"Oh, no," the Briton responded, with a shake of the head. "No such luck, you know."

"No clew at all?"

"Not the slightest."

"Well, I must say that is odd," and the chief shook his head as though it was the strangest thing in the world.

"Yes, I have taken advice on the matter, and I am advised, as I am unable to find the child, the legal presumption is that the heir is dead, and as the next of kin I am entitled to the estate."

"Of course, not a doubt of it!" exclaimed Kettleton, quick to perceive the strength of the position. "Now, if you had been a man eager for money and not particular how you procured it, you might have set up that claim in the beginning. And, instead of attempting to find the lost child, done your level best to prove that the child wasn't the right one if any heir had appeared to claim the property."

"Ah, yes, but, don't you know, I am not that kind of a man at all, my dear fellow," the Englishman hastened to explain, swelling out a little with the consciousness that his course in the matter from the beginning had been above reproach, notwithstanding the enormous amount involved.

"In the first place, I am a wealthy man and have as much money as any one man ought to have, and a great business besides, which is increasing every year and brings me in a princely income," he explained.

"If I was some poor devil, without a dollar to bless myself with, the case might be different.

"Then, perhaps, I shouldn't be so anxious to find my brother's heir, and would be deucedly inclined to secure the property for myself.

"Observe, my dear fellow, I do not pose as a perfect specimen of an upright man. I am only human you know, and humans, when a pot of money is in sight, are mighty apt to fight with one another like a lot of wild beasts."

"Very true," observed the chief, and he thought to

himself that he would have to be worth a heap of money before he would be magnanimous enough to allow five millions of dollars to escape him if, by hook or crook, he could possibly secure it.

"No, no, my dear sir, in the Macarthy family blood has always been thicker than water and we have always stood together, shoulder to shoulder.

"If I could find the slightest clew to the child I would never dream of claiming the money.

"Not only that, but I would spend freely of my own means to secure the property to the heir of my dead brother.

"But if the child is dead, as I now firmly believe, I shall not have any hesitation in claiming the money."

The chief declared that no one could possibly find fault with such a platform, and then the pair separated.

Kettleton took his way to his office feeling decidedly out of sorts.

"Durndest, strangest thing in the world that I can't get my finger into this hyer pie!" he muttered as he walked along.

"If I could have only managed to squeeze into the b'iling in some way I reckon I would have had my whack out of the five million!"

The chief could not keep the matter out of his mind, and even after he reached the office and took a seat at his desk the subject haunted him, until his meditations were interrupted by the arrival of an unexpected visitor.

It was no other than the charming song-bird of the Bella Union, La Belle Helene.

The chief received her with all honors; hastened to place a chair for her and explain how highly complimented he felt by her agreeable presence in his office.

La Belle Helene smiled as sweetly as usual as she

listened to his honeyed words, but for all that there was a serious look upon her face.

"A truce to compliments," she said, when Kettleton finished. "I did not come here for the purpose of hearing how well I look or how splendidly I sung last night, but my visit is strictly on business."

"On business?"

And the official looked astonished.

"Yes, and important business, too, as you will comprehend when I explain.

"But, in the first place, in order that you may not be puzzled by certain knowledge which you will soon see I possess, let me tell you that I overheard all the conversation between you and Mr. De Lormé the other night behind the scenes of the Bella Union."

The chief was amazed at this disclosure.

"I couldn't help overhearing, for you were right outside my dressing-room with nothing but a thin partition separating us, and I heard every word that was said just as distinctly as if you had both been in my room and talking to me."

"Let me see; what was the conversation about?" prompted Kettleton, with an innocent air, as though the particulars of the interview had escaped his mind.

This was a dexterous device on his part to ascertain exactly how much La Belle Helene really knew, for the chief was such an uncertain man in regard to the truth himself that he was apt to be apprehensive that everybody else was just as careless.

"The Macarthy estate—the five millions of dollars that here in California waits for an heir," the girl replied, promptly.

"Ah, yes, I remember; but what possible interest can you have in the matter?"

"I was the wife of Archibald Macarthy!"

"The deuce you say!"

And, leaning back in his chair, Kettleton surveyed the lady with the utmost astonishment.

"It is the truth!"

And then La Belle Helene proceeded to tell the story of how she had wedded Macarthy and separated from him exactly as she had revealed it to Andrew De Lormé.

When she had finished, the chief gave a low whistle, indicative of vast amazement.

"Well, hang me!" he ejaculated. "This is a regular romance!"

"Truth is stranger than fiction! But now, tell me, am I not entitled to a share in this five millions?" she asked.

"Most decidedly!"

"And will you aid me to secure it?"

"You bet I will!"

The chief was delighted.

At last he saw a chance to get at some of the Macarthy money.

"I was his legal wife, and therefore as his widow am entitled to a widow's share. But, of course, I shall have to prove that I was his wife, and, owing to the lapse of time it will not be an easy matter."

And then she went into the particulars of the case, which, thanks to the aid she had received from De Lormé, she was able to present in a perfectly clear manner.

"Oh, you have got a good fighting chance, as the lawyers say!" Kettleton declared. "Don't you worry about that. I can find the witnesses," and then he winked in a significant way, as much as to say if he could not find the right ones, he could procure others who would do.

Then he explained how the English Macarthy was preparing to claim the estate as the next of kin.

"If it was the direct heir, now, we wouldn't stand much show, but opposed to the brother, all the sympathy of the public will be with you, and, I tell you, that counts for a great deal in such a matter as this.

"Anyway, if we make a vigorous fight we can get a compromise, and the thing is big enough to stand a division."

And so they came to an understanding, and the two parted, mutually pleased.

But little did either of the schemers dream of the sleuth-hound so hotly on the trail up on the flats of the Stanislaus.

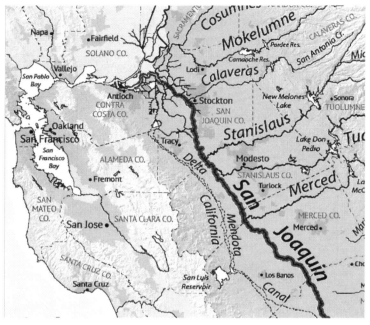

10. Present day map showing the relationship of San
Francisco and the Stanislaus River region.

CHAPTER XXXIX.
THE RECLUSE.

A good horse was purchased, saddle-bags packed, and De Lormé set out for the flats of the Stanislaus. He went in the guise of a speculator looking for opportunities to turn an honest penny and so quitted the beaten track, thinking that he might stumble upon what he wanted in some unfrequented spot.

And everywhere he went, no matter with whom he got into conversation, he adroitly came to speak of Archibald Macarthy.

At one time Macarthy had been a power in this region, being heavily interested in the mining operations then so extensively carried on, and in his travels De Lormé came across quite a number of old-timers who still remembered the dashing Englishman.

But not one of all with whom he spoke knew anything about his being a married man.

The invariable answer to De Lormé's inevitable inquiry as to whether he was a married man or not was that, to the best of their knowledge, he was not.

"Never heared of no wife when he was in these parts, stranger, so I reckon he wasn't hitched," was the usual answer.

But the fickle goddess, Dame Fortune, was disposed to favor the persistent inquirer in this instance. Chance brought him in contact with a courtly old gentleman who looked like a foreigner, and was introduced to De Lormé as being the proprietor of a still paying gold-mine located up in the foot-hills.

He was called Jerome Dumont, and when he learned that the stranger was in search of an opportunity to employ some idle capital, he invited the traveler to take up his quarters with him. As he stated, there were half a dozen good chances for investment in his neighborhood.

De Lormé had chosen a sturdy horse at Stockton before beginning his invasion of the Stanislaus region, and so he was prepared to accompany the stranger up into the rather wild region where his property was situated.

After leaving the hotel where De Lormé had taken up his quarters, the old gentleman began the conversation by saying:

"Both your voice and face are so familiar to me that it seems to me that I must have met you before."

"I think not, sir," De Lormé replied, "for I have an excellent memory for faces, and as yours is not familiar to me I do not think it is possible."

"Is this your first visit to this section?"

"Yes, to this particular part, but I was raised a few miles from this locality. I left here when a lad, went to San Francisco, and have made that my home ever since."

"It is probable then that I met you years ago, for I am certain that I have seen you before and conversed with you.

"Knowledge and remembrance of faces and voices are my strong points," the old gentleman continued.

"I am one of the oldest settlers in this neighborhood, having come here right after the first outbreak of the gold fever. If you lived as a boy anywhere in this neighborhood I should have been apt to have met you."

"It is possible, of course, that your memory serves you better than mine," De Lormé admitted. "And, by-the-by, speaking of old times, were you acquainted with the man who was once a great gun in this region, Archibald Macarthy?"

The benign expression upon the face of the old man

242

immediately disappeared and a stern look took its place.

"Archibald Macarthy?" he exclaimed, in angry tones. "Yes, I knew the man in the old time and to my sorrow. But don't speak about him, please, for it brings back to my mind a host of unpleasant memories.

"I thought I had buried them all in the sea of oblivion years ago, but the mention of the name of that infamous scoundrel brings them all back as freshly as ever."

De Lormé began to believe that he was in for a streak of luck.

Here was a man who not only knew Macarthy, but was intimate enough with him to be angry at the bare mention of his name.

But could the old man be induced to talk on this subject that he declared was so distasteful to him?

That was a question difficult to answer.

De Lormé thought over the problem for a few moments and came to the conclusion that the best way to treat the subject was not to press the old gentleman, but allow matters to take their own course. Possibly some favorable opportunity might come, and Dumont might of his own accord speak of the subject again.

The old gentleman entertained De Lormé like a prince, and showed him about the neighborhood in such a hospitable fashion that the conscience of the young man was troubled by the deception, innocent though it was, that he was playing on his host.

Dumont kept bachelor's hall, with only a couple of servants, man and woman, to keep things in working order.

One night, when they sat outside the house enjoying their cigars, De Lormé felt impelled to explain to his host what errand had brought him to the Stanislaus region.

The old gentleman listened attentively to the recital,

and when it was finished, said, gravely:

"Really, my dear young sir, there wasn't any need of your revealing your secret to me.

"Your quest was not an improper one, and a man may be pardoned for wishing to keep his business to himself.

"But it is fortunate for the success of your mission that you have chosen to confide your secret to me to-night, for I am the only man in the world, now that Macarthy is dead, who can throw any light upon this dark mystery.

"Archibald Macarthy was my brother-in-law. It was my sister whom he married."

"Is it possible?" exclaimed the young man, astonished by this unexpected declaration.

"Yes, my only sister, Louise," observed Dumont. "As you have doubtless guessed from my name, if you have any knowledge of such things, my family are of French descent.

"My father, in quest of fortune—he was a physician and of a roving turn of mind—came to this coast when he was a young man.

"Attracted by the charms of a Spanish-Mexican girl, he married and settled here.

"My self and sister were the fruits of that union. Just about the time of the gold discoveries death claimed my sire. And as he left no property to speak of, there wasn't anything to bind us to San Francisco, or any particular spot. So I followed the human tide to the flats of the Stanislaus.

"I joined the great army crazed by the lust for gold, and happening to make a rich strike in this neighborhood, resolved to settle here.

"My sister, whom I had been obliged to leave behind

in San Francisco, joined me as soon as I made arrangements for her to be comfortable.

"And she had scarcely been here a month when this man Archibald Macarthy saw her.

"My sister was a beautiful girl, and she fascinated Macarthy, who was then in the zenith of his riches.

"He sought for and procured an introduction, and immediately began to pay her the most devoted attentions.

"I did not favor his suit, for there were a great many things about the man that I did not like. But my sister grew to love him, and one night when I was called away from home on some important business, he persuaded her to go with him and be married.

"The rascal intended to trick her, for the man who married them was pretending to be a magistrate, but was in actuality a dissolute miner whom Macarthy bribed to perform the ceremony.

"After the marriage the pair fled to San Francisco to escape my vengeance.

"But the moment I returned, the miner came to me with his story. The trickster had been caught in his own trap, for the miner was a regularly ordained minister, though now under a cloud on account of his dissipation.

"But he had the right to perform the marriage service for all that, and Macarthy was legally married to the girl whom he would have betrayed."

CHAPTER XXXX.
AN UNEXPECTED DISCOVERY.

De Lormé had listened with the closest attention.

"'The engineer hoist with his own petard,'" he remarked.

"Exactly!" exclaimed Dumont, in grim satisfaction. "With the minister I hastened to San Francisco, and there succeeded after a long search in discovering the fugitives.

"I arrived just in time.

"The villain had already tired of his toy, and was about to abandon her.

"My appearance and the revelation that his tool was actually a minister came upon him with the force of a thunderbolt.

"Then, too, with my leveled pistol I held his life at my mercy.

"Finding that he was in the toils, he begged for grace, and at my sister's supplications—not because she still loved the villain who would have destroyed her, but because she did not wish to see me stain my hands with his blood—I spared him, but on these conditions:

"A certain sum of money must be paid yearly for the support of my sister and the child yet unborn. And while she lived he was not to attempt to procure a divorce so that he might be able to marry again.

"He agreed willingly enough, for he knew that I would kill him if he did not.

"Then, with my sister, I returned home. The child was born, but when it was about two years old the mother was seized with a mortal illness and died.

"Just one month after the mother's death the child

was stolen. Stolen by Macarthy, as I always believed. But when I found him in San Francisco and taxed him with the crime he denied it. Nor even after the most vigorous search was I able to discover the child or that he had anything to do with it, although in my own mind there wasn't any doubt that after hearing of the mother's death he had determined to secure possession of the child."

"No doubt at all that he was the man who did the deed, for I have discovered that he entrusted a child to the care of one Abraham Gwinnet, a saloon-keeper in San Francisco, some twenty-odd years ago," De Lormé remarked.

"That was the stolen child, beyond a doubt. I felt sure that Macarthy had the child, but when I came to think the matter over I determined not to trouble myself further about the matter, for he was the child's father and had more right to it really than any one else. It was only natural, too, that so rich a man as Macarthy was at that time should wish for a son and heir."

"A son!" cried De Lormé, in amazement.

"Yes, a son."

"But I have been looking for a daughter—I got the impression that the child was a girl."

"You are wrong: it was a boy: a fine, healthy little fellow named Lucian, after my father," the old gentleman answered.

"I have all the papers appertaining to the affair carefully preserved, so that at any time I could go into a court of law and not only prove the marriage, but also the birth of the child; and now, after all these years, I could easily identify the boy—although he has, of course, grown to man's estate—by means of certain birthmarks which he possesses on his body."

De Lormé thought the matter over for a moment,

touching his hand to his side in contemplation.

This was the strangest affair of which he had ever had knowledge.

The deeper he got into it, the more dense became the mystery.

He resolved to confide to the old gentleman the story of the tin box.

And when he had concluded Dumont exclaimed:

"That is the key to the mystery in my opinion! Obtain possession of the letter, which was in the box, and no doubt a clew will be found to the whole affair.

"It looks to me as if some trick had been planned at some time—take the name of this girl of whom you speak, for instance.

"Lucille! That is pretty nearly like Lucian, isn't it?"

De Lormé admitted that it was.

"But she is not the long-lost heir—there isn't the least doubt on that point."

"So I perceive," noted De Lormé. "Well, I will return to the city and try to discover what has become of the paper.

"The moment Irish Kate is able to speak, the mystery in regard to the whereabouts of the paper may be solved."

The next day De Lormé was on the road to Frisco, and when he arrived there his first visit was to the hospital.

The woman had recovered sufficiently to be able to converse, but she was as much in the dark as to what had become of the letter from the tin box as the young man himself. Nor did she know anything in regard to the contents of the letter.

She had sent for the little girl whom she usually

employed to read documents for her. But the child and her mother had unexpectedly left the city, and so the letter remained unread.

She had it in the bosom of her dress when she became involved in the quarrel with the two ruffians, and as her garments were badly torn in the struggle, it was probable that the letter had dropped to the floor and had been picked up by some one of the crowd attracted into the saloon by the fight.

As far as De Lormé could see, the only thing to be done was to endeavor, by advertising the lost letter widely, to recover it.

So from the hospital the Bohemian went straight to the office of the Alta California.

At the door he encountered the veteran actor, Batcliff, who, ever since De Lormé left town so unexpectedly, had haunted the newspaper office in search of him.

"Come up to your room right away!" the actor exclaimed. "A most astonishing document has fallen into my hands."

And when he got De Lormé safely into the privacy of the office, he placed in his hands a closely written letter, soiled with age. De Lormé had not read ten lines of it when he became conscious that he held in his hands the letter that had been contained in the tin box.

Then it suddenly flashed upon him how it had come into Batcliff's hand.

This was the trust confided to him by the ruffian, and which was to bring money to the "kid."

This fellow was the man who had taken the letter from the floor after it had fallen from the bosom of the assaulted woman, and he had sense enough to see, after reading the letter, that it was valuable.

The letter was from Abraham Gwinnet, and was

addressed to Lucian Macarthy, son of Archibald Macarthy.

In substance, the letter was a confession.

Having made all the arrangements with others for the abduction of the infant, Macarthy had entrusted the child to Gwinnet, the saloon-keeper. The father had known so little of his own child that he was not aware whether it was a boy or a girl, and Gwinnet had taken advantage of this ignorance to substitute another child, a girl, in place of the true heir. His idea being that in the time to come when Macarthy's property fell to her he would have a hold upon the heiress which would bring him in much wealth.

McCarthy's ruin upset the plan, and then the saloon-keeper, repenting of his crime, wrote the confession, placed it in the tin box while he sought the "flats of the Stanislaus." Intending to tell the man to whose care he had entrusted the boy to claim the box with the password when the child grew old enough to learn the truth.

But, death struck him down at the very beginning of his journey, and so justice had not been done.

Andrew De Lormé had guessed the truth long ere this.

His peculiar birthmarks proved he was in truth Lucian Macarthy and the heir to the five millions left by the dead man!

Thanks to Jerome Dumont's carefulness and Gwinnet's confession, he easily proved his identity.

De Lormé, as he still chose to be called, had no trouble in making good his claim, and the Englishman Maximillian Macarthy received him with open arms, impressed immediately in his favor.

Later, he was more than generous with his would-be

assassin's "kid."

And when La Belle Helene found that he was the true heir, she sent for him and confessed frankly that the tale she told was false. She had not been married to Macarthy, but had been engaged to him at the time his wealth so abruptly vanished, and that calamity ended the matter.

"You see, I am not altogether bad," she said, in conclusion. "I will not go into a court and by swearing to a lie interfere with your interest."

De Lormé appreciated the sacrifice.

"The moment the money is in my hands I will give you ten thousand dollars on condition that you go to Europe and learn to be the singer that you should be."

"And can't you give me anything but money?" La Belle Helene asked, bluntly.

"No. In the future let us be friends, but nothing more."

"Well, I'll take the money and live for my art alone then!" the woman exclaimed, proudly.

De Lormé's liking for the siren had passed away, for the fresh, young beauty and honest heart of Lucille Gwinnet had fascinated him.

"'He told his soft tale and was a thriving wooer,'" as the veteran actor remarked.

The dressmaker was not the lost heir, but she shared in the property eventually as his wife.

And the Bohemian always laughed when he told the tale of how diligently he had sought to find himself when lost in Frisco.

THE END.

Thank you!
Please join us at the Dark Lantern Tales web site, where you will find more contextual history, including our regularly updated Gilded Age Slang Glossary.
The Joe Phenix Series
Gilded Age Detective Stories
Steam-Driven Crime Stories

https://darklanterntales.wordpress.com/

Glossary of Slang and Period Phrases
as noted in The Frisco Detective

Alta California, the Daily Alta California was a newspaper that was published in San Francisco from 1850 to 1891.

Bedrock, in mining parlance, the bottom where no possible ore is to be found.

Bellows, in this story the word is used oddly, possibly meaning bellow, as in loudly and belligerently speaking.

Blood – perhaps originally from "pureblood," it refers to persons who claim the highest positions in society.

Billy-cock hat – a bowler hat, like a derby

Bung-starter, a mallet made of wood, used to loosen the "bung," or plug in the bunghole of a cask.

Chapter of accidents, a succession of unfortunate events

Come down, means pay up

Coves, guys

Dished, meaning screwed, or out of luck

Fly-cops, means plain clothes detectives

Gillies, possibly meaning young men with subservient jobs.

Go through, means to make a search of the person.

For money, or **for dollars** – means you can bet on it.

Hair-pins, whimsical slang when the speaker refers to himself, like saying, "people"

Halidame, by my halidame, halidom, an expression of emphasis, (possibly a corruption of halidome, meaning a place of worship or a religious relic)

Horny-handed means calloused hands.

I'll go bail, means I'll trust this.

In its wards, refers to a ward lock on a door, the ward being a plate that is cut out with the same cross section as the key.

In the toils, means captured or controlled by another.

Irish vernacular, it was expected of dime novel writers to provide characters with accents related to their ethnicity, country of origin, or the region of the US where they were raised. "Phwat" (what), "B'ye" (boy), and other examples are approximations of an Irish accent, at least as popularized at the time. "Spalpeen" is an Irish term for a scoundrel, or rascal.

Jehu, wagon or coach driver, originally a biblical reference

Laid by the Heels, means captured, arrested

Levant, period slang for run away, and possibly skip out on responsibilities, such as debts

Make a raise, means generate some funds

Modiste, a maker of fine women's wear, such as hats and dresses.

Of his kidney, means, of his type

Panned out, a prospector's term, meaning proven

Pidgeon-holed, means filed away

Papers, pasteboards, can mean playing cards

Quod, means jail

Rich lead, mining term for high value vein of ore.

Riffle – might mean task, or plan, and was derived from a mining term for a long "riffle" box that takes a flow of water with "pay dirt," and let's the gold settle into the space between slats on the bottom. These slats may be called riffles, and imitate a shallow, slow moving part of a stream that allows sediment to settle.

Salivate – as used in various popular stories from the 1870s to 1890s, "salivate" means to kill, perhaps by perforating with a weapon. "You'll get salivated in the worst kind of a way."

Sand-club, a weapon, described as looking like a sausage and made from cloth or leather filled with sand.

Sleuth-hound, an old name for a bloodhound, and a slang term for a detective.

Spencer "magazine rifle" must have been a reference to the Spencer Repeating Rifle developed during the American Civil War. It held seven cartridges in a tube form of magazine that was bored through the stock.

Stanislaus, the Flats of the Stanislaus, a river and area east of San Francisco where some of the richest gold discoveries of the California Gold Rush were found.

The whole b'iling (boiling), means, the whole thing

To take the rag off the bush, means to be the best, excellent and triumphant

Two bits, four bits, are terms that date back in the US to before the revolution. Spanish or Mexican eight Real coins were sometimes cut up into eighths, and these "bits" were roughly equivalent to a shilling in early nineteenth century America. Since two bits equaled a quarter dollar, a shilling would have been the equivalent of 12.5 cents. The Real was legal tender in the U.S. into the 1850's, along with denominations of money used today.

Whack, whack up, a share, to divide up the goods or money

Whist, Hold your Whist, means, silence, hold your tongue

Acknowledgements and Gratitude:

First for my wife, **Ann Wicker**, a professional writer and editor, who has tolerated my obsession with these old stories and helped review my editing.

Joe Rainone and **Bob Robinson** are two collectors and sellers who supply my habit for ancient sensational literature. I've learned a great deal from them both. Bob Robinson's web site can be found at: http://stores.imaginationradio.com/

Joe Rainone, with co-author **E. M. Sanchez-Saavedra**, created the deep reference source I rely on frequently, The Illustrated Dime Novel Price Guide. That reference book has a vast amount of information in a very readable form, and hundreds of illustrations. Visually, it is a mate to The Dime Novel Companion by J. Randolph Cox. https://www.youtube.com/watch?v=17e99w2zuqI

J. Randolph Cox, the recognized authority on all things related to Dime Novels and the popular press of the late nineteenth century, has been generous with answers to my questions over the years. When his Dime Novel Companion was published, it immediately became my first choice reference volume.

Pascal Storino, Jr., Criminal Investigator, Retired, is otherwise known as "Pat." This career detective has a fascinating website about the history of the New York Police Department at http://www.NYPDHistory.com and it is worth many visits. Pat has also been a great resource to help me understand more about the equipment and policies of the NYPD during the time of the Joe Phenix stories.

Martin Howard, collector and recognized expert in early typewriters. Martin was generous with his time and knowledge to help me learn more about typewriters in the Beadle and Adams' era. His web site is a delight to stroll through, so take a look: http://antiquetypewriters.com/

Demian Katz of Villanova University has been a great resource and helped with advice on many topics, including how best to take pictures of original material.

Northern Illinois University Libraries, in whose worthy hands the collections of Albert Johannsen and Edward T. LeBlanc are well curated and studied.

James Harper, MLIS, Z. Smith Reynolds Library, Wake Forest University, for helping me to locate some scarce text. They have an excellent library staff!

Illustration Acknowledgements and Sources

Frontis: Partial image, Historic American Buildings Survey, San Francisco, ca 1875, Library of Congress, http://www.loc.gov/pictures/item/ca0671.photos.016081p/

01. Page one of Vol. 4, No. 163, Banner Weekly, December 26, 1885, courtesy of Northern Illinois University Libraries, Nickels and Dimes from the collections of Johannsen and LeBlanc

02. Wood engraving from page one of Vol. 4, No. 163, Banner Weekly, December 24, 1885, courtesy of Northern Illinois University Libraries, Nickels and Dimes from the collections of Johannsen and LeBlanc

03. Wood engraving from page one of Vol. 4, No. 164, Banner Weekly, January 2, 1886, courtesy of Northern Illinois University Libraries, Nickels and Dimes from the collections of Johannsen and LeBlanc

04. Wood engraving from an 1897 issue of the National Police Gazette. Collection of the editor.

05. Wood engraving on cover of Beadle's New York Dime Library, Vol. 52, No. 665, of July 22, 1891, courtesy of Northern Illinois University Libraries, Nickels and Dimes from the collections of Johannsen and LeBlanc

06. Wood engraving from an 1879 issue of the National Police Gazette. Collection of the editor.

07. Image of an 1870 issue of The Daily Alta California newspaper. Collection of the editor.

08. Wood engraving from an 1883 issue of the National Police Gazette. Collection of the editor.

09. Line drawing of the Spencer Repeating Rifle, by Scientific American [Public domain], via Wikimedia Commons

10. Map section with SF to Stanislaus River, "By Shannon1, Map of the San Joaquin River basin in central California, United States, made using public domain USGS National Map data."

But wait!
There's More!

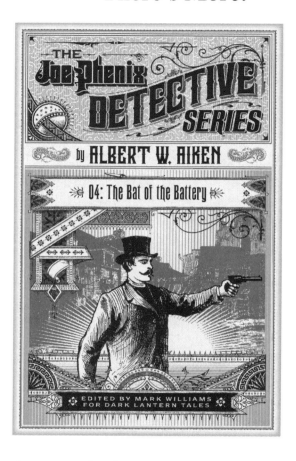

Turn the page to begin reading the first chapters of

Joe Phenix,
The Bat of the Battery

The Bat of the Battery;

or,

Joe Phenix, King of Detectives.

A Thrilling Story of New York Life by Day and Night

By Albert W. Aiken
Published 1883, Beadle's Weekly
Edited and Copyright 2018 by Mark Williams

CHAPTER I.
THE DEAD MAN.

It was a pleasant May night, the moon was up full and bright, and just as the clocks of the city marked the hour of twelve, the policeman whose beat extended along Battery Place had his attention attracted to a strange sight.

Battery Place is the square, which bounds the Battery Park on the north. The policeman had been sauntering leisurely along, swinging his club after the fashion of his class, when his eyes fell upon the figure of a man lying, extended at full length, in the center of the carriage-way which leads from Battery Place to the emigrant headquarters in Castle Garden.

At the extreme southern end of Manhattan Island and commanding a magnificent view of the beautiful New York Bay, The Battery has woefully fallen from its high estate in these, our modern times. Once it was the fashionable breathing spot of New York. Then, as the city expanded and the tide of wealth flowed up town, the Battery Park was for years neglected. Castle Garden, a round, wooden, castle-like building on the sea front of the park, was once a popular place of amusement. Within its walls Jenny Lind, the Swedish nightingale, first sang in the new world, but it is now transformed into a reception house for the adventuring souls who cross the seas to find a home in the land of the setting sun.

At such an early hour as the time of which we write, the streets were almost deserted, and so it happened that the policeman was the first to discover the man lying prostrate in the carriage-way. He immediately jumped to the conclusion that it was some emigrant who had been taking a look at the wonderful sights of great Gotham, then partaken of too much strong liquor. Overcome by the potent fluid, the man had lain down in the street to sleep off the effects.

"Oh, murther! Isn't that a temperance lecture for yee!" the officer exclaimed in a rich brogue which plainly betrayed his nativity.

"I'll be afther running him in, so as to give him a chance to pay for his night's lodging. Sure, five dollars is not bad for an elegant bed like that, patent pavement for a mattress and the whole of the beautiful sky for a blanket."

But when the vigilant guardian of the night came nearer to the supposed sleeper, he saw that it was no emigrant, for the man was dressed in an excellent suit of dark clothes, fashionably cut, and from his appearance looked like a well-to-do merchant. He was a tall, portly man, well advanced in years, with gray hair and a long beard of the same hue.

"Oho! Upon me life this is no small fish!" muttered the policeman, "I'll get a carriage for him, send him to his house or hotel and thin strike him whin he gits sober for ten dollars for me trouble. For 'I'm a dandy cop of the Broadway squad,'" he hummed as he came up to the man and knelt down by his aide.

The song, though, died away quickly when he placed his hand upon the stranger's person for the purpose of rousing him, and peered into his face.

"Mother of Moses! If he isn't dead!" he cried, startled by the unexpected discovery.

The policeman was right; the man was dead and had apparently been so for some time, for the body was perfectly cold.

"Phwat the divil is this anyway? Phwat kilt the man?" queried the officer. "Has there been foul play—is it a murther?"

But no signs of violence met his eyes; the face of the dead man was as calm and peaceful as though he was only asleep, and his clothing was not disarranged. Only one suspicious fact the metropolitan noted; there were no articles of jewelry visible; no watch-chain, no studs, although there were eyelet holes in the shirt bosom, which seemed to indicate that the man had been in the habit of wearing such things.

The policeman cast a rapid glance around and then hastily examined the dead man's pockets, but his search was a fruitless one; there was absolutely nothing whatever in them.

"Bedad! Some one has been here before me," the officer muttered. "That is suspicious! Be the powers! I belave the man was kilt by some murtherin' thaves, but who in the world did the job?"

And as he put the question he looked wistfully around. He had not the slightest anticipation of seeing anything, and therefore was not at all prepared for a sight which for a moment froze him with horror.

When he had approached the motionless man there

was not a living being in sight. On the left hand rose the walls of Castle Garden and the low sheds appertaining thereto. In the center was the sea-wall, and beyond that the waters of the bay, wherein rode at anchor vessels of all nations. On the right was the building of the Iron Steamship Company, and the approach to this building was partially blockaded by huge piles of freight, destined evidently for the Pennsylvania Railway's Freight Depot, which was the next building beyond.

As the policeman raised his head he looked directly at the huge pile of freight, and on the boxes stood a figure strange enough to startle almost any one, as it appeared, framed against the moon.

The officer, credulous and superstitious by nature, stared in alarm.

"Holy Moses! Is it a man or a divil?" he cried.

It was no wonder that he asked the question, for at a distance the figure, though evidently that of a man, bore a striking resemblance to a huge bat, being attired entirely in black, wearing a long, old-fashioned circular cloak, and just as the officer caught sight of the man, he had raised and stretched out his arms, and the cloak being thus extended, looked exactly like a pair of huge wings. The man wore too a small, soft hat, pulled in chapeau fashion down over his eyes so that it came to a point in front, it gave his head the appearance of a bird of prey.

The officer rubbed his eyes as if to make sure he was awake. When he looked again the figure had disappeared.

"Bad 'cess to me!" he muttered, "if the baste didn't give me quite a turn! Upon me wourd, I would have taken me oath whin I first saw it that it was a divil, but thin who iver saw a divil like that? Or a man a-gallivanting round in sich a rig? Mebbe it was wan of thim frog-eating Frenchmen—they do be afther making mon-keys of thimselves."

Then dismissing the subject from his mind, he turned his attention to the dead man. He felt absolutely certain that he had been robbed, but whether before or after death was a question. As far as he could see, there wasn't the least sign to indicate that the man had been the victim of foul play, and the officer finally came to the conclusion that the stranger had died a natural death, being attacked by some fatal stroke on that very spot, and some night prowlers had discovered the body and removed the valuables.

"Upon me conscience!" The officer murmured, af-ter completing his examination. "It's mighty odd that I never have the luck to pick up a boodle of this kind even once in a while."

Then he proceeded to summon assistance; the body was removed and the coroner notified, and in due time the inquest held, and then came a startling discovery.

The man had been murdered!

Right over the heart was a stab wound, so slight that hardly a drop of blood had come from it, inflicted evidently by a dagger whose blade was very little larg-er than a good-sized knitting-needle; but the wielder of this toy-like instrument of death had such an accurate knowledge of the human form divine, and knew so well where to strike his blow, that the steel had penetrated right through the heart. And then, too, on the left side of the neck, right over the jugular vein and under the ear, were two little punctures, hardly large enough to be classed as wounds, and which looked exactly as if they had been made by the teeth of some small animal.

This was really a wonderful case, and yet in a great city like New York so many mysterious deaths are constantly happening that even this occurrence created but little wonder in the minds of the public at large.

The newspapers briefly reported and commented upon the affair—mysterious death, murder evidently, where were the police, body unrecognized, something ought to be done and then the next day the matter was supplemented by some new horror, and the busy folks of New York forgot all about it.

There were some exceptions to this rule, however. There was a man who after the lapse of a few days came forward and identified the body. One of the representative men of the city, this gentleman, by name Redmond Lamardale, was a retired merchant and one of the millionaires of Gotham. The dead man was his brother Rufus, who had been engaged in business in Texas for some twenty years, and had come to New York on purpose to visit him, Redmond, whom he had not seen for years.

The New Yorker had been advised by letter that his long absent brother was on his way to the city. When time passed on and he neither saw nor heard from him, he became alarmed, and some morbid impulse prompted him to visit the morgue where the unclaimed dead bodies were kept on exhibition. There he found the man he sought in the gray-bearded stranger.

CHAPTER II.
A CONSULTATION.

In the private office of the superintendent of the New York police, in the white-fronted building on Mulberry Street, sat three men, who, from the nature of their position, were presented constantly to the public gaze.

One was the superintendent of police, another the Mayor of New York, and the third the Governor of the State.

The governor and mayor had just entered the office and had been received in due form by the police official, who, upon seeing his visitors instantly suspected that something important had occasioned their visit.

The mayor plunged at once into the subject.

"We have called upon you, superintendent, in relation to this mysterious death of Mr. Rufus Lamardale," he said.

"His brother, Redmond Lamardale, is one of my most intimate friends," the governor explained, "and I have promised to do all that I can to have the murderer, or murderers, of his brother brought to justice. He, himself, has not allowed the grass to grow under his feet in the matter. He has communicated with his brother's friends in Texas—he had no relatives there, being a bachelor—and has ascertained that when his brother started for New York he wore a heavy gold watch and chain, two valuable diamond studs, a diamond ring, and carried two or three hundred dollars in his pocketbook."

"None of which, if you remember, superintendent, were found upon his person," the mayor remarked.

"I remember, sir," replied the official. "In fact, there wasn't a single article of any description in his pockets.

267

He had been completely stripped of personal possessions."

"What can be done, superintendent?" the Governor asked. "Money in this case is no object, you know. Mr. Redmond Lamardale is wealthy enough to be able to afford to spend a hundred thousand dollars to bring the assassins of his unfortunate brother to justice, and for the sake of the good name of the city which you watch over, Mr. Superintendent, you ought to use every possible means to detect and punish the perpetrators of such an atrocious crime."

"Yes, this affair comes right home to both the governor and myself," the mayor added, "for while Mr. Redmond Lamardale is one of the governor's oldest friends, he is also a neighbor of mine and I have known and esteemed him for years."

"Your Honor, I have been doing everything in my power to get at the authors of this crime," the superintendent replied, earnestly. "Not only because the mystery that surrounds the deed has excited my curiosity and piqued me to action, but also for the reason that it is not the first time that this mysterious slayer has struck down his man right in the open street. This fact I have kept to myself for it isn't any use to make such a thing public. If the newspapers got hold of it they undoubtedly would make a great row about the matter. The assassin would thereby be put on his guard and so make the task more difficult for the detectives. Just listen to these notes which I have jotted down in my private book."

Then the chief procured his note-book and read aloud.

"No. 1. Horace Derwentwater, English, elderly, a stranger, tourist, man of means, stopping at Brevoort House, found dead, Jan. 5th, four o'clock in the morning in Ninth street near Washington park, all valuables removed from person. No signs of violence apparent on body on casual examination, but when stripped, death was found to have ensued from a wound made by a minute dagger piercing the heart. On the neck too, under the left ear, were two punctures seemingly made by a small pair of teeth."

Simultaneously the governor and mayor uttered a cry of astonishment.

"The resemblance of that crime to this murder strikes you, I see," the superintendent remarked.

"All the circumstances are exactly the same, with the exception of the place where the body was found," the governor replied.

"Yes, and the position in the street too, right in the middle of the roadway, as if the man had been assaulted in crossing the street, yet after a careful consultation with some of the most expert surgeons in the city, one and all assured me that it would not be possible, one time out of a thousand, for a man to inflict such a wound as caused death in these cases, unless the victim stood perfectly quiet, and then too, they were all of the opinion that the punctures in the neck were caused by the teeth of some small animal. Now, gentlemen, see how improbable it is that these tragedies occurring right in the public thoroughfares could take place without causing an alarm, even though at an hour when all the city is supposed to be asleep. But listen to the others…"

Then the official read his notes regarding three more cases, all alike in respect to the victims being elderly well-to-do men, strangers in the city, all killed by the same means, and all rifled of their valuables. One body was found in Madison Avenue, just above Madison Square, another in Wall Street, a few doors from Broadway, and the third on Fifth Avenue, within a stone's throw of the lower end of Central Park.

"You will perceive," the superintendent observed, when he had finished reading the notes, "that Mr. Rufus Lamardale is the fifth man who has fallen a victim to this notorious assassin, for that one man, and one man only, perpetrated these deeds of horror I feel quite certain. Another thing I feel sure of is that the murders were not committed in the places where the bodies were found. It is entirely beyond the bounds of probability for these murders to have been committed in such public places without exciting attention, even in the early hours of the morning when darkness shrouds the city. My theory is that the victims were all decoyed to some isolated spot where, even if a struggle ensued, no alarm could be given, and there the deed was done."

"But then, why should the assassin take the trouble to deposit the bodies in these public places?" the governor asked.

"That is one of the idiosyncrasies of crime," the chief answered. "I do not suppose, gentlemen, that you are aware of it, but I have a peculiar theory in regard to criminals, particularly those who commit great crimes. I think that all humans who sin against the laws of God and man, are in a measure diseased in their minds, not exactly lunatics, you know, but people whose heads are not well balanced.

"Now, in these cases, after the murders were committed, it was necessary for the assassin to get rid of the bodies. And let me tell you, gentlemen, that is no easy job in a big city like New York. Some of the most noted murders that the world has known have come to light through the attempt of the murderer to get rid of the remains of his victim.

Albert W. Aiken

"Depositing the bodies in these public places is pure bravado, defiance to the authorities. The author of these deeds is no common criminal, but a man of brains who has turned his talents in a wrong direction--a monomaniac, in fact. I cannot bring myself to believe that these murders are committed for the sole purpose of plunder, for I feel pretty well satisfied that in nearly all these cases, the victims' valuables could have been obtained without the robber being obliged to add murder to theft."

"The perpetrator of these mysterious murders is a sort or demon, then—a human fiend who kills for the pleasure of killing," the governor observed, thoughtfully.

"The idea seems rather far-fetched," the mayor remarked; "his honor" was noted for his practical ideas.

"Yes, Your Honor, that is very true, but there is an old saying, you know, that 'truth is stranger than fiction,' and I think it is quite safe to say that the imagination of man cannot conceive of anything stranger than the acts that some humans will commit. Take the case of this mysterious assassin, for instance; why, the records of crime do not contain a stranger case; we must go back to the old story of the crimes of Margaret of Burgundy in La Tour de Nesle, as told by Victor Hugo, or the tale of the vampire, who prolonged his miserable existence by stealing from his victims the remnant of the life which in the course of nature they would have lived if their career had not been brought to an untimely end."

"The vampire, by Jove!" exclaimed the governor, abruptly. "Of course, the idea is absurd, but don't these mysterious murders appear like the work of just such a creature? Although, I believe the vampire never took the trouble to drive a weapon though the heart of his victim."

"No, he bled them to death by biting them in the neck," the mayor remarked.

"The two little punctures in the neck of these victims would fill that bill," said the superintendent.

His visitors stared at each other for a moment, then looking at the official, shook their heads gravely.

"The idea is too steep for you to swallow, eh?" asked the chief.

"Oh, yes, the days of vampires have passed away," the governor, observed.

"Yes, yes, you can't come any La Tour de Nesle business on us in New York," declared the mayor.

"Well, gentlemen, I have got a clew, and I will leave it to you to say if it don't have the smack of a vampire about it," and then the superintendent related how, in prying into the circumstances of the murder, he had extracted from the policeman an account of the strange-looking figure which he had seen near the scene of the tragedy. At first he had taken it to be a huge bat, at the same time never suspecting that what he saw had aught to do with the dead man.

"Gentlemen, that bat, as the Irishman called it, is the party we want," the police chief said in conclusion; "and I have put some of my best men on his track. Whether he be man or devil, or vampire bat, I will bet a good, round sum that before a month is over I will have him safely locked up!"

Satisfied with this assurance the visitors departed, wondering greatly over the strange affair.

CHAPTER III.
A PRECIOUS PAIR.

Two young men sat in a cozy smoking-room of a sumptuous mansion on one of the fashionable cross streets of Murray Hill, as a part of the regions sacred to the golden kings of New York is often termed.

There was a strong contrast between these two young men, each to the other.

One was slender in build and short in stature, with an olive-tinged, foreign-looking face. He had peculiar eyes of uncertain hue, appearing gray at times and then dilating into jet black. This young man's hair was as dark as the raven's wing, and curled in little crispy ringlets all over his head. His face was smoothly shaven and appeared effeminate, yet there were certain lines around the eyes and the thin-lipped, resolute mouth which contradicted the otherwise sensitive appearance of his countenance.

This was the master of the mansion, Basilias Almayne, commonly called the "doctor," by his acquaintances from a tradition, which said he had once studied medicine in foreign lands.

Almayne was commonly supposed to be very wealthy, although really the world at large knew but little about him. He had only resided in New York about a year. And Almayne had not experienced any difficulty in gaining an entree into society owing to the fact that he was well acquainted with some of the leading young men of the upper ten, whom he had met abroad. His story, as told to them, in brief, was this:

Almayne was the only scion of an old Creole family, which had taken root years ago in Louisiana. He had never said much about his family, but from the fact that they were rich enough to send him to foreign lands to study for a doctor, and always kept him in funds so that he was able to gratify his slightest wish, his associates judged that the Almaynes were wealthy. And when studying in Europe young Almayne was, to use the language of his companions, "Satan's own boy!" The ring-leader of all the students in mischief and dissipation, it was often predicted that if the young Southerner did not die of drink he would get in some brawl which would end fatally for him.

As a student, Almayne easily held his own against his companions, for he was wonderfully gifted, and seemed to have the faculty of comprehending upon the instant what would cost another man hours of severe study.

In fact, he was a genius, all admitted that, and as more than one of his masters said, "He will be a great man one of these days, if he doesn't throw away his opportunities."

All of a sudden, right in the midst of his college studies, Almayne was called home by the death of his mother, and none of his companions saw or heard aught of him until he appeared in New York. Then, in answer to their queries, he said all his relatives were dead, and being his own master, he had come to the only city in the New World worth living in to enjoy himself.

From the style of the establishment he set up, and the manner in which he conducted himself, it was apparent that he had plenty of money. He pursued no business, although often in jest he would declare that he was a better doctor than nine-tenths of those who won princely incomes by following that profession, and so among his associates he was generally termed "Doc" Almayne.

His companion was called Francis Culpepper, a medium-sized blonde youth, with a face which, although fair to look upon, a good judge of mankind would not have been apt to form a favorable impression of.

This young gentleman, although not wealthy, moved in good society, for he came of an old family and was the cousin and confidential man of business of one of the richest men in the city, Redmond Lamardale, the retired banker.

Between Almayne and Culpepper a close intimacy existed, as will be perceived by what took place at this interview, the particulars of which we are about to relate.

"What is the matter; you seem out of sorts?" Almayne queried, after his visitor was comfortably seated and had his cigar in working order.

"There has enough happened to put me out of humor," was the sulky reply. "And I think that if you knew what I know, you wouldn't be in a very good humor yourself."

"Unfold yourself, although I doubt the truth of your statement, for I have such a deuced good opinion of myself, that it would take a great deal to worry me."

"Almayne, can I trust you?" cried the other, abruptly, and with a searching glance at the face of his host, who laughed at the inquiry.

"Well, as to that, Frank, my dear boy, you ought to be the best judge. You know what you can say and I don't, but if there is any doubt in your mind about the matter, give yourself the benefit of it and do not speak."

"Hang it, Doc, you and I ought to be in the same boat in this matter!"

"Yes, but, old fellow, two men can't very well pull together unless they have faith in each other; that is, to achieve anything, I mean."

"Well, you have as deep an interest in the matter as myself, and if you don't go in with me you are not the man I take you for. All I ask is for you to keep silent about the matter if you don't see your way clear to join me."

"All right, I give you my word that I will be as silent as the grave, so fire away!"

"In the first place let me get at your position. If I understand your game you are anxious to marry Miss Cassandra Lamardale, old Redmond's daughter and his heiress."

"I suppose I may as well own to that soft impeachment, though I trust you will do me the justice to believe that it is not altogether because Cassandra is an heiress that I am attracted."

"Oh, certainly; I understand that, but at the same time the fact that she is an heiress is no objection."

"Old fellow, with my expensive habits it would be sheer folly for me to pretend that a rich wife would not be a desirable thing for me to acquire, and I will go still further, Frank, and say that if Miss Cassandra had not been likely to come in for a good bit of money one of these days, it is not likely that I should have ever troubled my head about her, beautiful and attractive as she is.

"You know that the lady doesn't regard you with a favorable eye, and that if you win her consent it will be because she yields to her father's request."

"Oh, yes; she doesn't particularly fancy me, but then she isn't in love with any one else, and believes that she never will be, and so is not so much averse to marrying me as under other circumstances she might be."

"Now, then, I will come directly to the point. You know Batterhofer, the lawyer?"

The other nodded.

Albert W. Aiken

"He is Lamardale's adviser, and when the old gentleman announced at lunch to-day that Batterhofer was coming to see him on important business, my curiosity was excited and I determined to know what took place at the interview, for I will own frankly I am deeply interested. I am about the only relative, with the exception of his daughter, that the old man has, and I have always understood that at his death I was to be well remembered.

"The lawyer came in reference to the old man's will, as I suspected; I managed to overhear every word of the conversation, and now, prepare to be astonished! Cassandra is not Lamardale's daughter, but an adopted child, and at his death she is to receive only a small part of his fortune, and that so tied up that the interest alone will come to her; a few thousand dollars are left to me, also invested so that I cannot touch the principal—curse the old scoundrel; you see he doesn't trust me after all these years!"

"Too bad," and Almayne shook his head: but there was a look in his eyes which seemed to say that he did not wonder at it.

"And the rest of his fortune, his millions daily growing larger and larger, what do you suppose is to become of them?"

"I haven't any idea, unless like many another old man in his dotage he is going to make up for the sins of his youth by giving money to some charitable purpose."

"No, crossing from England to this country, and on the seas at this present moment as an emigrant passenger, is a young cud, without parents, without a living relative in the world, as far as she knows. She is called Lesbia Mardal, and is to be received by the old lawyer who was charged with the task of bringing her to this country. Lamardale is providing the money. The girl thinks that some friends of her dead father, moved by charity, have brought her over, and she comes here to earn her living. The lawyer is to find a place for her where she is to be put on probation, that fact being carefully concealed from her. Lamardale is to keep careful watch of her, and if she comes up to his anticipations, she is to be his heiress."

"The deuce you say!" cried Almayne, startled by this intelligence. "Why, what on earth put the idea into his head? What is the girl to him?"

"Nothing at all; she is an entire stranger; he has never even seen her. Why, Batterhofer, who as a general rule is not in the least curious, was amazed at the strangeness of the affair, but Lamardale said he had good reason for his action, and that in time he would explain."

"I'll bet a trifle that the old man means to marry the girl."

"My own idea, exactly, for he said she was a beauty, and splendidly educated."

"What steamer is she on?"

"The City of Chester, due here next Monday. Now then, if the old man likes the girl after she arrives, and carries out this idea, good-by both to your hopes and mine."

"We must keep a watch on the parties; the stake is worth some little trickery."

"You will go in with me then to put a spoke in the old man's wheel?"

"Oh, yes, for I want Cassandra, and I want a fortune with her, too. There are plenty of tools to be found in a city like this who for money will do anything. We will watch events, and when the time comes be prepared to interfere."

And so the compact was made; two strong men against an old man and an innocent young girl.

CHAPTER IV.
THE EMIGRANT GIRL.

Promptly upon the date expected, the City of Chester made her appearance in New York harbor. Only, being detained somewhat by fogs, she arrived in the evening instead of the morning. With night falling, she came to anchor off quarantine, at which the passengers grumbled loudly for one and all were impatient to reach the shore.

But it was not to be, and they were forced to content themselves with gazing at the dark outlines of Staten Island, rising plainly visible in the bright moonlight.

Among the steerage passengers, leaning over the bulwarks and looking at the distant lights upon the crest of Staten Island, was a beautiful young girl, who was so becoming that she had attracted much attention during the voyage.

This was Lesbia Mardal, the girl referred to by the two plotters in our last chapter.

In figure she was about the medium size, most exquisitely formed, and with a face of rare beauty, being pure Greek, a perfect oval, and lit up by as handsome a pair of great, brown eyes as ever dwelt in a woman's head.

She was plainly dressed, yet very lady-like in appearance, and quite reserved in her manners. Lesbia Mardal was so different from the usual run of single young girls who cross the ocean to seek a new life, that all of the officers of the ship who came in contact with her unanimously agreed that she was far more fitted to shine in the cabin than any lady on board of the ship. All wondered that such a girl should be obliged to cross the ocean alone, and in the steerage at that. But she had such a quiet, dignified way with her that no one cared to run the risk of offending her by questions.

The third officer, a good-looking, blue-eyed blonde fellow who answered to the name of James Blount, was especially interested in the girl. Late on this particular evening he happened to come across her, still gazing over the stern bulwarks at the distant land, and he plucked up the courage to say a few words.

They were almost alone on the deck, nearly all the passengers having gone below.

"It's a fine night, Miss Mardal," he remarked, as he came up to where she stood, wrapped in dreamy meditation.

"Yes, very pleasant, Mr. Blount."

The officer was pleased that she remembered his name.

"You will be glad enough to get on shore to-morrow, I suppose," he remarked.

"I shall not be very sorry, although the trip has been a pleasant one."

Blount hesitated and fidgeted about in an awkward way for a moment, and then said: "I hope you will not think me inquisitive, but I suppose you have friends on shore ready to meet you?"

"Friends," and there was a mournful tone in her voice as she spoke, and her eyes had a vacant look as she gazed upon the waste of waters, "yes, I suppose so, although as yet they are strangers to me."

"Oh, I thought it likely that you had relatives on this side of the water."

"I haven't a relative in the wide world that I know of, and I do not really think that any exist."

"All alone in the world?"

"Yes; although perhaps I ought not to say that, for

these strangers who have caused me to come across the ocean are acting like true friends; and as I have not had many so far in my life, perhaps fate designs to make up for the past by providing me with plenty in the future."

"Well, Miss Mardal, if you will allow me, I should like to be ranked among your friends in the time to come, although now I am merely an acquaintance. This is my last trip on the steamer, and I am about to embark in business on shore in New York. This will be my address hereafter, and if at any time I can be of any assistance to you, I hope you will not neglect to call upon me," and he handed her a card.

She placed it in her pocket-book, thanking him for the offer, which in her present condition affected her more than she cared to manifest.

"Yes, I am tired of a roving life, and have determined to settle down," he said. "I have secured a good business opening, and I think the chances are that I shall prosper."

"I am sure, I hope so!" Miss Mardal exclaimed, and this was no mere empty compliment, for the kindness of the young man had made a deep impression upon her and her wish for his success was sincere.

"What land call you that, sir?" asked a rather harsh voice at the ear of Blount; and turning, he beheld one of the steerage passengers, all muffled up in a long old-fashioned cloak, and with a slouch hat pulled well down over his ears. In addition to the cloak, he had a woolen comforter wrapped around his neck just as though he was cold, although the air was balmy and spring-like as became a pleasant May evening.

In person, the man was under the medium size, with a swarthy face fringed by coarse, black hair worn quite long; and a stubby, brown-black beard covered his chin.

Altogether he presented a brigand-like, although pictur-esque, appearance.

"That is Staten Island," responded Blount, taking a good look at the man, for he did not remember ever hav-ing seen him before, which he thought was strange, for he had an excellent memory for faces, and rather prided himself upon the fact. Then, too, the face of the man was an odd one—a face that once seen would not be apt to be forgotten.

"Staten Island," remarked the man in a reflective sort of way. "That is not ze New York then?"

"No; the city lies further up the bay. But you will ex-cuse my curiosity, I trust—where on earth have you kept yourself during this voyage? I do not remember to have seen you; but you are a passenger, of course."

"Oh, no; I have just dropped from ze clouds!" re-sponded the man with a laugh, speaking in a pleasant, flexible voice, now strangely at variance with his rough, uncouth appearance. From the slight accent, which there was to his speech, Blount came to the conclusion that he was a foreigner—perhaps a Frenchman or an Italian.

"By Jove! I must say I don't seem to remember you any more than if you did; and it's deuced odd, for we haven't a large passenger list this trip, and I didn't think there was a person on board of the ship whom I hadn't seen."

"Oh, you saw me often enough, sair, at ze begin-ning of ze trip, but after ze first day, I was attacked by ze dreadful sea malady and sought 'ze seclusion which ze cabin grants,' as your divine singers say in ze Pinafore."

The man was a gentleman, evidently, despite the fact that no one would have taken him to be one from his personal appearance. But, somehow, a strange doubt had seized upon Blount; he felt a sudden and most decided aversion to the man, and he could not get the impression out of his mind that, notwithstanding the assertion to the contrary, he had never set eyes upon his face before.

"How may I call your name, sir?" he asked, plainly betraying by his face that he regarded the other with suspicion.

"Leon Du Claire."

"You are a Frenchman, I presume?"

"A French Italian," responded the man, with that peculiar shrug of the shoulders so common to the Latin races. "French by descent, but born and reared in Italy."

Blount had watched the stranger with an earnest eye, and the more he saw of him the more convinced he became that he had never set eyes upon the man before.

He was not a passenger, for if he had been, Blount knew that he most certainly would have seen him. How, then, was it that he came to be on board the steamer?

He could not very well have dropped from the clouds, as he asserted, although it was possible that he could have gained access to the deck of the steamer by taking advantage of the darkness and coming alongside in a small boat; but then what game was the man up to that he should take such a course?

There wasn't anything to be gained by so doing, as far as Blount could see, and he dually came to the conclusion that the fellow was a stowaway, that is, he had stolen on board the steamer without a ticket before she left England, and had managed in some mysterious manner to conceal himself among the freight and live through the voyage. Such a thing had been done, but very rarely, for after a day or two in the dark hold the stowaways were generally glad to sneak out and throw themselves upon the mercy of the captain of the ship.

If the man was a stowaway, he had apparently

managed to endure the voyage about as well as anybody on board. Blount's curiosity was so excited by this strange circumstance that he determined to go instantly and examine the passenger lists and see if any such name as the man had given was registered, but without any intention of working harm to the stranger; for as long as the voyage was ended, and he was on this side of the water, it didn't matter materially how he had managed to get across.

"I imagined that you were either a Frenchman or an Italian from the way you spoke," Blount observed, and, with a remark about the beauty of the night, he sauntered away.

"How strange are these English-speaking people," the man in the cloak mused, speaking apparently to himself, and yet loud enough so the girl could hear every word.

"He doubts my statement; he thinks that I have fallen from ze sky, or else risen out of ze sea, and, in order to satisfy himself, he has gone to examine ze passenger lists so as to discover whether I have spoken the truth or not. How disappointed he will be when he ascertains that I am right in my account and he is weak in ze head for harboring such an idea. Ah! This world! What a strange world it is, eh, mademoiselle? Think how we poor humans go through life ever on ze watch against each odder!"

"Oh, I think you are wrong in your surmise," the girl replied, puzzled by the man's manner, and half suspecting that he was not quite right in his mind.

"No, no! I am quite correct as sure as that light burns yonder on ze land!"

Lesbia looked in the direction indicated, and then the man suddenly threw his arms around her, pressed one hand over her mouth, and with the other, applied a sponge saturated with some strange smelling liquid, to her nostrils. She was in the toils.

Chapter 5 is ready for you in your own copy of

The Bat of the Battery;
or,
Joe Phenix, the King of Detectives
from
Dark Lantern Tales

Joe Phenix;
the Police Spy

In 1878, barely a dozen years after the American Civil

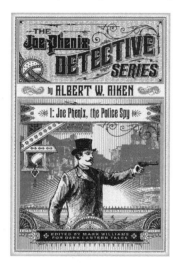

War, this origin story of ***The Joe Phenix Detective Series*** was published as a serial in the New York Saturday Journal.

This is Historical Fiction written when it was simply...Fiction!

Joe Phenix, The Police Spy, is essential as the origin story of Joe Phenix. It was written in a time when elaborate and decorative language was an important element of style, and a substantial serving of pathos was expected with melodramatic turns of plot. Given that framework, ***Joe Phenix, The Police Spy*** delivers a complex story with plenty of crime-fighting detective action!

Available as Print-On-Demand at Amazon Kindle, and as an eBook from Kindle, iBooks, Smashwords, and others. Look online at eBook listings to read a free sample!

Dark Lantern Tales
Rediscover Crime and Detective Stories of the 1800s
https://darklanterntales.wordpress.com/

Joe Phenix,
PRIVATE DETECTIVE;
or, The League of the Skeleton Keys.

There was a suspicious death, a marriage proven to be a sham, a grave disturbed at midnight, and all before Detective Joe Phenix has even entered the case!
Soon, in an underground New York City meeting place, an extensive criminal enterprise is revealed and infiltrated. Yet, the plot has only begun to unfold.

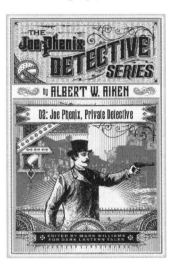

At the peak of summer, on July 24 of 1880, this second Joe Phenix adventure began as a serial in the New York Saturday Journal, a story paper published by Beadle and Adams. In *Joe Phenix, Private Detective,* he has become independent of the police force of New York City and has his own detective agency. **Written in 1880 to be read in 1880, this is Historical Detective Fiction created before it was ... Historical!**

Available as Print-On-Demand at Amazon Kindle, and as an eBook from Kindle, iBooks, Smashwords, and others. Look online at eBook listings to read a free sample!

Dark Lantern Tales
Rediscover Crime and Detective Stories of the 1800s
https://darklanterntales.wordpress.com/

The Wolves of New York;

or,

Joe Phenix's Great Man Hunt.

1881, New York City, and the Wolves are the worst of

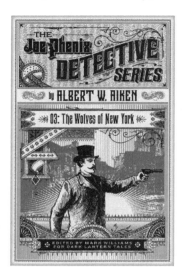

gangs. Their captured leader was sent to Sing Sing State Prison up the Hudson river, but made an astonishing escape. In frustration, the police superintendent calls in private detective Joe Phenix to hunt the man down.

The Wolves were a cold-blooded gang of criminals led by an androgynous mastermind called Captain Molly,whose mastery of disguise matched even the skills of Joe Phenix. Captain Molly was born of the Romani people, "Gypsies," a situation that in turns helps him and also helps his pursuer, the famous detective.

The mysterious Queen of the Gypsies guides with predictions, and Joe Phenix lives among the Romani to learn their ways while chasing Captain Molly through the most wealthy and the most foul parts of New York City.

Dark Lantern Tales

Rediscover Crime and Detective Stories of the 1800s
https://darklanterntales.wordpress.com/

Joe Phenix's Shadow,

or,

The Great Detective's Mysterious Monitor.

On a dark evening in 1890, a murderer strikes in the middle of New York City's Washington Square Park. Seemingly no one has seen the attack. Both the police investigators and private detective Joe Phenix are at a loss as to how they can proceed. However, Joe Phenix begins to get tips from a veiled woman who seems to have been mesmerized. The veteran detective doubts the powers of clairvoyance, mesmerism, and second sight, but his doubts are challenged as more mysterious revelations appear.

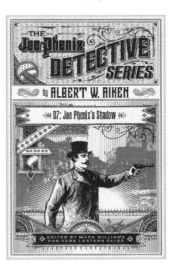

The Joe Phenix stories were intended for adults and contrast the seamiest side of New York with the elegance of the world of the wealthy. *Here is Historical Fiction written when it was simply, fiction.* And here also is one of the earliest detectives in popular fiction. Your first chapter is waiting for you.

Dark Lantern Tales

Rediscover Crime and Detective Stories of the 1800s
https://darklanterntales.wordpress.com/

Made in the USA
Columbia, SC
22 January 2019